CONQUERING PREHISTORIC

BOOK FIVE IN THE WEST OF PREHISTORIC SERIES.

ERIK 'TRACER' TESTERMAN

SEVEREDPRESS

CONQUERING PREHISTORIC

To those who risk much to battle evil on our behalf.
Stand fast.
Stay accurate.

CHAPTER 1

Many Years Ago...

"Take it," the man squatted down to look me in the eye and held out his pistol.

I stared at the revolver. It looked like the gun that my adoptive Father had taken with him when he left for the war so long ago.

"You know that I will not repeat myself," the man said with some measure of annoyance in his voice.

He wouldn't repeat himself. That was a fact. A painful one I'd learned with a little help from the back of his hand over the past two days since he'd taken me along with them.

Reaching forward, I took the gun. It was nickel plated, with ivory grips. I bet it was expensive.

It felt good in my small hand though.

"Shoot him," he ordered, pointing a thick finger at the gaunt gray uniformed man kneeling before us.

The Confederate sobbed; his rope bound hands raised in front of him as though in prayer.

I didn't know who he was. I didn't know what he'd done. As far as I could tell, nothing. But he was here now. We'd chased him down on the horses until his legs gave out and he lay gasping in a ditch alongside a field of unpicked cotton.

I blinked.

"We don't have all day," the officer warned as his horse stamped its hooves. The men and horses behind the Captain were growing restless and impatient. I knew that I had to do what I was told or face their wrath. And I'd seen their wrath. It scared me.

Raising the gun shakily, I pointed it at the top of the stranger's head. He was starting to go bald. There was a patch in his thin scalp that was already missing hair. I aligned the front sight of the pistol there.

"Do it," the Captain said. "Now."

The man looked up, tears streaking down his gaunt and unshaven cheeks.

The front sight was now between his eyes.

He trembled, sucking in a deep breath and letting it out in an attempt to calm himself.

"Child... please don't-"

The pistol bucked in my hand as I squeezed the trigger.

A large hand landed firmly on my small shoulder as the red-bearded Captain smiled down at me, flashing bright white teeth. "We'll make a man of you yet, Cato."

CHAPTER 2

Now...

I drifted in and out of consciousness as the pole sled dragged from behind the trike in the rocky sand.

I recalled falling from the wall of Whitesberg under the crushing weight of the dragon and waking on the sandy beach. My head throbbed and my ribs felt as though they were on fire. I stumbled, unsure of where I was or where I was going, just walking. Picking up one heavy foot and then the other, placing them in the sinking sand ahead of me, then taking another step. I was vaguely aware that I was leaving a visible trail behind me in the sand, but too messed up to care.

I walked for what felt like miles along that beach, but from what the Vikings later told me, it was only a few hundred yards over some sand dunes before I toppled over and passed out.

That's where the axemen found me as they returned to Novagant, victorious over the ape army at Whitesberg.

I guess I was lucky the giant crabs didn't get to me first. They'd strip a dinosaur down to bones in a couple of hours. A man in much less.

And now?

For the first time, I was without my guide, my mentor, my employer. He was gone. Dead. I was certain of that even though I never saw his body, but part of me knew he was no more, and I was free of him.

I didn't know how I felt about that.

The sled bumped over a rock, then another, sending twin daggers of pain shooting through my head and chest.

Gasping, I found myself drowning in the darkness of agony as I passed out again.

CHAPTER 3

I woke up in slightly less pain than before. My torso was bandaged tightly over my black button shirt. There was a pain in my hip, but for the most part, all the aches were familiar. Being shot multiple times over a couple of decades would give your body random aches for a long time to come.

Gingerly, I scraped my eyes with my fingertips, wiping off the eyelid crust so I could better see my surroundings. I was in a square hut built of stone and wood; the ceiling thatched with what looked like a thick covering of woven grasses. Hanging from the far wall near the door was my gun belt and pistols. That was a good sign. They hadn't been taken from me. There was a rough framed table with a pair of chairs in the center of the room, and a fireplace with no fire in it. I was lying on a makeshift bed in the corner.

"Ah, he awakens," came a gruff voice from a darkened corner. A man leaned forward into the light from an opened window. He wore a thick braided beard with a trio of lines inked diagonally across his right cheek ending before they intersected his mouth.

"Thought I was dead," I mumbled through cracked lips.

The stranger grinned broadly, "Not yet, my dark-skinned friend. Not yet."

I grunted in reply and gently pushed myself upright into a sitting position. It was then I noticed the backs of my hands. They were both a mass of dark scabs. Curious, I gently touched one, prying at the edge with a fingernail.

"Let them heal first."

"What is it?"

He smiled. "I will explain in time."

"Water?" I asked, my parched throat making it difficult to speak.

He leaned forward and placed a horned cup into my hand.

"Here is something better," he said with a sly smile and a wink.

I sniffed the handmade cup suspiciously; it smelled of fermented honey and spices. Shrugging, then regretting it from the pain that shot through my torso, I sipped from the edge of the horn. The unknown fluid was thicker than water, but rather pleasant on my tongue and slid down my achingly dry throat, coating it with a sweet taste.

"What is it?"

"Medu... or as you gunmen call it, mead."

"Gunmen?" I repeated, mulling the word over in my mind.

"Your people are of the gun," he pointed across the room at my brace of pistols, then patted the long-handled weapon at his hip. "Just as we are of the axe."

Grunting in understanding, I sipped from the horn again. "It's good," I admitted. "Do you have a name?"

"I am Thur Thaneson." He dipped his head in greeting then looked back up. "And you are Cato of the Black Plague."

"Just Cato's fine." I stared at him over the rim of the horned cup, suddenly realizing the obvious. "You speak English."

"Yes, some of us do. It helps to deal with the Shayana or the traders who come by ship. Now, stand Cato, let me see how you've healed," he ordered with a wave of his hand.

I passed the cup back to the strange, bearded man, and grabbing a nearby post, managed to get my feet under myself well enough to sway to an upright position without falling back on the bed.

"Ah, good. I was worried you'd grown weak and feeble." He passed me the horn again. From behind him, he pulled out a cane and handed it to me. The stick was decorated with strange etchings and drawings that I couldn't quite make out in the dim interior of the hut.

I rested my weight on it carefully, fearing the slender carved wood would break under my weight, but it held and felt surprisingly sturdy.

"How long was I out?" I asked as my stomach rumbled. The medu, or mead I reminded myself, was going to hit me hard on an empty belly.

He said something in his language that I couldn't understand, and sensing my bewilderment, showed me four fingers.

I nodded. Four days then. Four days since the battle and since the axemen had dragged my body to... somewhere?

"Where am I?" I croaked before sipping another mouthful of mead to slake my overwhelming thirst and hunger pains.

Thur stood and pushed open the wooden slab door, blinding me with sunlight from the outside.

"Novagant."

CHAPTER 4

Balancing carefully on the cane while still holding onto my horned cup, I followed Thur out of the hut.

I'd heard of Novagant from Reydan. Publicly, he had spoken of joining Whitesberg with the axeman town through the laying of rails. Privately, he planned to seek out what valuable resources they had that he could exploit as he did with the gold of the Shayana. Trading cheap trinkets for incredible wealth. And what he couldn't trade, he'd simply take through legal or other means. His army of Pinkertons, if there were any left after the Battle of Whitesberg, hadn't been for show.

Seeing the small, scaled drawing of the settlement that Governor Fredrick had made off reports was different than seeing the massive place with my own eyes.

It was busy. Very busy. Men and women walked around with dogs and children scurrying underfoot. All the men were armed with some sort of axe, a few carried swords, but only some of the women were armed with anything more than a knife tucked into a belt. I noted that those few women who carried an edged weapon had an air of confidence about them that the others lacked, even though for the most part they were similarly dressed and appeared to be doing equal work.

Interesting.

A crowd began to form around us, many of them speaking in a language I'd overheard a few times in Whitesberg. The mysterious coarse language of the Axemen.

There were some hardened stares from some of the warriors, including a few challenging looks, but mostly it seemed the people of Novagant were simply curious about the dark-skinned stranger standing in their midst.

"Ah, Elsha." Thur waved at someone in the crowd gathering around us as a small child swiped at me with a wooden play axe. In annoyance, I batted it aside with my cane, nearly falling in the process. People laughed, but it sounded more of good natured humor than any scorn at my weakness.

The crowd parted slightly, and a woman stepped forward.

The first thing I noticed was that she was beautiful. Freckles were splashed across the bridge of her nose, and green eyes stared at me with an unsettling intent. Her reddish blond hair was braided and hanging over her shoulder with a scrap of blue cloth tying off the end.

The second thing I uncharacteristically noticed was that there was a sword strapped to her side. As a man whose job was to protect another man with many enemies, weapons always drew my attention first. But this time, it was her beauty that had stolen my attention.

And finally, I realized that below her mesmerizing eyes her face was giving me a scowl.

She spoke in the same language that many of the others used, some words sounded vaguely familiar, but most were not. I stared at her in confusion as she pointed at me and spoke heatedly with Thur Thaneson.

After listening to her for some time, my tattooed guide cut her short with a swipe of his hand and a shout of 'Bah!"

Spinning on her foot, Elsha quickly walked away with the crowd parting before her.

Whoever she was, she commanded respect, or fear, from everyone.

Thur gently laid a hand on my shoulder. "Cato of the Black Plague, I see the stars in your eyes, but I'm sorry to say that Elsha does not like you. Not at all."

I didn't say anything as I suddenly recalled that I was holding a horn of mead. I sipped from the cup again, enjoying the feeling of warmth that spread from my belly and grateful for the movement to hide my embarrassment.

Now that the ruckus had died down, the crowd appeared to be losing interest in me and began moving back to whatever tasks they had at hand.

"Why doesn't Elsha like me?" I wondered aloud as the others moved away. "What was she saying?"

"She doesn't like anyone. Especially unproven outsiders who have no honor."

I raised an eyebrow at him. "No honor?"

He shrugged apologetically. "She believes gunmen have no honor, as their weapons kill from a distance."

"What does she know?" I scoffed as I gingerly ran a finger over my bandaged chest. The tan wraps were so tight that I could only take small breaths, which was fine since anything larger hurt like hell.

"She was with us when we found you, collapsed on the beach."

"She was at the battle?" I asked, surprised.

"Ja. She is…" he paused, as though searching for the word. "Shield-maiden. Woman warrior. She kill many hairy men. Also, very good with boats," he turned to face me. "You have these? Warrior women from where you come?"

I thought for a moment, thinking of Ashley James and Skyla Stratten at the battle of Granite Falls. "A few, maybe," I admitted. "Some only when they are mad enough."

Thur laughed and pulled down the collar of his shirt to point at a nasty scar below his black beard. It looked like someone had tried to slit his throat. "Angry women are fearsome!" he chuckled.

I carefully stepped aside to let an axeman and woman pull a two wheeled cart loaded with vegetables past. "A woman did that to you?"

He rubbed the scar thoughtfully. "Yes, and what a woman she was. She was shield-maiden also, like Elsha. But she liked me. Sometimes."

"What happened to her?"

He shrugged and sighed. "Married my brother."

I grunted and shook my head. Brothers could be real assholes. I knew that too well from Orville. Or Jed, as he went by these days. I wondered if he was still alive, but after a moment, realized he most likely was. He was harder to kill than a cockroach. And equally annoying.

"Where's your brother and his wife now?" I asked, looking around at the passing axemen and women. I was half expecting them to suddenly appear.

"Gone? Dead maybe? Missing." He shrugged and spoke with a hint of sadness in his voice. "They crossed sea with four boats and eighty men and women. Only one man come back. We found him wandering on beach, weeks later, naked and mad." He made a swirly gesture with his finger towards his temple.

That was interesting. But not my problem. "How far away is Whitesberg?" I asked, thinking maybe I'd get lucky and the axemen had a horse and saddle that I could buy. There were some gold eagles secreted away in my gun belt for such a time as this.

"Why?" Thur squinted at me with one eye. "Your master is dead."

So, I was right in my assumption. Orville must have finally gotten his revenge. Good for him, I supposed. It seemed to have meant a lot to him. I leaned on my cane and watched a pair of children play fighting with sticks. "He wasn't my master."

"Father?"

I looked at him sideways.

"Just because not blood doesn't mean not father," Thur said.

"No, he wasn't my father. I just... worked for him," I said. Which really meant, 'killed for him'. But such was my job, and I was good at it. And a man should be proud of what he's good at.

The two boys dropped the sticks and began fighting for real, rolling, shouting and scrapping in the mud. The men who I assumed to be their fathers began to urge their child to beat the other one. The mothers rolled their eyes, smiled at each other apologetically, and went on about their business trading with each other.

Thur slapped me on the shoulder with a chuckle. "Good! Then you can stay with us, heal, and maybe help in return?"

"Help?" I asked skeptically. "How?"

"When time right, you will see." He winked.

I dipped my head, wondering how I could possibly help them in return. Unless it had to do with killing.

Killing I could do.

A giant of a man bullied his way through the parting crowd. He had long shaggy hair pulled back with a ribbon, and a brown beard that touched his chest. A massive axe he carried over his shoulder, and two more smaller ones tucked into his belt.

I immediately disliked him. But then, I'd always disliked people bigger than me.

The two kids fighting stopped and stood, bruised and bleeding as they watched the large man stop in front of Thur and myself. Sniffing, he wiped the back of his hand across his face and frowned.

"This? This is the man Odin sent us?" He scoffed with a laugh. "He looks like nothing."

"Who's Odin?" I asked Thur, while keeping my eyes on the stranger.

The giant man roared in laughter that turned into a guffaw of sorts. With one hand he pointed the bladed end of his axe at me. "He knows not of Odin! Why would he be picked to champion us?"

The axe shined with a faint gleam of oil and the edge appeared to be sharpened well. I felt my left eye twitch, and suddenly wished I was wearing my pistols. Being unarmed did not suit me.

"Champion?" I asked, now very confused.

Thur stepped forward between us, the back of his hand gently pushing the axe blade away from my face. I saw his other hand slide down near the grip of his own axe. "We know not the meaning of the gods, only that we obey them."

"Bah!" Dropping his axe, he leaned on the shaft and spat at my feet. "When time comes, we shall see if he survives. And when he does not, you will know that it is I, Janse Borison, who the gods will champion." Turning his back, he rested the great axe back over his shoulder and the crowd parted to make way for the giant.

"That is the biggest man I've ever seen," I told Thur sincerely.

"Ja. But with large arms comes small head." He chuckled and his hand moved away from his hip. "Let us go. Even while healing, we can help you."

"Prepare me for what? Who is Odin? And what did he mean by champion?"

Thur gently patted my shoulder. "All in time. Now, you come with me and learn."

CHAPTER 5

For the first couple of weeks as my body healed, Thur was my guide. He translated much of what the other axemen and women said to me, as it seemed only some of them knew passable English. Luckily, I'd always had a knack for languages. I could speak Mexican fluently, along with Latin, and a touch of Chinese. So, I did as Thur said; I learned. Quickly.

First, he taught me about their pagan gods. The one-eyed but all-seeing Odin, trickster Loki, witch Frigga, goddess of war Freya, the mighty hammer-wielding Thor, and Balder. As I healed and rested, various Vikings came to me in my hut and spoke at length. I began to learn their names first, and then the words that were close to mine, and finally, the strange and odd words of theirs. Through this interaction, I learned much about their culture and way of life.

At night, when I was left to my own devices, I'd do pushups and various exercises to try and restore the strength and agility of my body that I felt robbed of from the dragon knocking me off the Whitesberg wall.

Then, when I was tired, exhausted and covered in sweat, I'd take the gun belt down from the wall and practice drawing and dry firing.

The movements brought back memories though.

Mr. White had me practice with them, for hours and hours, until my hands turned to leather and the actions of drawing and firing had become like clockwork. Very fast clockwork. The weapons had become extensions of my body and of Mr. White's will.

And I'd used them as such.

And now I wondered what I would do with myself.

In the meantime, the backs of my hands began to heal with the help of a salve Thur gave me. The scabbing slowly fell away, showing that I had been inked while unconscious. The symbols that'd been pricked into my dark skin meant nothing to me yet though.

One of the axemen who visited me to bring me food and speak of the gods, was an older warrior named Gundar the Wrathful. I'd learned of their nicknaming traditions, and that they were often either insulting or demeaning until the Viking embraced their name and made it fearsome and known. Gundar's nickname came from his youth, when his trike was ridden by another boy after he'd told him not to. He'd become angry and knocked the boy off the trike with a shovel, breaking his nose and knocking out his front teeth. That boy later grew to become a fearsome warrior, aptly named Ivar the Toothless, who was lost in the expedition across the sea. But the name Wrathful stuck to Gundar.

And it was Gundar who explained to me what the tattoos on my hands were.

"This," he tapped my right hand where a circle was drawn with what looked like eight tridents jutting outwards from the center, "is the Helm of Awe. The dragon Fafnir defended his treasure from man with it. It will give you might, and power, and strength."

Grabbing my left hand, he turned it over and looked at the needled ink in my dark skin with a frown. "This... this you should not have."

I looked down at the circular snake eating its own tail. "Why?"

"This is Ouroboros. It signifies the destruction of oneself and then the rebirth. This is not for one to give to another, but for one to choose for themselves." He tsked and let go of my hand. "It is a bad omen for Thur to have you inked so."

Turning both my hands over and clenching them into fists, I moved them together and looked at the two tattoos. I didn't like the idea of anyone marking me as I slept in a fit of feverish dreams. Especially on my gun hands. Without these hands and the power they held in them to hold a gun, I was nothing.

That evening, it was Thur who brought my meal of meat and potatoes. It was usually the same food every day, a stew of some unknown animal or dinosaur and some vegetables. But the food was pretty good here and there was always mead. The Vikings loved the drink so much that they protected their vast array of beehives with armed guards to fend off any pterodactyls that might make a try for them.

The axeman grinned as he handed over a wooden bowl to me and sat across from me with his own. "Cato of the Black Plague, how is your chest?"

Setting the food aside, I gently touched my ribs. The bandages had been removed, but my chest and sides were covered in ugly bruising, and they still hurt to touch.

I shrugged with one shoulder. "Fine."

Pain was nothing new.

"Good! Tomorrow we will try something else." He smiled broadly through his thick black beard.

I raised the inked backs of my hands to him. "You said you would explain in due time. Why did you mark me?"

Thur frowned and tapped his carved wooden fork against his bowl thoughtfully. "It is not yet time. Wait. And it will be revealed."

Spreading my fingers out, I looked down at the tattoos and shrugged.

I picked up the food, produced a blade and carved wooden fork from my pockets, and began to eat.

He watched me for a moment, as though unsure that I'd drop such a subject so easily. "You are... okay with this? Not knowing?" he finally asked.

I picked up a piece of meat with my fork and shoveled it into my mouth. "Yes. For now."

He watched me for a moment as I continued to eat quickly. "You always eat so fast. Your food will not vanish. You can eat slowly."

I kept eating at the same pace. Old habits died hard. As a kid under Reydan's command, I learned to move and eat fast.

Thur gestured with his fork at my gun belt that still hung from the wall beside the door. "Your pistols. You are good with them, no?"

Tipping my bowl up I drank the broth and small bits of meat and vegetables left over. Wiping my face with the back of my hand, I told him simply, "Yes."

With his hand, the bearded Viking patted the axe that hung from a loop of steel from his belt. "Tomorrow, you will learn these."

I lowered the wooden bowl. "Axes?"

"Ja! A warrior's weapon."

"Why?" I pointed at my matching pistols. "I have those."

"Ah, yes. But what do you do when you run out of... what you call? Shiny little metal things that go pow?"

"Cartridges."

"Yes. Cartridges. What do you do when you have no more?"

Shrugging, I set the empty bowl aside. "I reckon I'm shit out of luck."

He smiled broadly with crooked teeth. "You see? You need axe."

I didn't see the point in arguing with him. "Okay."

"Good." He stood and took our bowls. "Sleep well. Tomorrow, you will train with one of our best."

That night, I lay awake on my cot, thinking of what Thur had said about running out of cartridges. That'd never happened to me before, Reydan always made sure I had more than I needed. But now, here in the axe village, cartridges would be hard to come by. Once the bullets I had were gone, I'd be down to fists and my thick skull.

Thinking of fists made me frown and look at the freshly healed ink again. I wasn't a religious man, nor a superstitious sort either. I believed in myself and my abilities, knowing my limitations and constantly pushing at the boundaries of them to improve.

But the Helm of Awe and the snake, Ouroborus, felt ominous to look upon.

I wondered why Thur had me inked, and what they meant about me being a champion of Odin. It made no sense to me. But I'd seen how some of the axemen and women looked at me; they expected something of me.

I had my suspicions about what that was.

Their hospitality wasn't coming free.

I just wondered when the other boot would drop.

CHAPTER 6

The next day found me standing in a small field with a bunch of kids. To spare my dignity, they didn't have me out there with the youngest who were training with wooden axes in the open fields near a herd of grazing trikes. Instead, I was with a dozen youngsters who were probably in their early teens.

It was degrading, but at least we were using real axes and shields. The axes were dull. The shields beaten and battered, splintered in places and patched, and whatever had been originally painted on them was long worn off with abuse.

Holding the smooth handle of my axe, I took a couple of cautious swings with it.

"Listen up, you mangy curs! I don't have all day."

I ground my teeth as I saw the massive axeman taking a position in front of our scattered group.

Janse Borison.

Noticing all the others straightening into a ragged line, I joined them at the end. Even then, I still stood out. I was a foot taller than most of them and black.

"I should be out killing the remaining apes, but instead the Jarl wants me to train you." His eyes darted down the line at me. "So, I shall."

He picked up one of the shields from a nearby pile and thumped his large axe blade against the battered surface as if testing the beaten thing to see if it'd hold together. Walking down the line, he continued to thump the weapon and shield as he thoughtfully eyed each youngster in front of him with a frown. "This shield, it is to protect yourself from attacks. But it can also be used as a weapon itself." To drive home the point, he lowered his axe and thrust the shield flat in front of him, the metal edge jabbing forward. "Hit your enemy with a move like this, and it will crush their face or windpipe. Then you can take their life or leave them blinded and helpless as you move on to the next enemy, be it ape…. Or man."

Reaching the end of the line, his face twisted into a smirk as he stopped before me.

I stared back.

"This is Cato of the Black Plague!" he shouted to the others. "He has killed many men and apes! He is renowned amongst the people of the gun as a dangerous warrior. But today, he has left his guns behind and humbled himself to learn of the axe and shield."

His smirk turned malicious. He lifted his giant axe blade effortlessly with his arm outstretched, pointing the business end at my chest.

"Come. Let us see what you know. If anything."

So, this was it. Janse was going to humiliate me and probably try to kill me out of spite. I tightened my grip on my training axe.

Oh well.

Without giving the massive axeman a chance to adjust his stance, I swatted his axe blade away from me with the shield and swung my own axe at him.

His shield moved with startling speed and my blade thunked in deep as he blocked my blow effortlessly.

Grinning wickedly, he nearly wrenched the axe out of my hand as he twisted his shield back into position in front of himself.

"Cato is sly." He took several steps back and settled into a stance similar to that of a boxers, the shield held before him in his left hand, his large axe reserved in his right. "Come, Little Plague."

I lunged forward, bashing my training shield against his and swinging my axe overhead to split his skull.

Sliding his shield up, Janse blocked my blow with his while slamming his own shoulder against mine.

Off balance from the unexpected move, I staggered backwards with the shield against my chest as he went on the offensive.

Blow after blow he swung, hacking my shield to pieces as I desperately blocked and staggered under the onslaught. Splinters flew and fell away as the metal edge of my shield came loose and broke.

With a powerful swing, he knocked the remains of the shield from my stinging fingers.

Down to just my axe, I ducked beneath a shield jab that he'd just demonstrated and swung for his exposed leg.

Before my blade could hit, he hooked his own axe on mine and twisted, jerking the worn handle from my grasp, and sending the weapon flying.

I looked up in surprise just in time for him to slam his knee into my face.

Pain erupted as my lips burst and I fell onto my back in the thick grass.

Janse towered over me. "See? Even a renowned gunman can lose when paired against someone skilled in axe and shield."

The youngsters muttered amongst themselves, nodding and looking at me with skepticism.

Wiping blood off my face with the back of my hand, I winced at the pain from the split lips. From what it felt like, both top and bottom had busted. Considering the large amount of blood smeared on my hand, I expected I came away lucky that I didn't have my nose broken.

The giant axeman stepped back and looked down disdainfully. "Odin's chosen. I say not."

Gritting my teeth, I stood and picked up my axe from where it'd been flung.

Spitting a glob of bloodied saliva in Janse's direction, I walked over to the pile of training shields, picked up another, one that looked sturdier than the last, and returned to my spot in the line before him.

I didn't know about this pissing contest between Odin supposedly picking me over him, but apparently it was a big deal. And since I was currently unemployed and somewhat in debt to them for their housing, food, and care, I supposed I should play the part.

Slamming the axe against the front of the beaten shield, I stared at the larger man, ready to continue my lessons.

He grinned wickedly and swung his giant axe with one hand.

CHAPTER 7

Thur was waiting for me with a pair of meals in bowls as I gently lowered myself into the chair in my hut. Everything hurt. But I was glad that the hardened callouses on my palms protected me from wielding the smooth axe shaft for so many long hours.

He grinned at me through his braided beard. "How was Janse?"

"Rough," I muttered, while rubbing a sore shoulder. Holding up a shield and axe for so long was working muscles that had never been worked before. "You could have warned me."

"Sometimes it is best to learn by surprise. Speaking of which, you have a visitor." He pointed to the corner where a thin man dressed in black was staring at my guns on the wall.

The man turned and I saw he had the frocked coat and white button dress shirt of a preacher.

I snorted in annoyance.

He smiled at me while tapping his tattered bible against his thigh. "Cato Landry," he said softly. "It's a pleasure to meet you, formally."

I licked my busted lips; I hadn't heard my full name in a very, very long time. "Just Cato will do," I finally responded.

"Of course.... Cato," he leaned against the wall and pointed a finger at my matching guns in their black holsters. "Impressive hardware."

"Thanks," I muttered.

He straightened and tilted his head slightly. "Do you know who I am?"

"I know you're called Reverend and you're a preacher man... and you're also a friend of Jed's."

"Yes, and I am hoping to be a friend of yours as well."

"Why?" I asked bluntly.

He smiled slightly. "It's part of what I do."

"What else do you do?" I asked pointedly. "Especially with those scarred up knuckles of yours?"

He glanced down at the hands clasped about his bible, "You don't miss much, do you?"

"It keeps me alive."

"Yes, yes it does." He looked at Thur then back to me. "I'm here to bring the Word of the Lord to the people of Novagant. And to you."

"Pass."

He grinned widely now. "I hear you speak Viking?" he asked in rough axeman tongue.

"I do," I replied in the same language. I wasn't fluent yet, but I was getting pretty good.

"Good," he replied back in English. "I am learning, but it appears you are far ahead of me. Languages don't come easily to me, sometimes I struggle with our own." With a thin smile he moved towards the door. "We may be able to help each other, given time." He glanced at Thur and the axeman nodded at him. "Which you are short on. I suggest you train as hard with their weapons as you no doubt did with your pistols. You're going to need them."

"What for?"

"Can you use a spear?" he asked me unexpectedly.

"No."

He laughed heartily. "You'll learn fast, I expect." He nodded at the Viking across from me. "Thur."

"Reverend," the axeman dipped his head as the preacher left the hut and closed the door behind him.

"What the hell was that about?" I asked Thur, baffled.

"Reverend is here to convert us non-believers to follow his God to this place of Heaven," he chuckled as he fingered the small hammer pendant that hung from a leather cord around his scarred neck. "It doesn't sound nearly as good as Valhalla though... no drinking? No fighting? What's the point? Still, I'll listen. His God may have more to offer than mine."

"Ok. Why did he ask if I could use a spear?"

Thur grinned and handed me one of the two bowls beside him, then picked up his own. "We may be called axemen, but we use the spear as much, if not more."

"So tomorrow I'll be learning to use a spear?"

"You will see."

"Great. Another surprise."

CHAPTER 8

The boat shook as I held onto the edges. I'd been on ships before, big ones, but this longboat was something new. It was long, and the bottom was flat. It was strangely well balanced, except for the dozen Vikings who were intentionally rocking it back and forth with laughter as others used long handled oars to row it forward in the slight waves of the ocean.

Janse stood at the front of the boat, laughing manically as he held onto the carved prow of a half-naked woman.

"Cato of the Black Plague, today we will see how brave you are."

"What are we doing? Spear fishing?" I asked as Gundar the Wrathful handed me a spear with carved runes along the shaft.

He laughed and shrugged. "To feed a village, it takes many fish. But no, you will not be spearing any fish today." The old axeman grinned and lowered his voice to a whisper. "The others know, but I am certain Janse has not told you what you will be hunting. You will be near their nesting grounds, do not go deep into them. Stay on the edges, when you hear one, back up slowly and wait for it to come to you."

"Hear what? Whose nesting grounds?" I didn't like the sound of that.

He winked. "You will know soon enough. And be careful with that spear, it is my favorite."

It'd been an interesting morning already.

As the early morning sun glinted off the waves, we made our way across the beach to the longboats pulled ashore past the high tide mark where we'd run into Ajar.

Ajar was the axeman that Thur had mentioned to me my first morning here. The warrior who'd traveled across the sea and somehow returned, alone, naked, and stark raving mad.

He had cackled wildly as he squatted amongst the tall grasses by the boats as we walked down the beach. The mad Viking wore a breech cloth of sorts, a strip of cloth fashioned around his waist, and with his teeth wrenched a strip of flesh from a large, cracked crab shell.

The other axemen ignored him as we walked, but curious, I slowed and moved away from the group.

Gundar called out to me to not waste my time, but I gave him a wave and stepped closer to the madman.

I'd always found madness to be a curiosity. An infliction often created by suffering. One that I often thought I had myself.

Squatting on my haunches, I looked the madman over from several feet away. His fingernails were broken and dirty, his shaggy, unkempt hair and beard twisted together in filth, but it was his eyes that I lingered on. They were so light blue as to almost be gray. I'd always heard that meant the owner possessed exceptional sight and intelligence.

I didn't know how true that was, but it was something often said.

"What's your name?" I asked gently in his own tongue.

He lunged forward slightly, suddenly. Gnashing his crooked teeth with a mouthful of raw crabmeat.

Surprised, I rocked back on my heels to pull away.

At first, he laughed, almost manically.

But then he saw the knife in my hand, held low before my legs. Had he moved closer, he'd have impaled himself on the blade.

For a moment, the lunatic blinked as the realization sunk in. Then he laughed again and began shifting from side to side.

"You," he whispered, specks of pale meat flying from between his sunburnt and cracked lips. "You," he repeated, "are not one of us."

Considering the fact that I was black and stood out amongst the pale skinned axemen, I could see how he'd come to that obvious conclusion and kept my mouth shut, waiting to see what he'd say next.

"They will eat you," he said softly, his pale blue eyes darting back and forth as though afraid he'd be overheard.

"Who?" I asked, feeling an uncomfortable tingle running down my spine.

"They," he whispered. A trickle of urine streamed from between his legs, splashing against the sand and pooling between his feet. His body shook slightly. He was terrified.

Of what, I knew not.

"Who are they?" I repeated.

"Cato!" Gundar called. "Let's go!"

Startled, I turned my head to see the old Viking walking my way and by the time I turned back, the madman was gone, leaving behind him the gentle swaying of tall grasses from his passing.

"Dammit," I muttered to myself as I slipped the blade back into its sheath and stood. Stepping away from the dropped crab leg and quickly drying puddle of piss, I made my way across the sand to where the axeman leaned against a tall spear.

"What did Ajar the Mad have to say?" he asked while picking up his spear and hurrying with me to catch the others.

I shrugged, too deep in thought to answer. Who would eat me? Surely not the axeman, nothing about them indicated cannibalism. But then what? Pretty damn near everything in Prehistoria would eat a man.

"He's a wild animal," Gundar said before chuckling. "When he first appeared, we tried to talk to him. He'd just cackle and run away. We put food out for him still, but no one wants him inside Novagant."

"He's not allowed inside?"

"No. The first night we found him, we brought him before the old Jarl for questioning. He ran down the streets, screaming wildly and hysterically. Disturbed the hell out of everyone. For his safety, we brought him outside and left him there."

Considering what I knew of the Vikings, I could see their tolerance for such craziness to be small.

A loud splash of water brought me back to where I was.

Gripping the metal-tipped spear, I watched as Janse waved at the rowers of the boat to stop as the boat glided aground on the rocky beach. The Vikings had rowed for several hours, taking us north of Novagant along the coast, past a large river, and finally to a thick, lush forest edge that lined the rocky beach.

I gripped the spear tighter and looked at the youngsters that I'd trained with the other day; they were doing their best to look excited, but I could feel the underlying tension of terror.

Whatever this spear training was, it was going to suck.

Janse beckoned me forward. Standing carefully with my spear in hand, I worked my way forward, around the rowers, teenagers, and to where the giant psychopath waited. The others watched me walk as though I were doomed.

When I stood before him, he pointed with his spear towards the towering trees and thick underbrush of ferns and vegetation. "What do you see, Cato of the Black Plague?"

"A forest," I replied simply.

"Yes, and life and death. Today, you will learn to use a spear. Not to fight, but to gather." Reaching into the boat, he pulled out an arrow from beneath one of the bench seats. Running his hands along the red feathers, he held it up for us to see.

I got a sick feeling in the pit of my stomach as I realized what we'd be hunting.

Those were raptor feathers.

"Today we gather these. And we will see how brave you are."

One of the younger axemen pulled out a plain shield from where it was stowed alongside the outer edge of the boat and passed it forward to me. It was painted bright white, with a red dot in the center that reminded me of a bullseye.

Taking it in hand, I felt the weight. It was a solid one. Not a training shield, broken and ill-repaired. This one would hold under heavy use.

Janse leaned close to me and lowered his voice. "Feel free to die screaming, Little Plague."

Ignoring the giant Viking, I stepped off the boat and onto the small, pebbled rocks of the beach.

CHAPTER 9

I quickly made my way into the forest as the others disembarked and began to spread out. The youngster axemen all had an advantage; they'd heard of this trial before. They'd prepared and worked with a spear since childhood, probably since they were infants. And here I was, a gunman in a strange land with stranger weapons.

Gripping the rune-carved spear tighter, I promised myself I would not die today.

Slowly moving inland, I took my time as I left behind the scent of the ocean and sound of splashing waves.

Stepping around a thick tree, I heard a horrific scream to my distant right echo through the forest.

I reckoned someone just got eaten.

There was a rustle of leaves before me.

I crouched down on the edge of a small clearing, letting the shield cover my front while peeking around the edge. I didn't know much about raptors, only that I'd killed a few when the apes used them to attack. They were fast, vicious little creatures, and I suspected wild ones were probably even worse.

I glanced to both of my sides; there wasn't much to see but the last thing I wanted to do was get hit by a pack of the bastards. There was nothing before me, except for a single brown rat-like creature that scampered over a fallen log, gave me a dark look, then ducked into a hole in the ground.

Adjusting my grip on the spear, I carefully moved around the clearing to stay in the protection of the trees and undergrowth. Stepping between a large pair of trees, I turned the shield sideways to keep from hanging it up. Something muffled crunched beneath my foot.

Pausing again, I dropped to a knee with another faint crunch.

Setting the spear on the ground, I ran my hand through the fallen fern leaves. My fingertips brushed across something hard and hidden. Digging into the loam, I gripped around it and pulled it out.

It was a partial egg. Cracked unevenly around the edges, and a mottled brown color on the outside. I turned it over and saw the inside was a dark shade of dirty white.

I assumed this meant I was near the breeding grounds for the raptors.

Risking a glance away from my surroundings, I looked down and saw that there was a circular outline in the ground. This had been a nest at some point. But it hadn't been used in some time.

A long furry centipede-looking thing ran over the leg of my pants, and shifting my body weight I flicked it off into the leaves with a tiny thump.

That's when I saw something gleam in the sunlight filtering down through the treetops near my foot.

Keeping my eyes roving on my surroundings, I dug back into the ground with my free hand. This time I touched something cold and sharp.

Pulling it free, I glanced down and saw it was an old seax blade with little bits of rotted wood attached to where the shaft had been. This had been abandoned here for some time. All of the axemen carried one of these short swords hanging on the front of their belt in a sheath.

There was an engraving on one side. I ran my thumb over it, but it was too encrusted with dirt and rust to make out.

With a loud ear-piercing screech, a heavy weight hit my shield from the front, knocking me back against the rough bark on the tree trunk. The old steel point dropped, forgotten in the shock of the stealthy attack.

Claws scraped across the shield, sending splinters flying. A toothed maw snapped shut on the top band, digging into the metal with a shriek. Nostrils on the beast flared, sending the disgusting scent of rotting meat across my face. Red feathers on the top of its head shook as if to tease me.

Using both hands I pushed back against the weight, trying to get the raptor off me to free up a hand to get the spear lying on the ground.

The beast pushed back, its hind legs digging into the ground as the six-foot-long killer of man fought to get around the half inch of circular wood between it and its prey.

I was not in any position to fight. My back was against the tree, my feet tucked behind the shield with most of my body, and both hands struggling to gain room between myself and the beast and not let the feathered little monster twist it out of my grip.

Turning sideways, I used my shoulders to push between the shield and tree, gaining a precious few inches of breathing room.

The shield rotated back and forth in my grip with the feathered head of the raptor as it tried to shake it free. My fingers ached from the death grip I held onto the leather strap with, and I was growing truly pissed off.

Changing tactics, I rose slightly and punched the dinosaur in the face.

It snorted, let go of the shield and screamed before renewing its attack with an increased urgency.

"Okay, bad idea," I muttered as I wrapped my hand around the fallen spear.

I tried to pick up the weapon, unsure of how the hell I was going to use such a long thing in such close quarters.

One of the clawed feet of the beast raked down the shaft, barely missing my fingers, and gouging deep into the runed carved wood of Gundar's spear. The claws caught on the steel-tipped head and ripped the weapon free from my grasp.

"ARGH!" I screamed in frustration, anger, and a little bit of fear of being eaten.

The raptor flung itself against my shield again. This time the black claws of its front arms grabbed the top of the shield, digging into the wood on the backside and narrowly missing my shoulder. I fell backwards against the tree, pinned once again.

My hand landed on something hard and angular.

The old seax blade.

Grabbing it in my fist, I clenched the filthy abandoned steel close to my body.

This was bullshit, I thought.

Janse sent me out here to play axeman with a spear and shield against raptors. The giant of a man knew that a gunman wouldn't know how to use one well enough to be given much of a chance against a prehistoric dinosaur.

And here I was, about to get eaten and prove him right.

From somewhere deep inside me came a crazed thought born of anger, pride, and desperation.

I let go of the shield.

As it was ripped away from me, under the clawed arms and teeth of the red feathered raptor, I lunged forward after the vicious little bastard. A forgotten battle cry from the depths of my ancestral homeland in Africa screaming from my throat as I dove forward with the seax blade held tight.

CHAPTER 10

I walked out of that forest and towards the waiting longboat with the gutted body of a raptor draped across my shoulders.

I was covered in blood.

Most of it dried.

Most of it not my own.

Janse stood at the prow of the boat, a bow held in hand with a quiver of red feathered arrows beside him, watching, waiting. Other axemen lounged nearby; one whittled something that looked like an ape with a stone club. But most were gathered around the two axemen wrestling on the rocky beach. I guessed they'd gotten bored.

None of the other youngsters were back yet. I hoped that meant they were still looking for a raptor to kill and that I wasn't the only survivor of this test.

I stoically kept the heavy dinosaur burden across my shoulders to keep from showing the strain it was putting on me. Instead, I locked eyes with the giant axeman, walked in front of him and dropped the corpse with a wet, meaty thud.

"Ah, the Black Plague returns first," Janse said, as he looked away from me and back at the forest edge. "Victorious over the raptor."

"Odin should be pleased," I told him with a smirk.

He frowned slightly but said nothing.

Gundar walked away from the wrestling axemen and took his spear back from me. With a growl he ran a calloused hand over the fresh gouges from the raptor's clawed foot.

"You've ruined my carved runes. You owe me a fresh shaft."

"It wasn't of much help anyways," I told him while reaching into my belt and pulling out the seax blade I'd found. Dried blood still caked the dirt and rust, even though I'd tried to wipe it clean with fern fronds. "But I found this, and this did the job."

Grunting, he took the broken weapon and looked it over. "There's an engraving," he muttered.

Taking it back, I walked past Janse and the boat to the water's edge with Gundar following. Crouching where the waves splashed against the shore, I moved aside a few handfuls of rocks to get at the gritty sand beneath them. With the black and brown sand, I scrubbed the blade, occasionally dipping the spearhead back into the ocean to clean off loose particles.

At a shout, I glanced behind us and saw a couple of other young axemen making their way towards the boat from further up the beach. One dragged a dead raptor behind him, while the other had what looked like his shirt full of red feathers under his arms from his kill.

"That makes three so far," Gundar said before quickly grabbing the spearhead from my hands.

Surprised, I watched as his brow furrowed and he squinted at the weapon. He held it up, turning it slightly to catch the sunlight and I saw what I'd cleaned off.

It wasn't runes that'd been inscribed into the spearhead.

But a design.

A design of a snake eating its own tail.

Ouroboros.

I turned my hand over and looked at the dark ink tattooed into my brown skin. They'd been created by different artists, but they were the same design.

"It seems the gods remind you of your fate," Gundar said while tucking the broken blade into his trousers. "I'll see to it that it gets a strong handle. You may have need of this soon."

"Thank you."

Another shout from behind us.

Looking back, I saw more axemen youngsters were closing in on the longship. Many of them deprived of raptors or feathers.

"What happens to them?" I asked.

"Those who kill nothing?" Gundar chuckled. "Nothing happens to them. They keep training. This is just a test of the gods to see who they will bless and who they will allow to be eaten."

"So... I didn't have to kill a raptor?"

"Of course not." The old Viking chuckled, "But doing so will rub Janse the wrong way, and I heard what you said about Odin being pleased with your kill. Janse will fret for days over this feat."

Shaking my head in wonder, I scooped up water and began to try and wash off the caked raptor blood from my skin and clothing.

I was going to need a bath, and as the salt water stung harshly in a few places, I realized I was going to need a few stitches as well.

"When Janse did this... did he get a raptor kill?" I asked Gundar, hoping I'd bested the giant axeman.

My hopes were dashed as he rewarded my question with a sly grin. "He got two."

CHAPTER 11

Walking through Novagant back to the hut, I ran into Jed and Reverend. I was in the market. There was lots of trading going on around me, folks working with all sorts of bartered goods, including some modern things like pieces of glass and canvas. I was still a little wet around the edges from trying to clean myself off. The sun beating down on me tried to dry me out, but it fought a slow battle against the humidity of the air.

"I see you didn't die," Jed said as he shifted that big rifle he always carried on his shoulder.

"Don't miss a thing, do you?" I replied sarcastically while reaching out and tapping the Sheriff badge that was pinned to his vest. "Looks like they'll give anyone a badge these days. Even outlaws."

"I've been pardoned," Jed replied testily. "I'm not an outlaw anymore."

"Don't ask me to pretend the sun ain't shining," I squinted my eyes up into the bright sky in sarcasm.

A low animalistic growl came from Jed's scowl and his fingers curled into a fist. "Says the man who protected a Union raider for decades."

"How are you, Cato?" Reverend asked quickly, as if to cut off any potential fights between me and my brother.

"I'm alright." Ignoring my brother's barb, I dipped my head at the new Sheriff inquiringly while asking the Reverend, "Why's he here?"

"Building good relations with Whitesberg's neighbors," Jed answered in annoyance.

"You do that by killing Mr. White?" I asked him point blank.

The man of faith sighed and tapped his worn bible against his thigh, obviously not pleased with the direction the conversation was going.

"No," Jed said simply.

"That a fact?"

Jed squared up to face me. "The Maxim machinegun that fell on top of him killed him. All I did was watch him die, with great satisfaction."

I slugged him in the mouth.

It was a short right jab, not a lot of strength behind it, but enough to bust his lips and piss him off.

He staggered back, surprised.

I glared at him but waited as he unslung his fancy rifle, handed it to the Reverend, and then removed his badge. Clenching his fists, he raised them as a trickle of blood dribbled down his chin. "Bold move, Cato. Let's see if it pays off."

"Now gentlemen, there's no need for-" the Reverend began.

"There's every need for it," I replied before leaping forward and swinging my fist at my brother's face.

He jerked his head to the left, trying to dodge my blow, and my clenched fist glanced off the side of his skull.

A sharp pain burst from my freshly healed ribs as he punched me in the side.

"Ooof," I gasped while grabbing him by the shirt and pulling him in tight.

We were in close now, trading blow for blow.

I had a grip on his collar and was slamming my fist into his face over and over, while he had a hold of my black shirt and pounded me about the ear.

Staggering about clinging to each other, my leg managed to get behind his somehow and realizing it, I shoved my brother backwards, tripping him.

We fell together. I on top and him pinned below.

I thumped him in his left eye socket with a hammer fist.

Grunting, Jed bucked his hip upwards, making me lose my balance as he rotated under me like a slippery ass snake.

Next thing I knew, he was on top.

I grabbed him by the throat, pushing his head up and away from mine as his fingers clawed at my eyes.

"Are you two done yet?" A sharp feminine voice cut through the pounding blood in my ears.

Jed shook his head, seemingly coming to his senses and letting go of me, he lumbered to his feet.

Hawking a glob of bloody spit into the flattened grass, I realized there was quite the crowd of onlookers that'd gathered around us. One of them caught my eye as a head turned away and a long braid of hair tied with a blue ribbon pushed through the crowd away from us.

Elsha.

A hand reached down to help me up. Grabbing it, I saw that the Reverend was bent over me, a concerned look on his face.

"If you two idiots don't stop this nonsense..." he warned as he pulled me to my feet. "One of you is going to kill the other."

"That's the point," I mumbled while wiping the back of my hand across my face.

A mix of sweat and blood dripped off.

Looking at Jed, I saw Skyla had appeared from amongst the crowd, touching her fingers to a shallow cut on his check. It'd been her voice I'd heard asking us if we were finished.

A glint of light came from her hand, and I realized she was wearing a wedding ring.

"Congratulations on the wedding," I said while picking up my black hat and knocking the dirt off it. "I suppose I wasn't invited for a reason."

"We didn't know where you were," Skyla snapped. "And you threatened to kill me once, so you weren't exactly high on the invitation list."

"Fair enough."

Thur pushed through the throng of people that'd gathered around to watch us roll in the dirt.

"Ah, Huck Berry the Heart Eater," he said in English while dipping his head respectfully towards my brother who was reaffixing the tin badge back on his vest.

"Just Jed will do. Or Sheriff."

I snorted in amusement at the thought of him being a lawman. Fate had a sense of humor.

Thur turned to me and switched to his native language. "Fighting again? Is Janse not enough enemy for you?" He chuckled. "We'll make an axeman of you yet. Speaking of which, another lesson with the axe awaits."

Groaning, I tipped my hat towards Skyla and turned my back on Jed and the Reverend.

I was getting better with an axe and shield. Wielding them was coming more naturally to me over the weeks, but I still preferred guns.

I started to make my way through the displaced crowd, back to the training fields, when another axeman stepped in front of me with a raised hand. It was Asger, the right hand to the Jarl himself, and another friend of Jed's. The dark bearded Viking wore a pistol in addition to his sword.

Sighing, I wondered what now.

"Training can wait. Jarl Mikah would have a word with you."

"About what?" Thur asked, stepping beside me.

"You know what about." Asger jerked his chin towards me. "He's eaten our food, drank our mead, and trained with our children over the past weeks. He is healed. It's time he carried his weight."

"Ja." Thur dipped his head, then turned to me. "Remember your manners when you speak with the Jarl. But also remember that he is berserker first and a Jarl second."

I'd seen the Jarl a few times, but never up close. The one-armed Viking had never seemed interested in me before.

"Where is he?"

"In the Great House," Asger replied. "I will walk with you."

Thur nodded at me to go with the other Viking. "Janse's beatings can wait."

"Ah, Janse is training you? Good! You will learn much as your body hardens," the other Viking said with a broad smile. "Now, come."

CHAPTER 12

We walked together to the Great House on the highest hill inside Novagant. I'd never been in it before but had heard it was where a thing called a *thing* was held. A thing was some sort of great meeting between the axemen, where feasts were had, decisions made, disagreements settled, and challenges laid out. There had been only one thing since I'd been here, but as a non-Viking, I hadn't been invited.

Asger leaned against the heavy door and pushed it open before we stepped inside.

The inside was enormous and open with rows of tables, benches, and carved pillars holding up the roof. At the far end sat something of a throne. Not the sort a king in the past would have used, made of gold and jewels. This was made of hand carved wood and draped with dinosaur hides.

On it sat the only other person in the entire room, Jarl Mikah.

The one-armed axeman king held a horned cup in his hand and took a sip as he watched us cross the open room to stand before him.

"Honored guest, Cato of the Black Plague, it is a pleasure to meet with you," he said in the axeman tongue.

The thought crossed my mind that maybe I should kneel, or curtsey, or whatever someone does when meeting with Viking royalty, but then I figured I'd just do what we do in any saloon back across the Shimmer.

I dropped my chin respectfully and grunted in return.

Asger walked to the nearest bench and sat, adjusting his sword as he did so.

The Jarl smiled down at me. "Cato of the Black Plague-"

"Just Cato will do."

"Ah, yes. Cato. We will speak simply. You have eaten our food, healed in our homes, and trained with our warriors. Now we have need of you in return."

I reckoned now the other boot was about to drop and braced myself for it.

"When I became Jarl, I pledged to my people that we would cross the sea and expand. We tried once before, and only Ajar returned." He sighed and looked down at the cup in his hand. "I've known Ajar since we were boys together. He was one of the few who treated me as an equal with this," he gestured towards his missing arm. "He was a splendid warrior, a berserker who rivaled and occasionally bested me... and to see who he has become... the others call him Ajar the Mad now."

With a growl, the Jarl hurled the cup across the great hall. The horned container smashed to the ground, spraying mead and clattering against a table leg.

Asger wiped a frothy speck off his trousers.

"I will not let his name be ruined in vain," the Jarl continued with a shout. "The sacrifice of his mind will not go unanswered." Grabbing his sword from where it rested against the wooden throne, he swung the blade around to point at me with it. "We will cross the sea. We will find out what happened to the other ships, and we will conquer whatever lays before us. And you, Cato, will help us make it so."

"I will do this," I said grimly. I had expected as much. I was only good at one thing, killing. And since I was here and on my own with nothing to do, I might as well do what I'm best at.

Jarl pointed towards the black bearded Viking still sitting on the bench. "I will announce it tonight. We will send four ships across the sea to discover what happened. Asger, Thur, Janse, and Elsha will sail the ships, with Asger in charge overall."

Asger dipped his head in response to the Jarl's command.

"And me?" I asked, dreading the thought of being placed on Janse's boat for a long trek across the water.

"You will be on Thur's ship. He has vouched for you. Thus, you will fight with him."

"Good. Just one more question. Can I bring my guns?"

The Jarl grinned wickedly. "Yes."

CHAPTER 13

Later that evening, I sat in the Great House with the others towards the back. At the far end was the empty throne of the Jarl. The multitude of windows that lined the walls were open, letting in fading sunlight and fresh air. The benches were full of men and shield maidens drinking mead, laughing, and talking loudly.

Thur sat beside me, a horn of mead in his hands and a smile on his lips. I'd already told him what the Jarl wanted with me, and my axeman friend was ready to get on with the glory that came from conquest.

We waited impatiently as Jarl Mikah made his way through the entrance and to the raised platform where everyone could see him.

There was an air of excitement in the room.

Everyone either knew why we were here or had guessed it. We'd been selected by the Jarl himself to make the voyage across the sea to see what had become of the previous axeman expedition.

The Jarl raised his hand and quieted the room before beginning to speak.

"You have all been chosen, for your bravery and tenacity, for your willingness to fight, to overcome, and to explore." He paused for a moment as the crowded hall strained their ears for his next words. "Now you will have your chance. We do not know what awaits us across the sea, but it defeated four boats of warriors, and the only survivor came back with his mind gone. Tomorrow, we send four more boats. And I am confident that where the others failed, we will succeed." He raised his hand and pointed to the side where Asger stood leaning against a rough sawn pillar. "And the warrior who will lead you, is Asger!"

The crowd erupted in cheers and banged their cups against the tables. The Viking was well known and appeared to be well liked.

"His second," the Jarl continued, "will be Janse Borison."

Thur swore under his breath as he dutifully raised his fists and hammered the top of the worn table with the others in the room. He leaned over slightly towards me, "Watch your back, Cato. He will not tolerate anyone stealing his glory in battle or otherwise."

"He can have it all."

"And Elsha?" he asked wryly with a jerk of his head towards where the beautiful shield maiden sat with her sisters.

The pounding of fists stopped and Janse and Asger moved to stand beside the one-armed Jarl.

I stared at Thur, grateful that my dark complexion hid the embarrassed rising heat from my cheeks.

"I've seen the way you look at her. He looks at her the same," he whispered, a bit drunkenly.

Nonchalantly, I shrugged and took a long swallow of the mead that I'd left undisturbed on the table.

The Jarl waved his hand at Asger. The black-haired Viking stepped forward dutifully and shouted, "Men and women of the axe, sword, and spear. Enjoy your night, for tomorrow, we sail!"

Shouts and cries came from the men and women. Some hilarious and others coarse, with most of both coming from the table filled with shield maidens.

After a moment, Janse stepped forward, his great axe resting on his shoulder. He cast an imposing figure in the Great House. Even with a fire burning brightly and the shutters thrown open, shadows were cast upon his face menacingly.

Effortlessly, he raised the axe horizontally until the upper tip of the curved blade pointed at the crowd. "And glory we shall have! We will return victorious, with new lands to expand to and any riches we find. By my axe and Odin's beard, I swear it!"

Fists pounded tabletops again. Louder this time, creating a thunderous roar of approval.

Asger waited for the applause to die down while giving a grim look. He faced his chosen subordinate of the expedition. "And survivors? You forgot to mention them."

"Ah, trouble with the leaders already," Thur murmured drunkenly.

"Yes, yes. We will bring back any of our stranded brothers and sisters," Janse said dismissively as he swung the large weapon back to his shoulder.

"If they live," Gundar muttered from beside me.

"And the outsider? The gunman? Why does he sit with us?" Elsha shouted while moving to stand by her bench.

I stared at her.

Damn, she was beautiful.

And she was talking about me which was rather shocking.

Thur began to rise in my defense, but Jarl Mikah waved at him to sit back down. "Cato of the Black Plague is a great warrior of the gunmen and as such, has a place amongst us."

Janse scoffed and shook his head behind the Jarl as there was much muttering and talking amongst the tables of men and women.

"He is worse than the children with shield and axe!" Elsha laughed.

Without thinking, I stood swiftly to my feet.

"I am not one of you!" I roared to be heard over the mass of voices. It worked, and the room went silent as every face turned towards me. "But I am here at the Jarl's invitation, and in return for your hospitality, I have offered my services as a killer of both men and ape. I too wish to see this other side of the ocean and what awaits us and am willing to journey there with you."

Elsha scowled as our eyes met and I hoped she didn't realize that she was the reason I wanted to go. Even after all these weeks, we'd never spoken to each other. But I'd seen her, watched her train with her sisters, and watched her scowl in my direction whenever our paths crossed.

Thur was right, I had it bad.

"Why Cato of the Black Plague? Why should we trust you? When you were found, you were walking away from battle," Elsha retorted with a snort.

"I was knocked off a wall by a dragon," I replied. "After we killed dozens of apes with the Maxim machine gun."

"Ah yes, another gun. An unhonorable weapon," Janse said, egging me on as he scratched a fingernail against his large axe head.

Asger crossed his arms and watched with amusement. The Jarl had the same look. They both appeared curious as to how I was going to convince the other axemen that I was worthy of taking another Viking's spot on this expedition.

"A challenge then, to prove myself," I suggested.

"How?" a voice shouted from another table.

"We don't have time. We leave in the morning!" cried another axeman.

"Careful, Cato," said Thur with a hiccup. "You're asking warriors for a challenge. That's quite the invitation for honor, glory, and dismemberment."

Gundar leaned over to me, "Try a duel."

That was more of my style.

"Then a duel perhaps!" I shouted, thinking of how fast I was with my pistols. No one could beat me. Especially in Novagant.

The room went quiet for a moment, before erupting in a roar as dozens of men shouted agreements, challenges, and others shouted I was unfit to duel an axeman.

Janse began laughing heartily.

That concerned me.

Jarl stood and raised his hand to quiet the room. Then he grinned broadly, "A duel it shall be!"

Drunkenly, Thur climbed on top of the table. "Someone! Get a hide!" he cried out before staggering back down.

Gundar pounded his fist against his chest, and slowly the entire room began to as well. A loud drumming noise filled the interior of the Great House.

"What's going on?" I asked, suddenly concerned. I'd never seen them do this before.

"We're all offering to fight you."

"Why? No one can beat me with pistols."

Thur laughed so hard that mead came spilling from his nose as he choked on the drink. Gundar reached over and slapped him on the back, while also roaring with laughter.

"Pistols? Axemen don't duel with pistols!"

"Aw, shit," I muttered to myself.

CHAPTER 14

At first it looked like there'd be mass bloodshed over who got to duel me. But finally, the Jarl got involved and narrowed it down to the leaders of the boats. Janse, Asger, Elsha, and Thur.

I'd duel one of them, axeman style.

Gundar brought out a fistful of straws with one short and the rest long. Whoever draws the short straw wins the right to fight me.

It was Gundar that had to bring them, as Thur was already passed out on the table. My friend was snoring loudly, with his face lying in a small puddle of mead and drool.

I hoped it was him. I could probably take a drunk axeman...

And heaven help me if it was Janse. He'd probably decapitate me out of spite should the opportunity arise.

And if it was Elsha? Well, as long as I didn't have to kill her, fighting her might actually be fun. Unless she chopped me apart, I realized sourly. I didn't even know what the rules were. Is it to the death? Surely not...

Tables were moved back, spilling mead and drunken axemen as they pushed them aside. Another Viking brought in a large dinosaur hide. From the coloring, it appeared to be from a trike of the sort that the apes rode.

The hide was spread over an open space on the floor.

Other axemen produced all sorts of weapons to be laid on the hide. I swallowed hard as I watched pairs of spears, axes, swords, and the short sword seaxs. Some smartass even laid down a pair of carved wooden forks. Two brand new shields were brought in, unpainted still, but combat ready and of a far greater sturdiness than the training shields I'd become accustomed to breaking on Janse's axe.

Gundar held out a clenched fist filled with four straws.

I watched as Elsha grabbed the first straw and pulled it out. A long straw.

She threw it down and shouted something in axeman tongue that I hadn't learned yet. Probably the sort of thing that'd make a gunwoman blush.

Janse selected the next straw with his thick fingers. His hand looked large enough to completely cover Gundar's.

Another long straw.

"Odin is on your side today, Cato of the Black Plague!" he shouted with a laugh while tossing the straw over his shoulder.

I dared to breathe as Asger pulled the next straw. If he pulled another long straw, that would make Thur the holder of the short. I glanced at the unconscious axeman. Someone had brought a bucket of water and was standing ready to wake the man if needed.

Asger pulled the short straw.

He roared with happiness and the Viking with the bucket dumped it over Thur's head anyways.

"Wake, fool!" he shouted as my axeman friend sputtered awake. "Or you will miss the duel!"

"Is it me?" he asked drunkenly. "Do I fight the gunman?"

"No. Asger."

"Ahh, good," he burped before shouting, "more mead!"

CHAPTER 15

The Great House had turned into a mad house. Drink was flowing wildly. Word had quickly spread through Novagant what was happening; there wasn't a window in the building that didn't have a dozen faces peering through in excitement.

I glanced at Thur.

Once again, my axeman friend had passed out on the table.

Luckily Gundar stayed with me to help explain the rules, which were few and simple.

"First rule is don't get killed," the old Viking chuckled. "Second rule, you fight until someone's blood is spilled onto the hide. You don't have to kill Asger, just bleed him a little. And there are no other rules."

"Do we just grab whatever weapon we want?" I asked, looking at the array of them laid out on the hide.

Asger moved to his place on the far side. He had stripped down to the waist. The Viking's body rippled with inked muscle.

I decided to keep my shirt on. Anything that might help keep my blood in seemed like a good idea.

"No. The crowd decides what weapon you get."

I withheld a groan. There was no telling what that would mean.

One of the shields was passed to Asger while the other was pushed into my hands. I gripped the leather band on the inside tightly, moving it from side to side to get a feel for the heft of the defensive tool.

Jarl Mikah stepped onto the trike hide laying across the rock floor and raised his hand to quieten everyone down.

The room grew somewhat quiet. I think most of the axemen and women were too intoxicated at this point to manage completely shutting up.

"For Cato of the Black Plague… axe!" he said loudly.

The crowd booed and jeered, and only a couple of warriors shouted and raised their hands into the air to show support. As I looked around, I saw one of those hands jerked down by the Viking's friends in a fit of laughter.

I glanced back at the hide. That had been my better option.

"Spear!"

"Seax!"

"Sword!"

"Fork!"

And there it was. The crowd had already decided as they'd observed the weapons. In a burst of noise fit to shake the entire building, dozens of hands went up whereas for the previous weapons there had been few, if any. Elsha and Janse were the loudest, and I found myself more annoyed at that than bothered by what weapon I'd be dueling with.

"So be it!" The Jarl scooped up a fork.

Keeping my face as impassive as possible, I accepted the tiny carved utensil.

The Jarl then repeated the options for Asger. At first, it looked like I'd be facing an axe with my fork. But at the last offered weapon, the crowd went wild again.

Jarl Mikah passed the small weapon to Asger who raised it overhead as if already claiming victory.

Fork to fork it would be.

"You don't have to kill him, just get him to bleed on the hide," Gundar was telling me.

"With this?" I hissed as I shook the eating utensil at him.

"I don't know who laid out the forks, but my helmet is off to them. It was a grand idea," he replied. "This is the sort of duel that will be spoken of for some time... so long as you make it fun for everyone watching." He looked at me sharply. "You don't bleed easily, do you?"

I didn't answer. I was staring down at my fork and shield and trying to come up with a strategy.

I couldn't.

Except beat and stab away at the Viking until I got lucky.

CHAPTER 16

Jarl Mikah quieted the crowd down again. "Axemen and women... the duel will continue until the first drop... or the first spray... of blood is spilled! BEGIN!"

Asger roared and rushed towards me with his shield in front of him as the crowd went nuts.

Rising to the challenge, I raised mine slightly, put my shoulder behind it and ran at him screaming my name since no one else was.

Shield crashed against shield, and we both rocked back slightly, then planted our feet and pushed mightily against each other. The crowd roared around us.

Asger had better footing and vastly more experience than I, and I felt myself beginning to be pushed backwards.

Swearing, I pushed back harder.

My muscles strained and veins popped out as I fought to overpower the Viking.

It wasn't happening. I couldn't. I wasn't strong enough.

I stepped back abruptly, letting Asger's weight come forward unexpectedly.

As he moved towards me, I twisted my shield about and tried to let him go past me.

He was quick though. As his shield thrust forward, he twisted about to keep it between the pair of us. Wood scraped against wood, and I stumbled backwards, finding myself off balance.

Falling, I was caught by a laughing axeman with a braided beard. He shoved me back onto the dinosaur hide as Asger took the moment to smack a horn of mead out of the startled hands of an axewoman and in my direction.

My raised shield caught the alcohol and kept it from going into my eyes.

Apparently, Gundar was right, there really were no rules here.

Wood dripping, we slammed together again, and I could smell the stench of mead. The floor was growing slippery from it dripping off my shield.

He knocked me back again, this time sending me sprawling against a table.

I took my time getting back up as he raised his shield and fork and shouted with the crowd for my downfall.

Seeing a lit candle wobbling on the table, I took a chance and twisted my shield around to touch the flickering flame.

My hunch was correct.

With a violent whoosh the outside of my shield lit on fire.

Axemen and women jumped back to get away from me as I stood back up and swung the flaming shield before me and advanced towards Asger.

He began moving backwards, his loud boisterous shouts gone and his face now stern and serious as he watched my burning shield.

I had the momentum, so I pressed my luck and charged forward.

He ducked as I thrust the steel edge forward of my shield and splintered part of his. As he hunkered down defensively, I continued to use my shield to beat and batter away at his. Pieces broke and fell.

For a moment, through a small, cracked sliver, I saw one of his eyes peeking through. It was large and fearful.

That motivated me to continue bashing away.

Finally, with a great swing of my shield, I smacked his to the floor. It landed in front of the Jarl, and I realized the room had gone quiet.

Snarling, Asger raised his fork and began to charge my flaming shield as I hurled my wooden utensil at his face.

It struck him squarely between the eyes before falling to the floor.

Blinking rapidly, he paused his attack in shock.

And as he shook his head, a single drop of blood fell from his right nostril and landed on the hide.

"Huzzah!" shouted Thur drunkenly before the room erupted. Gundar was suddenly at my side, slapping my back hard while shouting in my ear that I'd won.

I stood in shock, looking around the room as the flames dwindled off my shield as the last remnants of the mead was burned away.

"Well done!" Asger yelled, as he threw his fork into the crowd behind him and embraced me in a bear hug.

"You've earned your place, gunman," he said into my ear as a trickle of blood dribbled down from his nose onto his chin. "And this was a duel that will long be told of."

Jarl grabbed my arm and lifted it. "Cato of the Black Plague has proven his worth and will sail tomorrow with Thur! Let no man or woman doubt his courage or cunning."

Looking around, I saw Elsha's beautiful face wearing a scowl as she turned, pushed through the crowd, and walked out of the Great House.

CHAPTER 17

The next morning, my pistols were wrapped carefully in oil-soaked cloth in their holsters and tucked away into the center of my bedroll. Thur managed to find me a Viking equivalent of a slicker and I wrapped the guns and blanket inside to keep them dry from ocean spray. The bundle would go into my sea chest that I'd sit on as I helped row when needed.

I wouldn't be able to get to them quickly, but once we sighted land, I'd dig them out and strap them on.

But I wouldn't be completely unarmed, I'd have my axe and spear. My plain, unpainted shield was attached alongside the outside of the longboat. It was tradition that it would remain unpainted until I had proven myself in battle with it. Mine wasn't the only one, there were several other unpainted shields from youngsters split amongst the boats.

My boots I'd left behind in the hut. I'd be going native for this trip and wearing the hardened leather shoes of the axemen. Riding boots wouldn't help me cross an ocean or fight on foot. And we weren't taking any mounts. Trikes wouldn't ride well in the narrow, shallow bottom boats for such a distance as we were expecting. Horses would probably work, but they didn't have any.

I did keep my black cowboy hat. I wasn't about to leave that behind.

A massive group had gathered to see us off. It appeared that almost everyone in Novagant had come to the docks by dawn. The atmosphere was a festive one, children were playing and laughing, women hugging their men goodbye, and the ones not picked for the expedition grumbled loudly that they should have been chosen. For those I'd be making the adventure with, there were many loud boasts of glory to be returned from whatever we found across the ocean. And should it be a civilization, then there would be many spoils brought back.

I thought it was bold considering we didn't know what we'd be facing. And in this crazed prehistoric world full of strange dead civilizations, there was no telling what we might come across.

Thur and I had spoken in length about what we may find. Neither of us were convinced that it would be just apes or men. Ajar had fought apes many times before, they wouldn't have turned the man mad. And men? What men could possibly have done such a thing to him? It didn't seem possible.

So, what then?

We didn't know. The only hint I had was what Ajar had told me weeks ago when our paths crossed on the beach. His mysterious claim that *they would eat me.*

From the crowd, I saw a pair of cowboy hats making their way towards me. The figures wearing them pushed through a throng of children playing with carved wooden axes and swords and stood before me.

I straightened slightly, facing the two taller men.

"Cato."

I stared at my former brother, turned former outlaw, turned current lawman. It was still a hard concept to grasp, that the man who stood before me was now a Sheriff. Fate wove a strange pattern with him.

But I supposed the same could be said for me.

Eugene stepped forward and clasped a hand to my shoulder. "Good to see you, son."

"You too," I said, stopping short of calling him father. It still felt strange to think that my father was alive after all these years.

Jed scuffed the toe of his boot in the sand for a moment, obviously uncomfortable. "We ah, brought you something," he said while our father passed me a leather scabbard with the open end flipped over and tied off.

"We aren't sending you off without proper weaponry to defend yourself," Father stated firmly as I took the heavy bundle. I looked over the scabbard; it was a simple leather wrapping, but from the smell and feel, it'd been heavily oiled and waterproofed.

Unsure of what to say, I turned it around in my hand, carefully rested the barrel end on my axeman footwear and untied the leather thongs that held the flapped end closed. From within I drew the hefty rifle out into the early morning sunlight by its walnut stock.

No, I realized.

Not a rifle.

A shotgun.

But of a design I'd never seen before.

Puzzled, I stared at it. The wood stock was familiar, but beyond that, the rest looked strange. There was a sharp hump where the receiver met the wood, and a knob jutted out from the right side of the weapon. The only reason I knew it was a shotgun was from the thickness of the barrel that extended past the tube underneath it. It was impossibly large for a rifle.

Jed smiled slyly at my baffled stare. "This is a new design of John Browning. Not just a shotgun, but a *repeating shotgun.* Like my rifle it's the first of its kind. From what I gather from Carson Skinner, the contract is still being negotiated for its production. Things aren't going well with Winchester, so it's likely someone else will be making it. But regardless, he's calling this the Auto-5 because it holds five shells."

Tossing the empty scabbard over my shoulder to keep it out of the sand, I tucked the shotgun into my shoulder and aimed away from the crowd into the open ocean. The heavy weapon settled naturally into my hands.

"12 gauge?" I asked, judging by the thickness of the barrel.

Father chuckled. "No, son. 10 gauge."

My jaw dropped slightly. This thing was going to kick like a beast. But it'd also hit like one too.

"Don't expect them to be produced in 10 gauge, this was just a test creation of Brownings to see if he could build it. They'll most likely be mass produced in smaller gauges." Jed hefted a leather satchel. "Got you some ammunition as well."

Father frowned. "Where you're going, there won't be any support except for what you have with you. No more reloads except what you brought. So, we brought you a shit ton of 'em. But you only got the one shotgun-"

"Which means don't lose it," Jed cut in.

I looked from one to the other, then back to the weapon in my hands. I could shoot a shotgun and rifle, of course. Reydan had seen to that during my upbringing. I just never carried either one often because I preferred my pistols. But this... this was something new and powerful.

"Thanks," I mumbled awkwardly.

"You're welcome," Jed said with a dismissive wave. "Now, I've got to go see the Jarl about a couple of his axemen eating someone's cow." As he turned to leave, he glanced over his shoulder at me. "Good luck, Cato."

Father and I watched him push back through the crowd until his brown and battered cowboy hat was no longer in view.

"He means well," he said.

"He's still an asshole."

"Yeah, well, he thinks the same of you," he laughed before turning to face me, suddenly serious. "I want you to promise me you'll come back. I lost you once. I don't want to have to cross a damn sea to find you again."

My throat suddenly felt constricted, and I looked away and coughed slightly to loosen it. "Don't worry about me. Jed's the one who needs babysitting."

"Yeah, I know. He's always been the hot-headed one."

We stood in silence, surrounded by family members saying goodbye to loved ones. We were still strangers, but we shared a bond of sorts, one that seemed as though nothing could break it. I supposed the same was true of Jed and myself.

Eugene coughed uncomfortably, "Look, son, if you ever want to talk about what happened after Reydan took you…"

"No," I said sharply, regretting my tone immediately. "No," I repeated, softer this time. "Water under the bridge."

"Sure, Cato… sure." Father's eyes had moistened, and he blinked rapidly. He looked down at the boat I was standing in. "You got somewhere to keep this?" He lifted the lumpy bag of shells with a grunt.

I took it from him, surprised at the heft of the satchel. They weren't kidding, from the feel of it, they'd filled it to the brim with shotgun shells.

"Got some ammunition for your pistols in there as well."

"How'd you know what caliber?"

"I've been shot with a .44 before." He rubbed his chest. I knew the bullet was still in there somewhere, rattling around inside him. I'd shot him twice, but the Doc was able to only pull out one.

I winced.

He laughed heartily at my reaction. "Just teasing, son. I had Jed sneak into your hut while you were off single handedly fighting raptors and find out for me. By the way, I heard you got one. That's supposed to be pretty big magic with these people. I'm impressed."

"Thanks." I opened my sea chest and pushed in the oiled satchel next to my wrapped pistols. "Thanks for all of this," I repeated, sliding the shotgun back into its scabbard.

Father held out his hand. As we shook hands, he leaned close and whispered, "Illegitimi non carborundum."

I smiled at the family Latin motto and repeated it back in English. "Never let the bastards wear you down."

"Exactly. Take care, son."

"Yes, sir."

He slapped me on the back once, firm and hard enough to sway me as I stood. With a smile, the old gunfighter turned and walked into the crowd and out of sight.

CHAPTER 18

"You ready?" Thur asked as I settled onto my chest in the longboat. There was a steady wind now which billowed out our sail and strained the boat against the ropes tying us to the dock.

"Ready as I'll ever be," I replied grimly while carefully securing the oiled shotgun and scabbard away. It wouldn't do to have the danged thing go overboard before I got a chance to use it.

"At least with this wind we won't have to row anytime soon." He grinned and showed me the underside of his hands. "Axes and shields build thick callouses, but working oars," he grunted a laugh, "those will build thicker skin than a man should have."

"Especially on your backside!" shouted another axeman from the back of the boat who'd already sat down on his sea chest.

The others laughed as they moved about the ship in preparation. The crowd along the port pushed closer, some throwing flowers at us while others smiled and called out to their loved ones, wishing them luck and glory. A man dropped his trousers and mooned us good naturedly while others jeered at who had been chosen to go. One fellow reminded another of a hefty debt he still owed, and that he wasn't allowed to die until he paid it in full.

Jarl Mikah pushed through the crowd until he stood on the planked dock between Thur's boat and Elsha's. Raising his hand into the air, he quieted the crowd.

"People of Novagant! Behold your brave sons and daughters!"

The crowd cheered.

I glanced at the shield maidens' boat. Elsha was standing at the front by the carved woman figure holding a sword in the prow of the boat. She was armed much like the men in my boat, a pair of axes tucked into her waistband, a sheathed sword, and a seax worn across her front.

Her head turned and I realized she was staring back at me.

Swallowing, I looked back toward the Jarl to catch the rest of his speech.

"Those who've gone before will be found. If they are alive, they will return, if they are dead, their vengeance will be swiftly carried out by the blades of their brothers and sisters."

"You will all die!" cackled a loud voice as the crowd murmured and parted.

"Ajar!" the Jarl called, with obvious frustration etched on his face. He looked pained as he searched the crowd for his childhood friend. "Have you something to say of worth?"

The sole survivor of the previous expedition strutted forward as the citizens of Novagant parted, still naked except for the loin cloth covering his privates. Wild eyed, with his unkempt beard and hair, he looked every bit his namesake.

"You..." he pointed a crooked finger at each ship in turn, "are already dead. They will kill you and feast upon your uncooked flesh."

He paused as his gaze fell on me. "You," he laughed maniacally. "Nothing will save your blackened hide. Not even the gods of Asgard!"

Janse stepped off the boat, pulling the protective leather sheath from the tip of his spear and walking across the dock towards where Ajar stood unevenly. "It is time to end his madness, before it infects us all!" he said loudly.

"Janse!" the Jarl shouted at the giant Viking. "No axeman blood will be shed today."

The axeman twirled to face his king, twisting the spear in his hands and pointing the steel tip at Ajar. "He is no axeman! He is a coward! Had he any pride, he'd have died with the others."

Ajar the Mad shrieked angrily and ran at Janse with his teeth bared. Men moved to intercept and grab at him, but the madman was too quick and nimbly dodged them all.

He leapt at Janse as the giant Viking twirled his spear around and slammed the carved wooden shaft against the madman's skull.

I grimaced at the sound of the weapon smacking the side of Ajar's face and dropping him like a sack of potatoes.

"And no axeman nor coward's blood was shed, my Jarl!" Janse called out as the men of his boat laughed.

Jarl Mikah smirked at the giant. "Bind him and take him with you, Janse Borison. He may be of value on your trip."

"For what? Feeding the great fish?" Janse thrust the sheath back onto his spear angrily. "He is dead weight, of no worth or use to us."

"I said take him." The Jarl stepped forward, his lone hand dropping to the pommel of his sword menacingly.

I rose and stepped forward without thinking. "We will take him."

Thur shot a dark look at me, and I realized I'd talked out of place as this boat was under his command.

"If we can get him to talk..." I whispered.

"He could be of use," Thur finished. With a sigh, he stepped up beside me. "We will take him, Jarl."

Janse laughed and nudged the unconscious axeman with his foot. "For what purpose?"

"He spoke to Cato before on the beach. He may speak again," Thur replied.

Jarl dipped his head at us and released his hand from the sword. "He is yours then, Thur Thaneson. Use him as you will."

Janse stepped back into his boat, shaking his head in disgust.

Thur and I moved over to the downed madman and gently picked him up between us. He weighed more than I would have expected, there was still muscle beneath his sun-tanned skin. But he strongly stunk of stale sweat and fish.

Jarl held up his hand as we walked past, and we paused in front of the axeman's leader. "Ajar the Bold was once a powerful warrior and protector of Novagant." The one-armed king untied the decorated short blade across his front and handed it to me. "Remind him, if you can."

"Yes, Jarl," Thur told him sincerely before we loaded the unconscious man into our longboat. We laid him down in front of our benches and sea chests.

Satisfied, Jarl Mikah nodded at Asger, and the Viking shouted at the ropes tying the longboats to the dock to be let loose.

With the sails unfurled, we began to glide away from the docks of Novagant to the cheering and waving of swords and axes from the men and women of the Viking village.

CHAPTER 19

With Novagant in the distance, Thur pulled out several strips of leather from his chest and handed them to me. "Better tie Ajar up, before he wakes."

Stashing the Jarl's fancy seax aside, I took the leather braids and kneeled beside the unconscious madman. With quick movements, I began tying his wrists and feet together. "You think this is necessary?"

"You ever had a madman loose on a boat before? Headed back to the place where he lost his wits?" Thur grumbled.

"Good point," I admitted.

"I hope you didn't take him on just to piss Janse off."

I hesitated a moment, thinking before answering. "No," I said finally. "If we can get him to talk, he can be of help. He's the only man who's been to the other side of the sea."

Ajar's eyes snapped open, and he began thrashing wildly against his restraints and screaming.

"Easy, easy friend," I told him while trying to avoid his kicking, bound feet. He still managed to get a couple of thwacks in with them against my chest and shoulder before I stood and backed away.

"Having a problem?" Janse shouted from his boat as the madman's shrieks filled the silence of the ocean. "Try gagging him!"

Ignoring the giant asshole, I waited until Ajar finished screaming and kicking to help him up.

It took longer than I thought.

But we finally got him somewhat calmed and seated on a bench.

Tears were rolling freely down his sunburnt cheeks and spittle hung from his mouth as his wide eyes roved over our boat and the open waters around us.

I offered him a sack of water. He grabbed it greedily and with tied hands, drank quickly.

Then he threw up.

The disgusting fluids and half-digested foods in his stomach stank horrifically. I gagged at the stench of raw fish and crab meat.

Thur growled, "You're cleaning that up, Cato." Then handed me another sack. "Try this, it's mead."

Shrugging, I handed the new sack to Ajar, and he drank again, this time calmer and with a smaller mouthful.

Licking his chapped lips, he looked from me to Thur as if seeking permission.

"Go ahead... just drink slowly," Thur told him.

The boat rocked gently on small waves as we watched him drink.

I sat on the bench beside him, ready to grab the crazed axeman should he try to leap overboard. "Ajar," I said softly.

He licked his chapped lips and looked at me from the corners of his eyes.

"Ajar, we need your help."

"No. Be eaten, you will. I will. All of us!" His voice rose in fear.

"I won't let that happen. Nor will Thur, or the others."

Thur stepped in front of the madman and looked down at him with a mixture of pity and curiosity. "I wonder what madness he saw on the other side."

"Teeth. Teeth and claws. Slippery and fast. Too many, we couldn't fight them!"

"Fight who?" I said, wondering what sort of dinosaurs could do this to a man.

He burped and took another gulp of mead. Tossing the half-filled sack at Thur, he lay down on his side and closed his eyes. "Fast. So fast," he murmured. "They will eat you."

"We are getting nowhere," Thur grumbled while resting his hand on the top of his axe.

"We still have time," I said, standing in the rocking boat. "How many days do we have? And how do you know there is anything across the sea anyways?"

The axeman stared back in the direction of his home, remembering. "I was with them when we saw land for the first time. We were four days on the water and about to turn about and head back to Novagant. And that's when we saw the land in the distance. It looked another day before we would reach it, and Jarl Mikah, before he was a Jarl, decided to turn us back and gather a force to investigate. That force of axemen is the group that we lost, with only him," he dipped his head at a close eyed Ajar, "to return."

"Did you know any of those who didn't come back?"

He frowned, and in his eyes, I saw a sudden sadness. "Novagant is not so large a place for those born and raised there, Cato of the Black Plague. We all knew those who didn't come back."

CHAPTER 20

The hours on the ocean seemed endless and turned into days. At times the wind would be against us, or not blowing at all, and we would pick up the oars and row. My hands began forming thick callouses almost immediately.

During the many hours of boredom, we played several Viking games and told stories. One of the games involved a wooden board and two sets of figures carved of trike horn. An outnumbered king with a small force would be surrounded by an army and have to navigate his way to safety without being captured.

It was fun to watch, and a few times I tried my hand at it only to lose terribly. Gundar was pretty good at it and was the only one who could thrash Asger at the game.

As for stories, I mainly kept my mouth shut. My past wasn't something I was keen on bragging about, regardless of how much goading came from Thur and the others. They wanted to hear of me killing men and apes, of my guns and what they could do. I stayed mum for the most part, only telling them small bits and pieces to get them to leave me alone.

At night we would pull the four boats next to each other, lash them tight, and enjoy each other's company after a full day of only our own boat to keep us occupied.

I tried talking to Elsha only once, but she gave me a short answer that implied she wanted nothing to do with me.

After a while, I mostly stayed near Ajar. Keeping an eye on him and enjoying the laughter and boisterousness of the Vikings from a slight distance.

The madman kept me occupied though. He tried to jump out of the ship and swim back at one point of madness. Asger's boat was closest, and they grabbed the axeman and tied him up until they could give him back that night.

It seemed the only thing he truly cared for was mead. And Thur wasn't pleased with how quickly Ajar was going through his boat's stash. But it kept him calm, or asleep. So, we kept him supplied as well as possible just to make things easier on the rest of us.

And at times, I would remove the large Auto-5 shotgun from its scabbard and practice dry firing and loading. After hours of doing this, my movements grew fluid and familiar. I caught Elsha watching me from her boat more than once. And I was always very aware of how she thought my guns were a dishonorable weapon. Luckily, the other Vikings seemed to be completely enamored with the guns and all wanted to know how and where to get their own.

We would also practice with axes, seaxs, and spears. Mainly the basics, as we didn't want to risk injuring anyone out here. But I learned more of how to use them and was beginning to feel like I could handle the axeman weapons without completely embarrassing myself.

CHAPTER 21

We seemed to be making good distance, and it was on the fourth day when we encountered the fog.

Ajar shit himself.

Literally.

Then he tried to jump overboard, twice.

After the second time, we tied him to the longship's mast. But after hearing him scream hoarsely for a good twenty minutes about how we'd all be eaten, Thur gave in to everyone's requests and had him gagged.

The man thrashed wildly, contorting his body in painful ways, arching his back, and trying to break free.

"Having some troubles with your madman?" Janse called from his boat with a belt of laughter as we sailed through the tendrils of gray fog that enveloped us like the open arms of a grave.

Staring at Ajar, I didn't laugh nor really hear Gundar's response.

Instead, I quickly turned away and opened my sea chest. Picking up the heavy water protected package inside, I unwrapped my gun belt and quickly slung it about my waist. With both hands I drew the pistols, twirled them, then slipped them back into their holsters. Satisfied that they were loose enough to draw and ready to fire, I reached down and picked up the scabbard containing the Auto-5 shotgun.

"What is it, Cato?" Thur asked, ignoring the giant in the other ship laughing and watching me get ready for battle.

"Ajar," I said, nodding my head in the former warrior's direction while pulling the heavy weapon from its leather scabbard.

He'd gone silent.

But now his eyes were wide as well. He turned his head from side to side, looking about intently.

"Trike shit," Thur murmured, before calling out, "Arm yourselves, men of the axe!"

The Vikings on our boat immediately scrambled about, either unsheathing the heads of spears or quickly stringing bows that'd been stored under the benches. Quivers of arrows were already placed along the inside of the longboat, near the shield-lined exterior. The archers and spearmen shifted into position, looking for a threat.

"What is it, Thur?" Asger called from our left side as we moved closer and closer to the mist.

"I don't know, but I've a bad feeling," he shouted back.

"Feelings? Bah! You've gone as mad as Ajar!" Janse cried as he walked towards the prow of his ship and its carved wooden trike. "It's just mist. All it means is we're likely close to land."

"I don't like your words, you big asshole," Thur said as he picked up his own spear and pulled the sheath off the steel-tipped head.

"Let's pull our boats together, and you can try to do something about it. But be prepared, I throw forks harder than Cato."

"Silence!" Asger shouted.

The men quietened down at our leader's command, and we heard only the creaking of the boats, the flapping of the sail, and a gentle splash from behind us.

Glancing back, I realized our rudder man was missing. The wooden shaft that he used to steer with swayed back and forth freely, and his seat was empty.

Except for his weapons that he'd set beside him.

"Hierto is gone!" I shouted, raising the shotgun to my shoulder.

"Women of the axe, prepare for battle!" Elsha cried from somewhere to my left as we slipped into thicker gray mist.

"Claws and teeth! CLAWS AND TEETH!" Ajar screamed, having worked free one hand, and pulled his gag out.

"Shut your madman up before he infects us all!" Janse twirled towards us, "Or by Thor I shall end him!" He hefted his spear to throw at our boat when something gray launched itself out of the water and tackled the giant axeman.

Thrashing, they fell out of sight to the bottom of the boat.

At the same time, all around us the ocean churned to life as dozens of gray beasts began climbing over the sides of the boats.

Jerking the barrel of the shotgun towards the splash closest to me, I saw what looked like a lizard clambering over the side of the ship.

Even in the muted light peeking through the fog, the scaly greenish silver face was hideous. Black eyes set close together, with two slits for a nose below. A wide mouth gaped open, and a pink tongue slipped over fangs and jagged teeth.

Grabbing onto one of the shields strapped to the boat, it pulled itself over the edge and hissed.

I pulled the trigger and the ugly face blossomed into a red mist as the Auto-5 kicked backwards into my shoulder.

The shotgun blast seemed to set everyone off.

Shouts and screams of men and women echoed through the fog.

Archers loosened arrows into the faces of the monsters while others jabbed with their spears.

But there were so damned many of them.

I shot one that was leaping at Thur's back as he used his spear to fend off an attacker to his front. The ugly lizard flipped out of sight, leaving a splatter of blood on Thur's armor.

This shotgun was amazing, I thought. Five shots, no lever to work, just point and pull the trigger.

With a sadistic grin, I twisted towards the next lizard only to have a clawed hand slap the shotgun from my grasp. The weapon clattered to the floor of the boat.

Kicking the scaly beast in the chest to get some distance, I dropped my hands, drew both pistols, and fired.

The monster toppled over the side with a pair of .44s in it.

"Loosen me!" Ajar roared from the mast behind me.

Without thinking, I spun and shot the back of the mast. The bullet sent splinters flying, but severed the ropes, and freed him from the thick wooden pole and sail.

The madman jerked free, grabbed a fallen spear, and thrust it, screaming, through the back of a lizard clawing at a downed axeman. Wrenching the steel-tipped weapon free, he drew back and hurled it across the boat. It pierced the chest of one of the creatures, and clawing at it, the beast fell backwards off the boat.

I turned away, leaving my back to the mast for what meager protection it offered, and began firing at everything scaly.

Several more lizards died from my bullets before both hammers fell on fired chambers, clicking loudly with no bangs.

I was out of cartridges.

Dropping the pistols into their holsters, I pulled the axe free from my belt.

A heavy weight hit me from the side, knocking me down. Thrashing to get free, I managed to roll onto my back as the lizard dug its claws into my clothing and pierced my flesh. The axe handle I managed to turn sideways and jam between myself and the creature.

Inches from my face, the fangs of the lizard separated. A pink forked tongue flicked over my face, rotten breath stinking of fish and salt water.

"Fear," it hissed.

I was shocked. Not only that it was speaking, but that it was speaking Latin.

Without thinking, I bit the forked tongue as it flicked over my face again.

The salty red muscle thrashed inside my mouth as I clamped my front teeth down as hard as I could and jerked my head from side to side.

Blood filled my mouth as the tongue came free.

Shrieking, the lizard rose with blood streaming from between its open jaws.

An axe cleaved through its skull, and the corpse fell on top of me.

Pushing it away, I dragged myself free while spitting out the slimy lump of flesh and oily blood onto the wooden flooring of the ship.

Ajar stood over me, holding out a free hand.

I took the madman's hand, and he pulled me up.

The battle was over as quickly as it started. Bloody water sloshed in the bottom of the boat from lizard and man alike. I heard splashes and saw several Vikings who'd been jerked into the ocean frantically swimming back to the closest boat.

One disappeared, jerked under the water by a creature.

A Viking hurled another axe, narrowly missing a shield maiden but impaling a lizard that was swimming after her.

Gundar quickly pulled her aboard.

"It spoke to me," I said, checking the tears in my shirt from the beast's claws. They'd dug in enough to cause bleeding, not too deep, but enough to be worrisome for infection.

"They do that," Ajar replied grimly as his pale gray eyes looked around the boat then down at himself. "Where are my clothes?"

"Your clothes?" Thur laughed as he wiped a smear of blood across his face and helped another wounded Viking up. "Madmen don't wear clothes."

"I'm not mad." Ajar looked around at all the staring faces. "At least, not anymore."

"Battle will do that, rattle your senses back and forth," Thur said as he clasped the madman on the shoulder. "Glad to have you back."

"And by Odin's beard, what are we doing here?" the former madman said while picking up a spear. He thrust it towards the thick fog around us. "Going for a sight see?"

"Just a casual sail to opposite shores."

Out of the fog the other boats pulled alongside ours. I stared at Ajar, baffled at the change in the man's personality.

"Don't look at me like that, Cato of the Black Plague," he warned.

"Well, well, it appears the madman survived." Janse's booming voice came from the side as his boat bumped against ours.

"Go mount a trike, Janse," he called.

"Ah! It appears that Ajar the Bold has returned from the land of the lost minds. Good to have you back, brother," the giant Viking growled with sincerity. "Pray tell, what are these dead monstrosities?" He picked up the severed head of one and held it up for all to see. "I lost three men to them."

"Four here," Asger replied as he lashed his boat to ours.

"One sister from our boat," Elsha called from the other side of Asger's boat.

"She's over here," Gundar replied.

Thur looked around the longboat and sighed. "Two dead."

"Cato's gunfire likely helped to scare them off," Ajar replied as he turned over a dead Viking with a face missing and began pulling his clothing off. "They weren't expecting that."

"You didn't tell us what they are," Janse said accusingly before tossing the head into our boat. It rolled against my foot and stopped, pink tongue flopping out from between sharp, pointy teeth.

I kicked it away.

"Lizards."

"What do you mean, lizards?"

"I mean we never had the chance to name the damned things. We were too busy fighting them," Ajar said angrily.

Gundar stabbed the severed head with his spear head and flung it back towards Janse. "Keep your lizard parts in your own boat."

The giant ducked as the lizard head flipped over his shoulder and splashed into the water behind him.

"Stop fooling around," Asger shouted. "Post some guards. The rest of you, clean up, or I'll put my axe up your ass."

Ajar turned his back to the shield maidens' boat and continued stripping the dead Viking of his clothes.

Reaching between a pair of sea chests, I picked up the shotgun and inspected it. The wooden stock had a slight gouge in it, but the metal looked fine. I racked the bolt on the side, ejecting the remaining shells and making sure it worked.

Picking up the shot shells, I inspected each one before reloading into the tube beneath the barrel. Sitting on the bench, I opened my sea chest and dug out several more shells to load into the weapon to top it off.

"That's a mighty fine gun," Thur said, sitting beside me as the other warriors began cleaning up. "I'll trade you my wife for it."

I laughed. "Your wife has one eye."

"Aye, and a beautiful one at that. Or, if you think about it, she'll only see you for as half as ugly as you truly are. But fine, keep your gun. It's likely I'll take it off your corpse before this expedition is over."

I chuckled, then realized he was serious. "Fine. But if you die first, I get that," I pointed at his rune-inscribed axe in his belt. It was a beautiful piece of axeman craftsmanship. Forged and built by the best axe maker in Novagant.

"Deal, Cato." He stuck his hand out and we shook on it.

"Speaking of weapons," Ajar muttered in front of us as he slipped a shirt on. "Whose axe is this?" He pointed at the one sticking out of the skull of the lizard whose tongue I bit off.

"Hjunir."

"Ah, where's he?" He stepped on the toothed face and wrenched the blade free with a sickening suction sound.

I sighed. "Naked. Behind you."

Ajar turned and looked down at the dead axeman he'd stripped. "Oh, well he won't have any need for this either then." He hefted the blade. "Not as fine as my old one, but it will do."

"That reminds me. Jarl Mikah gave us something for you," I reached under the seat and pulled up another wrapped bundle. Tossing it to the Viking, he caught it one handed and raised an eyebrow quizzically at me.

Unwrapping the seax, he whistled as he looked the decorated short blade over.

"This is certainly Mikah's." He sat on the sea chest across from me and Thur. Running a thumb lightly over the blade, he looked at the drop of blood that it cut with satisfaction. "He traded three captured ape trikes for it to be forged." With a frown he looked from the seax back towards us. "This is fit for a Jarl... not a madman who failed his brothers and sisters." He sheathed the blade and held it out to Thur.

The axeman reached out and gently pushed the weapon back at Ajar. "It is not for you to decide who is worthy of the blade. Jarl Mikah deemed it fit for you. Wield it with honor."

"Truth is in Thur's words," Gundar said from behind me. "Now stop bickering like old women and help us clean this damned mess up."

Laughing, we stood and started grabbing dead lizards.

"How much farther?" I asked Ajar as we tossed another lizard corpse over the edge of the boat.

It sank quickly out of sight, leaving a small red smear on top of the ocean water while vanishing into the depths.

"Not far now."

"When I told you it spoke to me, you said 'they do that'... what did the others say?"

"I don't know. We couldn't make sense of what they were trying to say. In part because we were too busy trying to kill them. But they didn't speak our language," Ajar replied.

"That's because they were speaking Latin. One of them said the word 'fear'... in Latin."

"Odd. And you think I didn't see you, but I did. You bit one of their tongues off," he said accusingly.

Gundar laughed darkly while scooping bloody water from the bottom of the boat. "It seems that you and your brother have something in common after all. You like to eat your enemies."

I glared at him but said nothing.

"How do you know this... Latin?" Thur asked.

"I'm good with languages. And Mr. White liked to speak Latin."

"Good. Maybe you can negotiate the lizards' slaughter," Ajar said. "Wretched things killed over a dozen of us. And took my mind for a bit. I'd like to get even."

"I suspect we will have our chance," I told him sincerely.

"How did you find your way back to Novagant?" Thur asked the former madman as he pulled an arrow out of a lizard, inspected the shaft and red feathers, then set it down to be cleaned and reused.

Ajar paused while reaching down to grab the next corpse. "I... don't know."

"What do you remember?" I asked him before grabbing the legs of the lizard and straining my back to lift the beast. We found out you didn't want to grab them by their short tail, the damn things would come off when you went to pick them up.

"There are gaps in my memories. Or just fragments. I remember bits and pieces..."

"Getting smacked on the head will do that to you," Janse rumbled from the boat opposite us. He hurled a lizard over the side by himself, showing off his strength.

Thur lowered his voice and wiped a bloody and gore-smeared spear tip off on the leathery skinned lizard. "What of those in your boat? Did anyone else survive?"

Ajar looked away and shook his head slightly. "I don't know. I remember rowing through the mists and being attacked by these damn things. And then attacked again once we landed... nothing else."

Thur kept silent. The mystery of the last expedition was personal to him. He'd spoken little of his brother and his brother's wife, but from what Gundar had told me, they'd all been close.

"Land ahead!" came a cry from Asger's boat that was several lengths ahead of our ship. The ocean grew quiet as everyone stopped cleaning up and stared ahead, straining to see through the gray mist.

And then, there it was.

A rocky beach. Gray and brown, and drab looking.

As the boat glided forward, a thick forest edge was revealed past the beach.

No one spoke. We only watched as we sailed closer. I felt like everyone was thinking the same thing… what awaited us ashore?

CHAPTER 22

Leaving the fog behind, we slid the boats onto the pebbled sand. Then, grabbing onto the sides and using our legs to run the shallow bottomed boats up past the high tide mark and onto patches of grass struggling to grow from the gray sand and rock.

There was nothing in sight up and down the shoreline, but the lush, shaded forest ahead of us was inviting to get out of the sun beating down on our skulls and backs.

Ajar walked forward, alone, with a spear and shield taken from the dead Viking in hand and the Jarl's seax strapped across his front. He stared at the shadowed forest edge with a frown.

"Any of this coming back to you?" I asked while approaching him loudly from behind. The man was on edge, and I didn't want a spear tip through my ribs if I could help it.

"Just something about the nights. That's when it's most dangerous here."

"Good to know," I muttered.

"We'll send out a few scouts to check the area around us," Asger was telling the ship captains nearby while gesturing towards a high peak overlooking the sandy beach we were standing on. "But I suspect someone can make it up there and back before dark."

"I'll take three shield maidens and go," Elsha said quickly, as if to speak before anyone else had a chance to offer.

Janse chuckled without humor but said nothing.

Noticing that I was close enough to overhear their conversation, Asger pointed at me with his unsheathed sword. "Cato of the Black Plague. Go with Elsha."

"We don't need him," she hissed defensively.

"He has guns, and unlike most of us, knows how to use them well. Take him."

"He-"

"It was not a suggestion," Asger said, visibly annoyed. "Take him, two of your sisters, and go. The rest of us will begin to build a camp and await your return."

Elsha nodded curtly, then spun and walked away quickly, disgust evident upon her face.

Thur moved to my side, grabbed my arm, and pulled me towards the boats. "Be grateful. You'll be spending time with Elsha while the rest of us are felling and shaping trees."

I ignored the barb about the beautiful shield maiden and answered honestly, "I'm better with guns than axes."

"I know. But be careful. Something wiped out an entire expedition and turned Ajar mad." He pointed a finger at my pistols. "Sending you was a good idea; if we hear those firing, we'll know you're in trouble."

"So, you can send help?"

Thur laughed. "No."

I frowned.

"Well, we won't know where the hell in the nine realms you are," he said defensively. "But we will prepare ourselves for an attack. You'd be saving lives."

"At the cost of my own," I said sarcastically.

"And the gods will look upon that sacrifice favorably, even your Christ Jesus."

Reaching our boat, I pulled myself over the edge and moved back to my sea chest. The shotgun was resting beside it.

I slung it over my back.

"Best hurry," Thur said as he reached over the edge of the boat and picked up a large, bladed axe that he'd brought along for felling trees. "The women are leaving."

Swearing, I leapt over the edge, landing softly in the sand and fast walked after Elsha and her two shield maiden sisters as they left their boat with bows and spears in hand.

Catching up to them, I was breathing heavily from trudging through the loose sand.

"Keep up, Cato of the Black Plague, or we will leave you behind to find your own way," Elsha said over her shoulder without looking back.

Wordlessly, I straightened and followed them into the forest as the sounds of axes chopping into trees echoed from behind us.

CHAPTER 23

The trees here were the same as in Prehistoria I noticed as we trudged through the forest towards the mountain peak in the distance. I hadn't grown up receiving much of an education past what I needed to know to protect Reydan White, but I was observant. That'd saved the man's life a few times. The last time being when my father and his gunman friend tried to ambush him.

Stepping over a raised tree root, I swallowed hard remembering the shock after I'd shot the man twice before recognizing him as my father. I hadn't been very observant then.

Gritting my teeth and pushing the thought from my mind, I looked at the three women in front of me. They were all fearsome warriors. They had to be to be considered a shield maiden and the honor that came with it. Elsha led the way, her thick braided reddish hair thrown over her shoulder, exposing a faint tattoo on the back of her neck that I'd never noticed before. I couldn't make it out as we walked, but I was curious about it and the meaning.

Then there was Ingrid. She was a black-haired warrior of exceptionally plain looks. But her biceps and forearms were corded with sinewy muscle. She talked very little, but I'd heard her laugh once during a particularly hilarious story of Janse's on the boats.

Her laugh sounded like a donkey braying.

After Ingrid came Helga.

Helga had been beautiful... once. As beautiful as Elsha, from what I'd been told. But she was short tempered and quick to fight. The scars over her nose showed where it'd been broken several times, and she was missing a front tooth. Her face was heavily inked, and she looked every bit the savage barbarian Viking woman you would expect.

As I watched she hawked and spat at a large green ant on a leaf.

With uncanny accuracy, the glob of spit knocked it off.

Elsha held up her hand, and I stopped a moment after the shield maidens did.

Quietly unslinging the shotgun, I cradled it in both my hands while straining my ears to hear anything that may be close.

There was only the sound of chittering prehistoric bugs and the distant screech of a pterodactyl.

The leader of the warrior women looked back down at the ground, then knelt.

We moved closer, and I saw what she'd seen.

It was part of a skeleton. A human arm. The bones had been gnawed and worried on by beasts. Thin, shredded strips of dried skin remained attached to the few crooked fingers still left.

Elsha reached down and gently moved the finger bones apart. From between them, she picked up a small blade with a dark carved handle. I recognized the handle as trike horn. Before I could get a better look at the knife, she slipped it away into a pocket.

"Is that-" Helga began to speak.

"Let's go," Elsha whispered softly as she rose.

Slinging the shotgun back over my shoulder, we continued to follow her, silently working our way forward through the jungle.

An hour later, sweat rolled down my face, and my shirt was soaked with it. The humidity in the forest had to be a hundred percent, it felt like we could swim in it. As bad as it had been back in Whitesberg, this was even worse.

"You sense the quietness?" Helga asked Ingrid as we edged our way around a large field near the base of the mountain. She was right, I realized. The towering trees had gone quiet around us. The pterodactyls and various background insect noises that we'd become accustomed to were gone.

The muscular shield maiden nodded and drew an arrow from her quiver. Swiftly, she notched it, but left her bowstring unpulled.

Elsha looked back at us, raised a single finger to her lips, then crouched and gestured for us to come forward.

We quietly slid into position around her, Ingrid and Helga on her left, I on her right with my shotgun held in both hands. We all leaned towards her as her lips moved slightly, "I hear breathing."

Straining, I tried to listen for what she heard, but my ears weren't the best. Gun fire will do that to a man. Especially lots of it.

Helga nodded, and pointed as her other hand grasped the hilt of her sword.

"It's coming from our left."

"Stay here," Elsha commanded before she moved forward, staying in a crouch, concealed by the thick underbrush of the jungle that surrounded the opening. Within seconds she was out of our sight, her passing visible only from the trembling leaves that she'd gently pushed aside.

Minutes passed as prehistoric gnats swirled about pestering us. Even this lost period of time wasn't free of such nuisances, except here, they were much larger. Some were big enough to buttstroke.

Growing annoyed at the wait, I shifted my sweaty grip on the Auto-5 and wondered what the shield maiden leader was up to.

A terrific roar split the quiet, much louder than needed to be heard through my own shot out ears. It came from the left, the same direction that Elsha had gone.

Startled, I leapt to my feet to charge forward.

Before I could make it two paces, Helga grabbed me and jerked me to a stop. "No!" she hissed in my ear as we both looked in the direction the leader of the shield maidens had gone.

Another roar, this one closer. Now we could hear the sound of breaking branches and thudding of heavy footsteps as something giant approached.

I shrugged free of Helga's grasp and raised the gun to my shoulder, muzzle pointed in the direction of the noise.

Undergrowth snapped and broke, moving closer and closer. Small trees shook and trembled as something pushed them aside.

Something very large and very tall was headed our way.

I raised the barrel higher.

Elsha burst forth from the brush, her cheeks reddened, her strides long. Her bow was strapped over her back, and she cradled something large and white to her chest with both hands.

"RUN!" she shouted before casting a glance over her shoulder. Behind her a dead, half rotten tree toppled over with a booming crash. She deftly leapt between a gap in several tightly intertwined trees and sprinted forward.

I hesitated while Helga and Ingrid moved.

"RUN!" Elsha shouted again as she passed by me in a rush. The other two warrior women didn't wait. They followed their leader in a sprint.

I hesitated, curious at what was coming our way.

Thick tree branches twenty feet high burst apart in a shower of leaves as the monstrosity appeared. Its head slipped through the twin trees that Elsha had leapt through, but its shoulders slammed into them with a loud crack that made leaves fall from branches.

The dinosaur's snout was long and lined with teeth, very much resembling an alligator. But monstrously sized in comparison. And the brown and black colored body was huge. A long neck attached to thickly muscled shoulders jammed between the trees, and a large fin rose from behind them into the air, pushing apart more branches as its back legs leaned forward against the twin trees.

It was trapped.

Jerking the large muzzle of the shotgun up, I fired, rode the heavy recoil, and fired again.

The long, toothed snout roared again. The stench of its breath was wet and nauseating.

I had hit it though.

I knew it; at this distance I couldn't miss.

But like most things on this side of the Shimmer, it didn't give a shit about being peppered with double-ought buckshot.

The beast roared again, twisting its head about to the side, then staring down at me with what could only be described as raw, unbridled hatred.

I fired again as it reared back and lunged.

There was a small splash of blood as the trees buckled, pushing forward while the beast's clawed feet churned up the ground in an effort to push the dinosaur's body through. The thick trees withstood the force, bending, but not breaking.

I did what I should have done earlier, I turned tail and ran after the women.

CHAPTER 24

Catching up to the shield maidens as they paused beside a small stream, I rested the shotgun against a tree trunk, bent over, and gasped for breath.

Running was not a strength of mine. That's why I carried guns.

Elsha laughed at me, even though she was leaning against a boulder taking deep breaths of air herself.

"Next time, do as I say," she said, this time her tone lacking any sort of snarkiness that I'd grown used to.

I grinned at her, nodded, and straightened with my hands on my hips. Ingrid and Helga were with her, both resting against the same boulder as Elsha. They looked beat as well. I figured we'd run half a mile at least, until the angry roar of the giant beast had faded into the background.

"Have any of you ever seen such a thing?" I asked breathlessly.

"Never," Elsha replied as the others shook their heads. "This is something new to this place."

"What were you carrying?" I asked the leader of the shield maidens.

Smiling, Elsha reached down and picked up a large off-white pebbled rock at her feet.

No, not a rock.

An egg, I realized.

"You stole its egg?" I asked in surprise.

She nodded, "There were several in the nest, but I could only carry the one. It looked to be the freshest."

"No wonder the beast is angry."

"Its loss. Because we will eat well tonight. Here, Cato of the Black Plague, it's your turn to carry it as we climb the mountain."

She waited for me to pick up and sling the shotgun across my back before handing me the egg. I took it in both hands, it was heavy, and warm. The pebbled shell felt thick and sturdy.

I hoped like hell the damned thing wouldn't hatch as I was carrying it.

Elsha froze, and I realized she was staring at my hands.

"What?"

She leaned closer, a frown on her face. "I'd heard you were inked while you slept, but not *what* was tattooed on you."

"Yeah, well, I didn't get to choose. Why?"

70

"The snake eating its tail, has anyone explained what that is to you?"

"Gundar did. It's Ouroboros, symbolizing rebirth."

"Yes. It's a very rare tattoo. Most people are too afraid to have it inked on them because of what it represents."

"What does it represent?"

"Suffering, hardships, rebirth. All required in order to be remade."

I didn't have anything to say about that, so I remained silent. After a moment, she sucked her lower lip and turned away, deep in thought.

Helga and Ingrid stepped closer and looked down at my hands cradling the dinosaur egg.

"Helm of Awe," Helga muttered. "That's a good one. Much strength and power will come from that."

"But Ouroboros? There is only one other who I know of who dared to have such a tattoo," Ingrid said grimly.

"Who?"

"Thur's brother."

CHAPTER 25

By the time we hiked to the top of the mountain, the sun was setting through the trees, and it was obvious that we'd be spending the night in the jungle.

My arms ached from carrying the wretched egg. I set it down less than gently before stretching my arms and shoulders out and then cracking my neck from the weight of both the heavy shotgun slung across my back and that heavy damn egg.

"Let's have a look," Elsha said as she moved close to the cliff edge of the mountain top, the rogue strands of her red hair blowing against her face and rustling the bit of blue cloth that tied her braid. Leaving the beast egg behind, I stepped forward to stand by her side.

The view before us was breathtaking.

Far below, waves crashed silently against the shore. The only sound this high up was that of the pterodactyls flying past and the rustling of the grass beneath our feet from the strong breeze that blew against us.

Turning around, I looked away from the ocean and inland. The land stretched for miles, a thick forest near the shore turning into an open prairie spotted with clumps of trees farther away before disappearing from sight.

"If this is an island, it's a damned big one," Helga declared.

"There." Ingrid pointed. "Ships."

Turning back towards the shoreline, I followed her extended finger. There was something down there. It could have been trees, but the chances of three trees falling in as straight of a row as that was doubtful.

"There are only three of them. I thought the previous group took four longboats," I said.

"They did. But Ajar had to return somehow," Helga muttered as if I was an idiot.

Elsha glanced back in the direction we came. "We have two options. We either go back, or we go search for survivors."

"Survivors," Ingrid said firmly.

Helga clasped her sword sister's shoulder gently. "If he's alive, we'll find him," she said softly.

Ingrid nodded.

"Then let us go see the boats," Elsha said, having already made her mind up with none of my thoughts being included in her decision.

I shrugged to myself. It didn't matter. We were already going to spend the night out in the jungle, not completely unexpected. And if we followed the shore back tomorrow, we'd probably be back to the boats by nightfall.

This time Helga picked up the large egg to carry it.

CHAPTER 26

We made good time, heading downhill in the direction of the previous expedition's boats. Surprisingly there was little life to be seen. Mainly the small brown rodents scurrying through fallen leaves, chittering at us angrily, then disappearing into their burrows. It was a relief to not have to fight dinosaurs the entire way, but also concerning. There should have been more animal life around and I wondered if it was because we were still in that long snouted, fin backed, monster dinosaur's territory.

Eventually darkness overtook us, and we were forced to find shelter for the night.

Shelter turned out to be a pile of rocks that nature had piled close enough to provide some measure of protection.

"Not much room in here to swing an axe," Helga muttered as she sat the dinosaur egg down.

"Better than being eaten."

Silent, I found what looked like a comfortable place and sat down, the long-barreled shotgun resting beside me against the rock at my back.

Ingrid sat down across from me, and I shifted my legs slightly to give her room for hers. It was tight quarters between this jumble of uplifted stones. None of us would be lying down to sleep tonight.

"Tell us, Cato of the Black Plague, why are you here? Truly?" Elsha asked as she pulled together some fallen branches and began breaking them into smaller pieces.

"I was asked to come."

She stared at me for a moment before looking back down at the twigs in her hands. "Many would have loved the honor of that ask, especially coming from the Jarl himself."

I shrugged and pulled an oiled rag from my back pocket. As the women watched quietly, I drew each pistol, carefully wiping it down before holstering the weapon. Elsha had an amused look on her face, a nice change from the typical scowl she carried for me, but I knew it meant our talk was not over.

Finally, taking the shotgun and beginning to wipe it down, I asked, "What is it?"

The shield maiden leader stacked the sticks into a small teepee. "Many of us are here because we knew the axemen and women who went before. Why did you say yes?"

I sighed and ran the rag along the thick barrel. "Because I'm good at killing, and I've nothing better to be doing."

"Yes, because your master, Reydan of the Train, is dead."

I burst out laughing. "Reydan of the Train? Oh, he'd have loved to have been called that. But he wasn't my master."

"Tell us of this man," Ingrid asked, as she drew a honing stone across the edge of her sword.

I stopped laughing and looked at the oil-soaked rag in my hand. "Not much to tell."

"We understand he had a great blood feud with the new Sheriff. The Heart Eater."

Nodding slightly, I gave the shotgun a final wipe then tucked the rag away. "He did."

"Why?" asked Helga.

"Whose knife was that you found?" I asked abruptly, uncomfortable with the direction this discussion was heading.

Elsha reached into a pocket and pulled it free. The small blade shone in the fading light and peering closer, I could tell I was correct earlier. It did have a handle carved from a trike's horn.

She looked at the knife for a moment, before reaching over and handing it to me.

I took it in my hands and looked it over. The forged blade was about six inches long. There were runes etched into the handle, but I didn't know what they meant.

"Give that to Thur. It will give him comfort," she commanded.

"Comfort for what?"

"That his brother, Leif Thaneson, now resides in Valhalla."

Turning it over in my hands, I looked at the knife differently now. Thur was the closest person I had to a friend. Letting him know that his brother was dead should be my task.

"And what of Leif's wife? Didn't she go with him?"

Helga grimaced as if I'd asked something I shouldn't have. The movement made her scarred and inked face look even more fearsome.

"Yes, she did," Elsha replied curtly as she tucked tinder into the small stack of thin twigs and sticks and produced a flint. "Hopefully, she is with other survivors down by their boats. Or the boats will give us some idea of where they've gone."

I tucked the blade away into my belt, careful to do so in a way where the unsheathed blade wouldn't cut me. Elsha was back to being short with me, but I supposed bringing up one of her missing shield maidens would do that.

"Wake me when the egg is ready," Ingrid said, pushing her bow to the side and curling up slightly.

"I'll take first watch," I offered as my stomach grumbled. Standing, I stretched then climbed to the top of the rock pile that surrounded us. I hadn't had a chance to grab any food for this scouting trip. I was willing to bet none of us had as we expected it to be brief and not an overnight trek.

It was a good thing we had that giant dinosaur egg.

Below me, Elsha struck sparks to the tinder and began to gently fan the flames as I settled into a comfortable position.

Helga passed my shotgun up to me, handling it as carefully as though it were a newborn that would wake at any moment and kill someone.

Holding onto it, I looked around the dark forest. Thin streaks of light that trickled through the leaves were fading away with the setting sun. It would be pitch black soon.

I glanced back down at Elsha gently arranging the fire and more sticks around the egg.

What was it that Ajar the Mad turned Bold again had said?

At night was when it was most dangerous… and they will eat me.

CHAPTER 27

A little while later, in the early hours of the night, we feasted well on the dinosaur egg by the flickering light of our small fire.

I think that we were all worried that there would be a dinosaur in it ready to hatch, but we lucked out and the yolk was pure yellow and cooked to perfection by Elsha.

Mr. White had always had his eggs over easy, and I always ate the same way he did. This was a nice treat to have them different for a change.

And I was glad to be done carrying the heavy damned thing.

After that, it was my turn to sleep and Ingrid's turn at the watch. We all got as comfortable as possible while she worked her way to the top of the rock outcropping. I managed to sleep in bits and pieces. A restless sleep full of bits and pieces of dreams that made no sense.

A little while later, I woke to a sound and the dropping of bits of pebbles about my head.

Confused, I picked one of the small pieces up from where it landed in my lap. By the firelight, I turned it over in my hand, one side was tainted red and rubbed off on my finger.

Holding it close to get a better look, I sniffed it.

Blood.

"Wake up!" I shouted, grabbing for the shotgun as claws reached down and thick nails dug into my shoulders.

With startling strength, I was lifted upwards, pulled by an unknown opponent towards the top of the rocks where Ingrid was supposed to be keeping watch.

Elsha's eyes popped open.

With incredible swiftness, she grabbed and hurled her axe.

It thudded into something above me, and I fell back down as a horrendously painful screech pierced my ear drums.

Diving to the side, I grabbed the shotgun and twirled around ready to fire.

A pair of lizards hissed at me from where they lay down on the rock top. The pair had been dragging me upwards when the axe slammed blade first into one of their backs.

I pulled the trigger and the first lizard's face turned into chunks of red meat as the close-range dose of double-ought blew through it.

Jerking the barrel back down I fired again, hitting both the axe handle and the second lizard. The handle shattered from the force of the buckshot and splintered into the beast's scaly hide.

"Hey!" Elsha shouted at the destruction of her weapon.

Another lizard leapt down from the rocks, landing in front of Helga who promptly ran her spear through it.

From the side, a scaly beast tackled Elsha, raking its claws across her armor and snapping fangs towards her throat.

I buttstroked the creature from behind, slamming the heavy shotgun into where its back and shoulders met.

Spinning around, it hissed in Latin, "Die meat!"

Elsha drew and hacked her sword into the lizard's side, sending a spray of red blood streaming down its lithe body. The lizard toppled over with a screech and the Viking shield maiden slashed down with her sword to silence it.

The lizard Helga had impaled was pulling itself forward on the spear, clawed hands gripping the shaft and dragging it through the thin body as it lurched at the shield maiden.

I spun the shotgun around, thrust the muzzle between Helga and the lizard, and pulled the trigger.

A fist-sized hole punched through the clawed monster. Something that looked like an organ splattered against the end of the shotgun muzzle.

I flicked it off and looked for more threats.

There was nothing but the crackle of flames, our labored breathing, and the twitching lizard corpses.

"Ingrid!" Helga shouted as she dropped the gore-covered spear and drew an axe from her waist.

Slinging the shotgun across my back, I climbed to the top of the rocks.

There was nothing but a small smear of blood.

Helga hoisted herself up beside me, followed by Elsha who carried a makeshift torch in hand.

"We have to find her," Helga said, then she shouted the lost shield maiden's name.

"Silence! And listen for her," Elsha commanded as she waved the flaming torch over the rocks.

There'd been no scuffle here. I wasn't a good enough tracker to make sense of it, but it was obvious she'd been caught off guard by the lizards.

In the darkened forest, not too far off, we heard a woman's pain-filled scream.

"That way!" Helga leapt off the rocks to the ground and charged through the dark underbrush alone.

"Curses," Elsha muttered in frustration before sliding off the pile of rocks to follow.

I jumped down as well, pushing through the foliage and trying to keep up with the flaming torch that created flickering shadows before me as it raced through the jungle floor.

Fifty yards in, and another scream. Closer this time. From the right.

The waving torch moved before me, and I followed a good dozen paces behind it.

Elsha stopped, and I pushed through towering ferns and branches beside her.

She held the light overheard as she looked around the ground.

There was a splatter of blood on a small stone, more dripped on a few leaves to our left along with a trampled clump of grass.

"They went that way," she said breathlessly, pointing with the tip of her sword.

Another scream of tortured agony. Close.

"It's a trap," I told her with sudden realization.

"I won't leave them behind."

I drew my right pistol, cocked the hammer, and snatched the torch from her hand.

"Then allow me," I told her astonished face as I began to drag the flames across the dry grass and twigs on the ground.

"What are you doing?" she hissed.

"Creating a distraction."

Flames leapt up, first small, then larger as they quickly consumed the dry material on the underbelly of the jungle.

I flung the useless torch away and began moving in the direction of the last scream as fire danced higher behind me.

Moving quickly, I covered about twenty-five yards in a crouch with the pistol pointing in front of me. From the last scream, it sounded like she was close. And if I was lucky, the fire distraction would either make them leave her to flee or investigate.

Amongst the distant crackling of flames, I heard a rhythmic hissing sound and saw leaves being gently parted.

There.

A splash of gray moving towards me in the firelight.

Closer it moved.

The snapping of a twig being stepped on.

Closer.

The lizard passed beside me, walking upright and twisting its body in a shifting back and forth motion as it looked at the growing forest fire.

With teeth bared, I leapt at him while swinging my pistol.

The round barrel smashed across his pointed face, and I saw a broken fang go flying.

On top of the scaly lizard, I used my heavier weight to hold it down while it thrashed beneath me.

Jamming the muzzle of my pistol against its head, I asked in Latin, "Where is she?"

It growled at me.

A sword lopped its left outstretched hand off at the wrist. The lizard shrieked and Elsha dropped to a knee beside me, the blade pressed firmly against its throat.

"WHERE?" I shouted.

With its right hand, it pointed. "Nearrrr," it hissed.

I pulled the trigger and splattered skull and brains several feet to our left.

Elsha darted around me in the direction the lizard had pointed.

The fire was quickly growing behind us. Smoke was getting thick, and I held back a cough.

Moving after the shield maiden, my pistol stayed pointed ahead at all the darkened shadows before us.

We reached a large tree with outstretched roots. While she went left, I went right.

A second later, Elsha let loose a ferocious scream followed by the sound of her sword hitting flesh.

By the time I leapt around the mass of tangled roots, it was over.

Two lizards lay dead with bloody slashes across their bodies. Helga was sprawled awkwardly to the side with her axe nearby. She appeared unconscious as her chest rose and fell gently with her breathing. A bloodied rock lay near one of the dead lizards. It had been a trap after all.

But frozen in place, I only had eyes for Ingrid.

The muscular shield maiden was propped against the tree. Her bowels had been ripped open and bluish-purple intestines were loosely draped around her neck.

Her eyelids flickered.

I dropped to a knee before her.

She moaned and I leaned in.

"It hurts," she murmured softly as a tear rolled down her face.

"Valhalla awaits you," I said gently. Using my free hand, I covered her eyes, and shot her through the heart.

"Cato! Hurry!" Elsha said while pulling Helga to her feet. The warrior woman had a nasty cut above her right eyebrow and was moving groggily.

Flames crackled, and I realized the fire I'd started had grown massive and was moving quickly through the dry underbrush.

Thrusting the shotgun into Elsha's hands, I quickly grabbed Helga about the waist and threw the muscular woman over a shoulder.

Coughing from the smoke, we ran from the advancing flames.

CHAPTER 28

After what felt like an eternity, I stumbled to a stop and dropped Helga onto the wet sand of the beach. She was not a light weight. Dry heaving, I wretched and bent over, gasping for air to fill my lungs. The smoke and running had taxed them beyond their limits. I felt lightheaded and weak. The muscles in my arms and legs burned with exertion. I felt like puking or passing out.

Fifty yards behind us, the forest burned.

"What is it with gunmen and fire?" Elsha asked as she quickly moved to check her shield maiden's forehead. The wounded woman groaned at her touch but said nothing as Elsha quickly wiped a finger through the gash to clear out any debris.

"It will need sewing to close," the leader of the shield maidens chided her charge.

"Men of worth appreciate battle scars," Helga said faintly with a grimace.

I accepted the shotgun back from Elsha. Racking the bolt slightly, I checked the chamber to make sure it was still loaded. The lizards were sneaky bastards and after seeing what they did to Ingrid, I had no intention of ever being taken alive by them.

"Can you walk, Helga?" Elsha asked after we'd spent some time resting and watching the fire begin to burn itself out. "The boats are not far."

"Did you see what they did to her? Our Ingrid?" Helga asked, ignoring her boat leader's question while staring off into the burning flames.

"Ja. I saw," Elsha replied softly as she wiped her bloodied hand against her pants.

"Such beasts. I hope they all burn to death. Screaming."

"Let's go," the shield maiden leader said while helping her friend to her feet. "The others' boats are not so far from here and the sun is rising."

With the shotgun cradled in my arms, I slowly led the way up the beach. Judging from a large nearby rock formation that I'd spied from the mountain crest, we were about halfway to the trio of longboats that awaited us.

CHAPTER 29

The sun had just risen over the edge of the sea, illuminating our shore as we reached the boats.

They'd been pulled ashore, out of reach of high tide, resting on the pebble and sandy beach in rows.

And they appeared to have been abandoned in a hurry.

Elsha headed directly for the boat in the middle, the one with a raven carved as its figurehead. From what I'd learned, ravens were supposed to be good luck. Odin used them to go out into the world and report back to him what the mortals were up to.

Following the shield maiden leader, I peeked into the closest boat as I passed and noted the sea chests had all been opened and things pulled out and scattered. There weren't any bodies, but I supposed corpses didn't last long in Prehistoria anyways. But there were many dark stains, which I suspected was from spilled blood.

Then I remembered Ajar the Mad's words from many days ago on the distant beach, "They will eat you."

A shiver ran up my spine and I tightened my grip on the shotgun.

The shield maiden leader climbed into the boat and looked around, frustration etched across her pretty face.

"What is it?" I asked as Helga stepped around me and climbed onboard also.

"This was Leif Thaneson's boat," the heavily tattooed Viking said, with her hands on her hips.

"Yes, and we found his body," I replied, patting the trike-horned knife tucked into my waistband.

"But not his wife's body," Elsha snapped.

I glanced at Helga, puzzled.

She leaned towards me, nodded at Elsha, and whispered, "Sif. Her sister."

"You have a sister?" I blurted out.

"Ja. If she still lives."

"We'll find her."

"How do you propose that, Cato of the Black Plague?" Elsha asked sarcastically as Helga moved towards the back of the boat.

"I've found that once you start killing things, others will offer up information," I muttered to myself before speaking louder, "Let's look around a bit, maybe we'll find some hints as to what happened to them."

"They were attacked, probably by those lizard people," Helga said, her hand on the rudder as she leaned over to look at something.

Elsha quickly moved down the length of the boat. A small pterodactyl squawked at her from the bottom of the ship, and she kicked it out of the way.

Helga pointed at the seat that stretched across the back end for the rudder axeman to sit and steer on.

I grabbed the top of the boat and scrambled my way into it.

Stepping over opened sea chests and spilled belongings, I reached the women. They were looking at runes that'd been scratched into the seat. They were rough and hastily written. From the curvature of several of them, I guessed someone used an axe blade to do it.

"What does it say?" I asked. "And why would they scratch it there?"

"Anyone who found the boat would check the rudder to make sure it was still seaworthy," Helga muttered.

"And the writing?"

Elsha gently ran her finger along the grooves scratched into the wood. "It says they lost a dozen in an attack. Several were taken. And they go to find them."

"All of this," I waved my hand about the mess inside the boat, "was from the lizards?"

"I think so," Elsha said while straightening upright to look around.

"Does it say which direction they went?"

"Yes." She pointed towards the north. Back into the jungle.

Figures.

Helga had lost her spear in the night attack and found another to replace it. Elsha managed to find some food that hadn't been sniffed out or gone rotten for us to fill our bellies with and an axe to replace the one I'd shotgunned to pieces.

"Here, Cato of the Black Plague, you'll need this." Elsha reached under her seat as we ate and pulled out a ring mail shirt like several of the other Vikings in Thur's boat wore. "I found this in the bottom of a chest."

I stared at it. I knew the value of such a shirt, ring mail was slow work to build, and few axemen could afford such a luxury in a place like this where it would come in handy against biting and scratching foes.

"Why don't you wear it?" I asked, not moving to accept the armor. She wore the traditional leather scale armor with studs that was most common amongst the axemen.

"Too big. And too heavy." She flashed me a smile, "I prefer to be quick and nimble with my sword. Heavy armor slows that down. But you, with your shotgun… you could use this well should anything get close to you."

Tipping my hat at her in thanks, I took the bundle. It was heavier than I thought it would be.

"Go ahead, put it on. You never know when we may be attacked again," Helga said while gingerly touching the fresh stitches across her forehead.

I chuckled, we were all sitting in a circle with our backs to each other, Elsha and me facing towards the sandy beach while Helga watched the water behind us. We were certainly prepared for another attack.

Standing, I set my hat down and pulled off the bandoleer of shotgun shells.

I found the arm holes in the armor and began to slide my hands through.

"No. You cannot wear that over your gunman clothing. It will chafe." Helga stood and walked down the boat, glancing at the runes on each sea chest before stopping near one. "This was Erikson's, he was about your size." She dug around the belongings strewn near it and picked up an off-white shirt. "Put this on underneath."

Taking the shirt from her, I began unbuttoning my black shirt. Once undone, I pulled it off, folded it, and set it to the side.

Elsha gasped and reached out to touch my side. "What are these from? Bullets?"

Glancing down at my body, I turned slightly, looking at the small circular burn marks.

"Cigars. Reydan White didn't take to repeating himself or allowing failure."

"He burned you with fire?" Helga said, shocked.

I shrugged. It was no big deal. "A few times."

"Cato," Elsha said softly as her fingers traced a trio of burns. "That is not a few times. It looks like dozens of burns, or more."

"I deserved them. I didn't do as asked." Slipping the leather shirt over, I realized it would hang over my guns.

The two shield maidens exchanged a look as I removed my gun belt, pulled the chain mail on, and strapped my pistols back on over top.

"What?" I growled in annoyance while practicing a quick draw. The chain mail slowed me down a bit, but I supposed maybe the protection was worth it.

After all, it wasn't like I needed to worry about being shot on this island.

"This Reydan of the Train, he sounds like a real bastard," Elsha said with a scowl.

I paused, looking down at the two women. "You don't understand. He raised me the best he could."

"No father should burn their child," Helga growled angrily.

"I wasn't his child. I was his bodyguard, and his life was mine to protect. In the end, I failed."

Elsha frowned but wouldn't meet my eyes. "I'm sorry," she said with a rare sincerity.

"It's nothing." In annoyance, I slung the bandoleer over my head and shoulder. It was a bit snug with the added thickness, but the leather strap didn't cut into my shoulder from the weight of the shells as it did before. "Are we ready to go?"

"Yes." Elsha stood. "But we go there," she pointed at the forest before us.

"What? No. We need the others first," I protested. "Back down the beach."

"The others are at least a day away and I will not wait any longer to see what happened to my sister." Straightening, she looked me in the eyes.

Hers were beautiful. I felt like I could get lost in their green depths.

"Tell me you do not fear death," she demanded. "If you are truly the champion of Odin."

"I'm no champion and I'm not an axeman. I won't go to Valhalla if I die."

"Where will you go?"

"I've been told a place called Hell."

The shield maiden smirked. "I've heard the Reverend speak of such a place. You would like Valhalla more. Perhaps you should earn your death."

I forced myself to break eye contact and looked back at the forested edge of the beach. The fire I'd created appeared to have burned itself out. And every now and then, when the wind turned just right, we got a scattering of white ash drifting down on us.

Well...

Why not?

It's not like I had anything better to do. I was an unemployed killer of men and ape. I supposed I could add lizards to that list now as well.

"Alright. Let's go."

CHAPTER 30

We left the boats behind and entered the forest. With the rising sun came the humidity, and once again we found ourselves quickly soaked in sweat and misery under the shade of the towering jungle canopy.

Helga stopped and swatted a large fly away from her stitched-up face in annoyance. "Do we have to cross that?" she asked grumpily.

Without a word, Elsha looked back at her for a moment, then stepped into the burnt field of ash from my nighttime fire.

Grimacing, I followed.

Every footstep billowed ash that stuck to our clothes and exposed skin. After several hundred yards, we were covered in a thick layer. I pulled my bandana over my mouth and nose, thankful that I'd kept the blue piece of fabric.

Taking note of my success in not coughing and gagging on the foul ash-filled air, both shield maidens decided that I wasn't a madman after all. They took the squares of cloth that I'd cut from my black shirt before leaving the boats and wrapped it around their faces, covering everything but small areas for them to see through.

"Told you so," I muttered. Helga, I think, smiled under her black makeshift bandana, but not Elsha. The further we left the boats behind, the quieter and more withdrawn the warrior woman had become.

Another hundred yards, and Elsha stopped by a large tree with several broken branches jutting from the trunk near chest level.

She pulled one of the branches out, and I realized it wasn't a branch, but a burnt arrow.

I stepped closer, curious.

What was left wasn't the thick monstrosity of an arrow that the apes used. Elsha must have been thinking the same thing, as she pulled an arrow from one of her quivers and compared the two.

Looking closer, I noted it had a small steel tip, protected from the fire by being driven into the tree trunk.

It was certainly an axeman arrow.

"Spread out," she said, her voice slightly muffled from the black cloth. "Look for signs."

I moved away, looking at the ground and trees nearby for anything out of the ordinary. With most of the underbrush burned away, we quickly found an axe head and burnt spear.

Nothing else. No remains from human, ape, or lizard.

"They passed this way," Helga said when we gathered back together, stating the obvious after pulling her makeshift bandana down so she could speak around it. She stared at the soot-covered axe head and what was left of the handle inside.

"Let's move," Elsha replied, dropping the burnt arrow to the ground.

'They will eat you,' Ajar had said.

Is that why we hadn't found any bodies yet? Just a lone severed arm of Thur's brother?

I dreaded the answer as a large pterodactyl screeched ominously overhead.

Not too much further, we passed gigantic footprints. Three big toes forward, and a small one to the rear. Even my basic tracking skills could tell by the burnt material pressed into the soft ground forming the track that they were relatively fresh.

I thought of the large alligator faced dinosaur whose egg we ate. The dinosaur had been massive, certainly large enough to make these tracks.

But there was no telling what was on this island. Back in Prehistoria, the axemen knew most of the dinosaurs, but here on this damned island, it was different. There could be anything out here. Perhaps something worse than the lizards.

Clutching the Auto-5 shotgun tighter, I followed the axewomen.

We found some trikes not too far away. They were wandering through the burned area, bellowing unhappily in their never-ending quest to eat.

These trikes were different from anything I'd ever seen before. While the axemen had a varying assortment of their own, these looked unlike anything they'd ever seen before.

"Look at those horns," Elsha said, pointing.

The beasts had twin horns tilting forward on the top of their heads like cattle. Below was a smaller nub, not much of a horn, but something to give their faces some more character.

The herd of trikes saw us and decided they didn't like our ash-covered looks and began to wander away.

"They are wild," Helga said as she eyed them cautiously. "If these were ever ridden, it has been a long time."

One of them butted its horns sideways against another, urging it to move faster or get out of the beast's way.

A young one bellowed softly as it fell behind the others, then jogged through the ash to catch back up to the herd.

"Let's go," Elsha demanded as she began walking around the cattle horned trikes, obviously unwilling to wait for them to move out of our way first.

We followed.

And soon we crossed out of the burnt area and headed back into the lush jungle.

It was at the very edge, between the small fires still smoking as they smoldered along, and the still thriving forest, that the lizards attacked us.

CHAPTER 31

It was Helga who saw them first.

We were a hundred yards from the edge of the open jungle, with smoke billowing in our faces, when they sprang their trap.

"Ambush!" she shouted, hurling her spear at the closest of the ash-covered monsters that popped up from where it'd been lying still in wait.

She'd hurled the spear with such force, that the spear went through the lizard's body and pinned it to the ground writhing in pain.

Elsha slashed her axe at the lizard that appeared out of the smoke before her, slicing it open from thin neck to waist as it twisted in a vain attempt to dodge the weapon.

I had my own troubles. A split second after the shield maiden shouted her warning, I'd heard a stick snap behind me.

Spinning around, I pulled the trigger. The right arm of the closest lizard was severed, and the screeching beast fell out of sight behind a charred tree. A second lizard was in the air, already leaping forward as I pulled the trigger on its friend.

Knocking aside the outstretched claws with the large barrel, I drew my left pistol and fired while still holding onto the Auto-5 with my right. The bullet hit, center mass, punching a large .44 sized hole through it.

The lizard kept coming though.

Even as its life drained from the hole, it fought to get me.

Claws ripped across the chain mail about my torso, snapping teeth from its pointed face bit down on my shoulder and I dropped the shotgun from the crushing pain.

I fired the pistol again and again, letting the lizard eat the bullets at close range and blowing large chunks out of its back from the exit wounds.

The lizard sagged, its strength fading fast.

Shifting the weapon, I fired another round into its mouth and put him down for good.

Twisting back towards the front, Elsha was down with a lizard on top of her fighting to keep from being clawed or bitten. Helga was hacking at another with her axe.

Drawing the right pistol, I thrust my hand outwards and shot the lizard trying to eat Elsha. It twisted, snapping at where the bullet had connected. She drove her axe blade down through its collarbone and into its scaly chest.

More were coming at us, running on all fours in leaps and bounds. Damn, but there were a lot of them this time.

We were all going to die.

I shot the pistol empty, dropping the lizards at the head of the pack.

The hammer dropped on a fired cylinder as one tackled me, and I fell. Jamming the barrel of the pistol barrel first into its gnashing mouth, I fought to get the beast off me.

The pistol was empty. I knew it. But it was the only thing keeping the lizard from biting my face off.

With my other hand, I drew Leif Thaneson's knife and began stabbing wildly with it.

Vaguely, I felt a pounding through the jungle floor, as though something... or somethings approached at a heavy run.

In the back of my mind, I doubted I'd be alive long enough to face the new threat.

The lizard lifted off me in a spray of blood as a large spear pierced through its side.

A heavy footstep landed inches from my head.

A trike foot.

Above me, mounted on the back of the trike, was a massive ape. Its thick fur was splotched bronze and black, and with both arms he lifted the dead lizard on the spear and flung it aside.

The ape growled something at me, and pulled on the reins, urging the trike to move away from my face.

Rolling over to my feet, I saw a half dozen mounted trikes slaying lizards with spear, club, and bow.

Baffled, I snatched the Auto-5 shotgun off the ground, strode forward two paces and blasted a lizard charging a downed Elsha.

Blood splattered across her pretty face, and she spat a glob of it out as she leapt to her feet, her green eyes blazing with blood lust.

Drawing her seax from the sheath at her waist, she slashed the short blade across the back of the final lizard that Helga was chopping up. Screeching, it tried to turn to face the second attacker, only to have an axe lop off its head.

Breathing heavily, I looked around the small battle ground as the ape mounted trikes began to move into a circle. The heavy twin horned beasts grunted and bellowed as they were rotated to face us. Obsidian-tipped spears and notched arrows were held steady towards us by the apes. Not pointed at us, strangely, but prepared to kill us should the need arise.

I tried to remember how many rounds were left in the shotgun as I eyeballed the apes over the large barrel pointed at them.

Certainly not enough to take them all.

I stared at the ape leader. The bronze and black-haired one that'd saved me.

But maybe him.

As long as I had a round in the Auto-5, he was going to get his.

Elsha growled from beside me, poised with her bloodied seax. Helga's back was pressed against me, her axe held in two hands, ready to go to Valhalla.

I wondered what the big apes were waiting for.

The ape leader growled something, and the other apes lifted their spear tips into the air.

The bronze and black beast passed his bloodied spear to the next ape, slid from the back of the trike, and walked inside the ring of horned dinosaurs to stand before me.

He looked me up and down, and I could feel the tension from the shield maidens beside me. Hell, I could feel the tension in my body as the urge to fight or run kicked in.

"Elsha," I whispered. "Don't kill him, yet."

"Why not?" she asked, staring the ape leader down.

"Because I'm curious."

"You mean stupid," she hissed.

I lowered my shotgun.

Maybe, just maybe…

This hairy bastard wanted something else other than our lives.

Slowly moving one hand away from the shotgun, I tapped a finger on my chest. "Cato."

The ape grunted noncommittedly.

I pointed my finger at him. "Monkey." Then back to me. "Cato."

The ape leader tilted his head slightly, raised a giant hand and pointed a dark finger at himself and coughed. "Achooks."

Helga leaned her head back towards me. "Did he just say his name?"

"I think so." To the big ape, I repeated the sound the best I could, "Awshucks." Then I pointed back at me, "Cato."

Awshucks shook his head and coughed again while pointing at himself in what could only be described as annoyance. "Achooks."

Elsha was still staring at the ape. "Is he going to kill us now or not? Valhalla awaits."

"Awshucks," I repeated again, trying to repeat the guttural ape language with great difficulty.

A couple of the other apes laughed. An odd sound to hear coming from seven-foot-tall hairy beasts with a pair of large canines in their mouths.

Awshucks shook his head in defeat, then said," Cato," in a clear, yet deep, gravelly voice.

Elsha's eyes widened in surprise. "You've a friend."

"Let's hope he prefers his food without names," Helga muttered.

The bronze and black ape appeared to relax. He pointed at a lizard corpse next to him, then another while repeating, "Buscha."

"Buscha," I said with better luck than the ape's name.

Several of the apes nodded, and the trikes began to move away from the circle. The apes were still on guard, but now their eyes were looking away from us. I wondered what other threats we had to worry about.

Elsha jabbed her seax into the ground, then bent down to pull her sword out from under a buscha body. "Looks like we live to fight again," she said while trying in vain to wipe the blade clean of soot and blood.

Awshucks stepped closer, his body relaxed, and held his hand out to Helga.

The shield maiden pulled back slightly, confused and still on guard.

The bronze and black ape leader pointed at her axe, then back to the large stone axe strapped to his trike. It seemed like he wanted to compare the two.

Relenting, Helga handed it to the ape. "Axe," she said as she did so.

"Axe," Awshucks repeated as he touched a large black thumb to the blade, testing the sharpness. He seemed impressed with the small weapon. Flipping it around easily, he handed it back to Helga, handle first, while repeating, "axe."

"I wonder if they know on the other side of the sea we've been killing them on sight?" Elsha asked.

"Let's not tell them that," I warned while looking at the dead buschas around us. They were all coated with ash.

"Smart," Helga said while pulling her spear out of the pinned dead lizard. She cursed when she saw the tip had bent slightly from hitting a rock in the ground.

"Yes, too smart," Elsha agreed. "They must have watched us coming this way, and instead of attacking, they covered themselves and waited for us to get close."

"These aren't mindless lizards, they are cunning and crafty."

"As shown by what they did to Ingrid. Luring us by tormenting her," Helga growled before spitting on the corpse at her feet.

I frowned, thinking of how I had to end the Viking warrior's life.

"We will have to be careful," Elsha said, glancing warily at the buschas and the apes that were cleaning up their weapons after the attack. Our group had come through mostly unscathed, but I saw a couple of apes with bite and claw wounds they were tending with chewed up purple ferns being applied. Next time I came across some of them, I'd pick some leaves for myself. Just in case.

Drawing several shotgun shells from the bandoleer, I began reloading the Auto-5 one round at a time.

Once it appeared we had our weapons in order again, Awshucks motioned for us to follow as the apes turned their trikes and began to walk away from the scene of the battle.

"No," Elsha said while shaking her head. She jabbed her finger to the north, "We go there."

The apes slowed their mounts and began talking amongst themselves. After a minute or so of confusion, Awshucks dismounted and walked back to where we stood.

I tightened my grip on the Auto-5 shotgun, unsure of what this disagreement might lead to.

The big monkey rubbed the bronze streak under his chin in a thoughtful manner, then squatted to the ground and brushed away a clear spot.

With a finger, he drew in the ash and dirt. A large squarish shape.

About a foot away from the square, he jabbed his finger in the dirt while saying something in ape speak.

"I think that's supposed to be where we are," Helga said, squatting down beside the beast. She pointed at the dimple in the ground from his finger. "Here. We," she gestured at us and the other apes, "here."

Awshucks grunted. "Here."

"Good. We go," she drew a line from the dimple to the rough square outline, "here?" She pointed at we three humans, "more of us here?"

The ape shook his head back and forth before giving what I assumed was a toothy frown.

Around the large square, he drew many rectangles with the edges touching.

Then he pointed at Helga's spear laying on the ground beside her and jabbed a finger angrily at the rectangles.

"Bad?" Elsha asked, leaning over her shield maiden sister to get a better view.

Awshucks grunted again, coughed, then repeated, "bad."

"He speaks better axeman than you do, Cato," she muttered, before pointing at the axe on her side. "Axe?" Then she pointed at the three of us and pointed at the rectangles. "Axemen?"

The bronze ape shook his head again before saying, "Axe." Then with his big hairy hand, he drew a line from us to the rectangles, then abruptly smeared away the end of the line where they met.

"I think he's saying if we go where these rectangles are, we die," I offered. Kicking a nearby buscha corpse, I pointed towards the rectangles. "Buscha?"

Awshucks nodded with a grunt.

"Why's he drawing that shape to mean lizards?" Helga muttered, obviously annoyed at the drawings.

"What about us? What about axemen?" Elsha picked up her axe and shook it. "Axeman here?" She pointed at the large square and many rectangles.

Awshucks nodded again with another affirmative grunt.

"Gods be good, the buscha have them," Helga swore and grabbed up her spear.

They will eat you, Ajar the Mad had said.

And the realization dawned on me that this was what he'd meant. The lizards were eating the axemen. Which meant we needed to get moving. If there were any left alive, we had to save them as quickly as possible.

But the ape leader shook his head again, jamming his finger at the mass of rectangles, obviously frustrated at our attempts to communicate.

We were still missing something.

With the edge of his hand, Awshucks wiped away the drawing, leaving a clean and uneven dirt and ash slate.

One at a time, with slow and deliberate effort, he began to draw again.

"What's that supposed to be?" Elsha asked. Helga shook her head in confusion.

Staring at it, I moved around and stood beside the hairy ape. He smelled like a wet dog.

Realization dawned on me. Of course, the axemen couldn't understand. It was in letters, not runes.

I read them off slowly.

"S.P.Q.R."

CHAPTER 32

"What does that mean?"

I ignored the question, looking around us with new appreciation for the dangers we were in.

"Cato," Elsha grabbed my arm and spun me around to face her while repeating herself, "What does it mean?"

"It means the damned Romans are here."

"Who?" Helga asked.

I stared at her, trying to recall what little I'd learned of them during my Latin lessons. Reydan White had taught me Latin once he found out I was good with languages, mainly so we'd have a secret way to speak that those around us would be unlikely to understand. Dead languages were good for such things.

"Those weren't rectangles, they were shields. Big ones, locked together to protect the men behind them with spears and swords. Like your shield wall, but bigger."

"These Romans, they are bad?" Elsha said with a frown.

"Very," I muttered as Awshucks stood from his crouch, watching our interactions carefully.

"Why? And do they have our brothers and sisters of the axe?"

"Romans were… are… a great warrior tribe. And they captured them most likely."

"If they are alive, we must get them back."

Sighing, I turned to Awshucks. Behind him the other apes had become bored waiting. Several had slid off their trikes and were watching two others that were wrestling in the ash.

"How many?" I asked. I pointed at our small group, then pinched my fingers close together. Then I pointed at the letters in the ground and asked again, this time moving my fingers and hands to different positions.

Awshucks stretched his arms out as far as they'd go.

"Shit," I muttered.

"I swear by Freyja, if they hurt them, we will kill them all," Elsha swore.

"You don't understand. Rome was vast. They had many armies of thousands of men and horses. Awshucks is saying there's a lot of them."

"If Sif is alive, I will not leave her. Nor the others," Elsha insisted as she made ready to begin walking away.

One of the apes moved to stop her with a raised hand.

Her sword made a hiss as the shield maiden leader drew it from the sheath.

Awshucks grunted something deep and guttural, and the ape moved away.

Helga shrugged at me, then began to walk after her leader with her spear resting on her shoulder.

"You want to help?" I asked the bronze and black ape. "Maybe kill some of them?" I pointed with the muzzle of my shotgun at the four letters scratched into the ground then towards the dead buschas.

The enemy of my enemy… and all that, I thought to myself.

Awshucks stared at me for a moment, before gesturing towards the ape who had tried to stop Elsha. This one was a brown and white mottled color, a head smaller than Awshucks, but an imposing beast just the same.

The ape had begun to mount his trike, but at another word from the lead ape, he stopped and handed the reins to another. Reaching behind the mount, he grabbed his stone club in one hand, and pulled an obsidian-tipped spear off where it was strapped to the back of the trike.

Awshucks did the same, readying his weapons, but him with a stone axe and spear.

The bronze and black leader spoke to the other apes as they mounted their trikes. After a few moments of back and forth talking, they rode away while Awshucks and the other ape began walking on foot after Elsha.

CHAPTER 33

As we walked towards the Roman encampment, we talked to the two apes. The white and brown ape was named Thathas. Or something like that, it was the best we could repeat. We worked on teaching them more of our words and tried to learn some of theirs. It seemed easier for the two apes to learn the axeman tongue than for the shield maidens to learn the ape language, although Helga seemed to have a knack for it. Maybe it had something to do with the large canines that the beasts had in their mouths.

But I began picking up words and meaning from their rough grunts and speak almost immediately.

Walking through the forest, Awshucks led the way and soon we headed up a mountain that reached above the treetops. It seemed that the ape leader wanted to show us something and this small mountain was between us and the Romans.

After several hours of sweat, swearing, and pausing, we crested the top.

From our vantage point, we could see the entire Roman fort. It was rectangular in shape, and massive in size. They'd dug an entrenchment, using the dirt to build ramparts that they topped with stakes. At regular intervals, there were watch towers. People, like ants, moved through the encampment in straight streets laid out between tents. It was a town unto itself.

"How many do you think there are?" asked Helga in awe.

"Thousands," Elsha replied quietly.

Awshucks jammed his spear butt into the ground and sat beside it, watching as though the sight below us was nothing new to him.

"And look," I said pointing towards the large corrals, "they have horses. Hundreds of them."

Helga spat to the side. "Trikes are better than horses."

"Horses are weaker," I agreed. "But also, faster and nimbler."

"Not with a trike horn through their guts," she grinned evilly. "Then they are tasty."

"There," I pointed, "buschas." The lizards were easy to separate from the men even at this distance, some walked on two legs while others crawled, or perhaps loped, along on four. But interestingly, it appeared none of them were inside the Roman fort. They were all outside of the earthen built walls.

I glanced at Elsha, wondering what she was thinking. The shield maiden leader was chewing on her lower lip thoughtfully.

"We can't defeat them," I told her. "They are too many."

"Anyone can be defeated," she said sternly, never taking her green eyes off the earthen fortress.

"We don't even know if the other axemen and women are still alive," I told her softly.

"They are. Awshucks said that's where they took them."

I looked at the sprawling Roman encampment. "We can't attack an army with five of us."

"Then you will go, and you will ask for them back," she turned and fixed me with a thoughtful stare.

I looked at our little group of people and apes, baffled. "What? How?"

"You knew what those markings Awshucks drew in the ash meant. Do you think you can talk to them?"

I sighed, not liking the direction this was going. "Yes, they probably speak some type of Latin. I can likely talk to them."

"Good," she said while Helga looked at me with newly found concern.

Thunder rolled overhead ominously as dark clouds began to form on the horizon.

"It appears Thor is on your side," Elsha said with a smile. "He offers you help if needed."

"This is bullshit," I muttered to myself in English.

"What?"

I switched back to axeman. "Nothing."

CHAPTER 34

"This is bullshit," I said in Latin to myself again as I carefully worked my way through the dense jungle towards the Roman fortification.

The prideful bastards might kill me before I had a chance to utter a word. But I was banking on their curiosity and perhaps even bureaucracy to keep me alive. For a time.

Then I was on my own. There was no plan to get me out. Two axewomen and two apes against thousands of Roman troops and cavalry, plus however many buschas... not a snowball's chance in hell.

It'd be up to me to talk my way out.

If possible.

I gripped my shotgun tighter. Thank goodness for gunpowder.

Pushing through a thicket of ferns, I found myself on the edge of a well-traveled path. I paused for a moment, looking both ways while taking in the construction of the wide makeshift road. It weaved with the terrain, taking the easiest path while still maintaining a general straightness to it. On each side of the road brush and small trees had been pushed aside, cut from the path with saw or axe.

I didn't know much about Romans, except what little I picked up while learning Latin from Mr. White. Occasionally, the man would throw some tidbit of knowledge out there as we practiced, as though to show off his higher education. And through those tidbits, I realized that he was quite taken with the Roman's way of doing business. I supposed the ruthlessness of S.P.Q.R in both military and politics was like the way he ran the railroad business. If it hadn't been for that, I supposed he'd never have gone as far in life as he'd gotten... before Jed killed him.

I shook my head.

Jed.

Damn that man. But he was a problem for another day.

Today had its own measure of problems.

Sighing, I stepped out onto the road and began walking in the direction of the fort.

I hadn't gone more than perhaps five hundred yards when hoofbeats sounded from behind me. Awshucks had managed to communicate that there were regular patrols on this road, and I was about to meet my first Romans.

Moving aside on the path, I clenched the Auto-5 tightly, and tried to put a smile on my face as a couple of dozen riders rode to an abrupt stop before me. Confusion was evident, as they looked at me and around the area, as if expecting an ambush. Two of the horses were empty of riders, but one had what appeared to be a cloth-wrapped corpse strapped to the back of one of the mounts. Judging from the shape and blood stains soaking through the fabric... a man.

One of the Romans, a man with a bronze helmet wearing a short ridge of vertical hairs across the top, dismounted, and briskly walked within several paces of me before stopping with a hand resting on the hilt of his sword. He was tall, a handsome fellow with hawklike features, and white.

Looking past him, I was pleased to see that at least one of the riders was of a darker complexion closer to mine.

That might make things a bit easier. I was worried I'd stand out like a sore thumb and be considered an escaped slave or some such.

"Who are you to stand in the way of the glory of Rome?" the man asked in Latin as he casually adjusted the bright layered armor that covered his upper arms and torso with his free hand.

It took effort to not roll my eyes as I responded in the same language, "My name is Cato. I am here to speak to you about peace."

"Peace?" the man sneered. "Is that why you are unarmed except for that axe and strange mace?"

My brow wrinkled for a moment until I realized that the Romans had yet to encounter firearms.

"Not a mace." I patted the shotgun with my right hand. "This is one of the tools of my trade."

"Tools?" He squinted at the Auto-5 thoughtfully. "For what trade?"

"Hole punching."

He smirked in condescension, "Ah, a leather craftsman. And what tribute do you have to offer, and from where do you come?"

Right now I knew I could only tell him two things without inviting the axemen to be raided or slaughtered, Jack and Shit.

And Jack had already left Prehistoria.

"I want to speak to someone who can offer terms," I replied, having absolutely no idea what title their leader might have.

"I am Decurion Albus Livianus. You will tell me."

I didn't respond, instead wondering how many of them I could kill with my five shot shells before having to draw my pistols.

Even grouped together like they were, there were too many of them though.

But this arrogant Albus asshole was going to get cut down first.

He snorted in annoyance at my silence while looking at me up and down thoughtfully. He seemed to be making up his mind on whether to kill me or not.

"Mount then. And let us see what our legion's Legate thinks of your peace." He stepped back and waved at the dark-skinned man holding the reins to the two riderless horses.

He moved them forward, and I mounted the one without the corpse across its back. It was difficult because they didn't have stirrups. Instead, I had to sort of pull and leap into the saddle to mount up.

They waited impatiently as I fumbled my way to the reins and picked them up. At least those were like our modern ones. Looking down at the horse, I noticed there were several claw marks along its neck. Not deep, but enough to cut shallow gashes which were caked with dried blood.

They'd run into some sort of dinosaur. Or an unhappy buscha lizard.

"Let us go, barbarian," Decurion Livianus said as he remounted effortlessly and began to ride down the trail.

CHAPTER 35

Together we rode several miles before reaching the heavily fortified encampment.

I had intentionally taken my time walking towards the camp more than necessary to meet one of their patrols. Because Awshucks, Thathas, and the shield maidens had gone ahead. Once I stepped out onto the road, they were already far ahead of us, slinking along through the dark jungle undergrowth, growing ever closer to the Roman's camp.

While I would speak with their leader, Elsha and Helga would scout the outside and look for any weaknesses in their defenses that could be exploited, or perhaps a glimpse of their missing axemen and women.

As for Awshucks and Thathas, I didn't know what the hell they'd do. We were still struggling to communicate. For all we knew, they thought we were going to attack the fort with just the three of us and wanted to watch the show.

The encampment was massive. The ditch that surrounded it appeared a good five feet deep, and almost six feet across. The earthen berm built beyond that stood a good six feet tall with a single row of sharpened stakes topping it off. Sentries paced the top of the rampart, and at each corner was a watch tower putting the guards inside another dozen feet higher and that much more able to view their surroundings. Inside the watch tower, some sort of large crossbow-looking weapon was mounted. It looked strong enough to fling a bolt through a trike.

"Gaze upon but a whisper of the might of Rome," the Decurion told me with a wide smile of superiority.

If only he knew the power of my weapons, I thought with some amusement. I could easily blow the armored man out of his saddle.

But might and power was more than the barrel of a single shotgun.

It could also be the steel swords wielded in the hands of thousands of men intent upon your death. Especially when those men followed an almost fanatical belief of superiority over every living thing.

A pair of buschas loped forward on all fours, coming to a halt near the horses as we approached the eastern entrance to the encampment and giving us reptilian hisses.

Decurion Livianus waved them away with his hand, and obediently they turned and walked off.

"Such savage beasts, yet so docile once you know how to control them," he said. "Much like men. When you have what they want, you can make them do all manner of things that may not come naturally to them." He smiled coldly and gestured at the lizards. "Much like these animals. They fought us, tooth and nail, and we slaughtered them. But once we discovered what they wanted, they came to us willingly, and now do as we request. They are our auxiliaries in this strange land. Our guides, scouts, and when needed, fodder for our battles."

"Battles against whom?"

"Whomever has the poor happenstance of crossing us. Take the hairy men, you have seen them, no?"

I nodded.

"This was their land when we arrived. With the help of the buschas, as they call their natural enemies, we defeated them. And now there are few hairy men who remain, hiding from our patrols as we slaughter them on sight and feast on their horned mounts." He turned slightly to face me as our horses walked towards the fortified entrance. "You see, barbarian, terms of peace are hard to come by. As you will find out when you speak with the Legate."

Sentries moved to shift the wooden stake barriers out of the way for the Decurion so we could ride inside.

And thus, I entered Rome.

CHAPTER 36

The encampment was huge inside. From the raised ramparts with sentries, to the first tent was probably a good sixty feet of open space. Men and horses flowed through this and through the other streets laid out between the tents. But it was in this large open space that they appeared to be forming up for training or patrols. The rest of the streets were for individualized movement, men carrying weapons and equipment, the ringing of blacksmith hammers on steel, the laughter of women and men intertwined in the tents. This place was a small city.

Following the Decurion's lead, I dismounted and passed the reins of the horse back to one of the riders. The riders had visibly relaxed upon entering the encampment, and I wondered what their fighting had been like against the apes and dinosaurs so far.

"Follow me, and we will request council with the Legate." He pushed through the throng of men, leading the way.

I followed.

After a few minutes, I wasn't lost, but I was overwhelmed. Everything was neat and tidy in the camp, and while the smaller of the tents appeared to be for the men to sleep in, anything larger than that had various signs or flags flying from tent poles to designate the area. I could still see back down the street to where we had entered over the heads of the multitude of people moving inside, but we were deep inside Roman territory.

Decurion Livianus quickly led me to the largest tent and told me to wait outside with the sentries before removing his helmet and entering.

For several minutes I stood, waiting, while I took in the sights, sounds, and smell of the camp. I'd been to several Army forts on the other side of the Shimmer with Reydan, they were nothing like this.

This place was completely self-contained, and the discipline with which the men moved made me wonder what sort of brutal training regimen could create such strictness and obedience.

Overhead, dark clouds moved ominously in the wind as thunder rolled in the distance.

It seemed the axeman's Thor was still with me.

The Decurion stuck his head out of the tent. "You may enter. And you may bring your strange tools, but you must leave your axe behind."

I slid the axe out of the steel ring that kept it on my belt and set the weapon down on the ground. The two sentries looked me over, and while looking confused at my pistols and shotgun, they gave the Decurion a quick nod and one gave me a push on the shoulder towards the tent flap.

Allowing myself to be herded inside, I stepped foot into ancient history.

Thick robes of rich red cloth decorated the walls, giving the illusion of warmth while no doubt also muffling the sounds of the camp outside. On the floor, lush rugs were layered so that inside the door no bare ground was left uncovered. A large table was centered in the middle, with what appeared to be a sleeping area off to the side. Laying on the table were neatly scrolled documents beside quills and ink. To the right was a pedestal, with a bust of someone important. Perhaps the Emperor of Rome? Most likely, I thought.

On the left of the table stood a thick spear with a large golden eagle on the top. No, not a spear. Some sort of standard. Like the carved bust of the face on the pedestal, this standard reeked of importance from the way it was racked. As if it were somehow holy.

My eyes snapped to the man in front of the table. He wore intricately detailed red and gold armor, protecting his torso and upper hips without immobilizing him. A red cape flowed from his back and a sword with decorated pommel was sheathed at his hip. In his hand was a helmet of even more absurdity than the Decurion wore that stood next to me.

"Legate Leo Cassius Augustus, this is Cato. A barbarian leather craftsman we found on the road seeking council with Rome for peace."

The Legate snorted in disdain as he looked me over. "A leather craftsman? Who is he of rank to seek terms of peace?" He stepped closer to me, peering from his hawkish eyes at my attire. "He is dressed like a savage with simple armor but complicated looking tools." Reaching out he flicked my shotgun stock. "And you say he was armed with only an axe?"

"Yes, Legate. And he speaks our language."

Augustus looked at me with what bordered amusement. "Let's hear it, barbarian. Speak our tongue, if you can."

"I speak it," I told him in my rough Latin.

"Hideous attempt. But it will suffice. For whom do you speak?"

I hesitated for a moment, thinking. "I speak for the gunmen tribe of America."

"Must be a small tribe, to send a simple craftsman to seek terms of surrender."

I ignored the barbs and replied simply, "We seek peace."

For now, I thought to myself. The chances of us being able to coexist with these arrogant bastards was slim to none.

"And what are your terms for the Gunmen of America?"

"Just that. Peace for both sides. You don't attack us, and we won't attack you in return."

Augustus laughed heartily with the Decurion and even the Roman guards outside who'd been listening were laughing. Finally, the Legate wiped a tear from his face, chuckling.

"We are Rome. You stand before greatness, and you yield, or we will erase you from the annuals of history."

It was my turn to laugh, and I did so in the smug bastard's face, "This ain't Rome, buddy, this is Prehistoria."

He snarled and stepped closer. I could smell the stench of wine on his breath when he spoke, "Where we go, Rome is."

"As I said, we seek peace." I fixed him with a stare. "And for our allies, the axemen. You have them. And we want them back."

I was bluffing here. I had no idea if they were all dead, but I figured it wouldn't hurt to ask.

"Ah, the axemen. Now there is a worthy foe." Augustus glanced at the Decurion. "How many are left?"

"Seven."

"Seven... a shame. Of how many?"

The Decurion shrugged. "Around forty."

Somewhere in the distance was a boom of lightning followed by a ripple of thunder. The storm was gaining on us.

I gripped the shotgun harder, my knuckles going nearly white. "What'd you do to them?"

"We did nothing," the Legate shook his head in mock sadness as he spread his arms innocently. "And we give them the occasional opportunity to leave."

"How?" I asked through clenched teeth.

The Legate laughed again. "It is almost time for this evening's sport. Come, I will show you."

CHAPTER 37

Decurion Livianus left us, and after picking up my axe, I followed Legate Augustus out of his tent and through the camp towards the back side from where I'd entered. His armored guards followed, never allowing more than six feet or so between them and their Legate. The soldiers we passed all stopped, slamming a fist to their chest and dipping heads in respect as their leader walked through their midst. He stepped quickly, nodding here and there, occasionally stopping to slap a soldier on the shoulder with a smile. The man was excited, and I wondered what this sport of theirs had to do with the axemen and their opportunity to leave.

But suddenly, he turned right down a street at a brisk walk. I tightened my grip on the shotgun as I followed, wondering where he was leading me.

He stopped before a tent. It had no difference from the others, except for the six legionaries standing outside of it in full armor with spears in hand.

Glancing at me, Augustus ducked his head and stepped into the tent.

I followed, gasping at the stench that assaulted my nostrils. It smelled of feces and urine, mixed with raw meat and sea water.

Blinking, I waited for my eyes to adjust to the dark interior.

There was nothing in the room. Except a large, forged metal cage surrounded by six more heavily armed guards.

Chained inside was the biggest and ugliest buscha I'd ever seen before.

"Behold, the first denizen of this land to be subjugated under the might of Rome," Augustus said with disgust.

I stepped forward to get a better look.

Like the others, it was hideous. But what made this one different, other than its size, was its unique coloring. Instead of a grayish green, this one was a vibrant blueish white. There were numerous wounds along its body, some old and others fresh. They'd tortured it.

Opening its mouth, a forked tongue ran over jagged teeth. Then hissed. "Free," the beast said in guttural Latin.

Legate Augustus laughed darkly. "No, my old friend. No."

"What is this?" I asked while suddenly feeling the urge to get a bath and blow this massive buscha away with the shotgun.

"This is the queen of the lizards. It is how we are able to use them for the glory of the empire."

"They fight for you because you have their queen?"

"While she is no beauty, the other lizards think the world of her. We've made it quite clear. They fight for us, or we kill her."

"Why do you show this to me?" I asked, already knowing the answer.

"Should we not come to terms... This is who I will feed you to."

Over my dead body, I thought.

"Come, we are going to be late," the Legate said cheerily as he turned and left.

Rain drops began to fall as we walked through the back gate, around the semi-circle fortification that protected it, and towards a field full of men. Beyond the group of men, I could see a large herd of trikes fenced in. The horned dinosaurs bellowed gently, and I wondered if they knew they were going to be eaten.

At a shout from one of the guards, the large crowd of men quickly parted to allow us to walk through them.

We reached the center of the crowd, and there was a large hole in the ground. Surrounding it were stairs of varying height that men stood on to get a better view inside.

From the snarls coming from the pit, I knew what was in there before we stopped at the edge and looked down.

A trio of raptors glared up at us.

One snapped at the other, then leapt, his claws digging hopelessly at the sides of the pit in a vain attempt to climb out.

The Legate laughed and kicked a nearby rock into the pit.

It bounced off the top of a raptor's head.

"This is your sport?" I asked as the crowd began to shout and jeer.

"Our part of it."

The men on the opposite side of the hole shifted aside, and among the jeers I saw a familiar face being pushed through the crowd.

Frozen in place, I stared as Elsha was dragged towards the pit.

Only when she reached the edge did I realize it wasn't the leader of the shield maiden. The looks were close, but her face was more stern, harsh, and her hair darker and shorter. Her armor was different as well; where Elsha wore studded leather, this woman wore steel plated leather armor with both muscular arms exposed.

Which meant it was her sister, Sif.

I swore in English under my breath.

The Legate glanced at me to make sure I was watching, then raised a hand to point at the shield maiden.

Sif glared back defiantly.

"This is why we are down to seven. Every day we throw one into the pit to fight, but not before they are asked a simple question." Looking at her, he raised his voice, "Where is your home?" He asked in Latin.

She spat into the pit.

He pointed at the men holding her by the arms. They were dressed identically, in armor of a higher status than most of the soldiers. And their sharp Roman features looked the same. Twins perhaps? Either way, they were big men. Big scary men. "Dominic, Titus... do us the honors."

Laughing, they shoved her forward and with a snarl on Sif's lips, she fell into the screeching pit.

I moved without thinking.

BOOM! BOOM! BOOM!

The raptors were dead, and the barrel of my shotgun was oozing smoke.

Grabbing the Legate by his armored collar, I let the shotgun fall on its sling and drew my right-handed pistol. Whose barrel I promptly jammed under his chin.

Everyone stared at me from around the pit, and from in the pit, Sif stared with her raptor blood-splattered face in surprise.

"If you think that was impressive, you should see what this little leather hole puncher does," I told the shocked Legate.

He paled slightly.

"Tell your men to get her out."

He didn't move or speak, and the crowd of angry Roman legionnaires began to inch closer. Every single one of them was armed with at least a sword. I'd never get out of here alive in a fair fight.

I moved the pistol and shot Titus in the chest.

"No!" the Legate cried.

The big Roman looked down, touching a finger to the small hole in his armor as blood bubbled through his lips from a punctured lung. The rest of them backed up as Dominic grabbed the man by his arm and eased him to the ground.

"I said... get her out," I growled, placing the hot muzzle back under his chin with enough pressure to singe his skin.

"Get her out," Augustus stammered.

A soldier moved out of sight and quickly reappeared with a ladder that he lowered into the pit.

Sif climbed out and took the legionnaire's sword from its sheath. Twisting it around in her grip, she slammed the hilt of the blade against Dominic's head and dropped him beside a dying Titus.

"Who is next?" she demanded as the soldiers backed away from her.

I spied the Decurion Livianus among the crowd. "Tell Livianus to fetch the horse I rode in on, and I want the other six axemen brought here. Now." I shook the Legate with his leather collar to drive home the point.

He gave the orders, and we stood around awkwardly as Titus died across the pit and the others ran to fulfill the Legion Commander's orders. I could have asked for any horse, but I didn't want to ride out of here on a mystery mount that might throw me a dozen feet down the road. But the one I rode in on, that one I trusted to listen to me... as much as a horse without stirrups could.

Shortly, I had two more shield maidens and four axemen standing with Sif, and Livianus holding the reins to my horse. Dominic was sitting up now, a large knot forming on the side of his skull. He looked like he wanted to murder us all with his large bare hands.

But I didn't give a shit.

We were getting out of here.

"Bring the horse," I ordered Livianus while pushing the Legate in front of me towards the trike pen. At another shout from the Roman leader's guards, the soldiers backed away to give us room to walk through them.

"Mount the trikes," I told the remaining axemen and women.

They did so, and a shout of alarm came from across the open field.

Awshucks and Thathas emerged from the jungle with Elsha and Helga at their side. The big apes looked positively tickled as they lumbered towards us with weapons in hand.

The Legate snarled angrily. "You are allied with the hairy men? The audacity! You shall be crucified for what you've done here today."

"Shut your mouth, worm."

"We heard your shotgun," Elsha said as she rushed over and embraced her sister.

"Good. Now mount up and let's go before they decide to rush us," I told her in the Viking tongue so the Romans wouldn't understand. "I can't kill them all."

They listened, opened the corrals and the two apes picked out a pair of larger trikes for their own mounts.

"Get out of here," I told the trike mounted group. "Don't wait for me, just go."

"No! We won't leave you," Elsha said firmly.

"You're not. I'll be behind you. But I want you to have a head start before this entire army comes after us."

She nodded in understanding, turned her trike and they rode away in a large group as fast as the big bodied dinosaurs could carry them.

Switching back to Latin, I whispered in the Legate's ear. "These are my terms of peace. Let us ride away, and we won't kill you all. Come after us, and it will be the last thing Rome ever does before I burn it to the ground."

"You killed my brother," he said coldly.

"Who?"

"Titus."

"Let me guess, Dominic is also your brother?"

"Yes."

I looked around for him, but the crowd had grown significantly larger as word had spread through the encampment. I was willing to bet there were almost a thousand pairs of eyes on me now.

I suddenly got a bad feeling about the missing twin. If I were him, I'd have gathered a group and headed out another gate to get a head start after us.

And most of the Vikings were unarmed.

Grabbing the horse reins, I mounted quickly while keeping the pistol pointed at the Legate.

"Remember my words."

He spat at the ground. "The word Cato will be cursed on every lip of Rome. Until you die. Then it will cease to exist."

"Then you'd better get it right, asshole. The name is Cato of the Black Plague."

I wheeled the horse around, knocking the Legion Commander to the ground. Firing a shot into the air to keep the other soldiers back, I kicked heels to flanks and the horse surged forward in the direction the trikes had gone.

"I want them alive!" I heard the Legate scream from behind me at the top of his lungs.

I hoped that meant they wouldn't send the buschas after us.

CHAPTER 38

I left the shouts and cries of thousands of men arming themselves behind me as my horse raced across the jungle floor. A dozen trikes left a hell of a path behind them. It'd be easy to follow.

I was worried about the Roman cavalry coming after us. Even a dozen armed men could wreak hell on us. Or a dozen of those toothy damned buschas.

Once out of sight of the watch towers of the encampment, I caught up to the other riders as they paused and waited for me against my demand.

From there, we rode as fast as we could in the direction of the shore. Awshucks led the way; he and Thathas seemed to have an uncanny ability to find a path wide enough for the trikes to move through and apparently knew the direction we wanted to go in.

And we were making good time, even skirting around the small mountain that we'd watched the Roman camp from.

Until the trikes came to an abrupt stop.

Pawing and bellowing softly to each other, they refused to go forward more. I slowed my horse and wheeled it back around, riding back towards the others to see what was the matter.

"What? What is it?" I asked Awshucks as if the big black and bronze ape knew what my words meant.

Getting the gist, he pointed ahead of us and grumbled something while cupping a hand around his ear.

Then I heard it, a loud, rhythmic sound… like something massive breathing.

I glanced behind us, no sign of any Romans yet. But they were back there, I knew it. And likely gaining on us. We were having to forge a path, although at times it seemed Awshucks had taken us on old trike trails. The Romans behind us simply had to follow the tramplings of a dozen trikes and one poor horse.

"Take them around," I told Elsha in a loud whisper, pointing to our right where the jungle looked more sparse and easier to ride the herd of trikes through.

"What will you do?" she asked hesitantly.

"Slow down our followers."

"How?"

I grinned at her, knowing full well I was about to do something stupid.

She sighed, then jerked her head to the right and pulled her trike in that direction. The others walked the horned dinosaurs slowly at first, as if unsure of where they were going, then quicker as they moved away from the spot where I sat alone on my horse.

Elsha gave me a final look of disapproval before following Sif and Thathas out of sight.

I waited after they disappeared into the jungle, leaving me alone with the heavy breathing from something monstrous not too far ahead.

Once satisfied that they were far enough away, I rode my horse forward slowly. He hesitated at first, but with some gentle coaxing, he began to walk.

Overhead the slight trickle of raindrops was beginning to come down in earnest. The storm was about to sweep over us. I prayed it'd give everyone the opportunity to escape the Romans.

A hundred feet further, we pushed through a screen of small bushes and ferns and were rewarded with the sight of the giant sleeping dinosaur.

It was the same one that we had stolen an egg from. That seemed like weeks ago but had only been a couple of days. I guess running into an extinct civilization of arrogant humans would make time seem to fly.

There were a few wound marks on its snout from the shotgun. Small, puckered holes that had clotted and were in the process of healing. The Auto-5 hadn't had much of an effect on him, but I had it loaded with buckshot at the time. A heavy 10-gauge slug would punch through a good bit deeper. I glanced down at the remaining shells in the bandoleer across my chest, half of them were slugs. But I'd loaded the shotgun with buckshot prior to meeting the Roman patrol and on the ride away from the encampment I hadn't bothered to change the shells out.

Just in case I needed to pepper some people and their mounts.

But it was still surprising, here my horse and I were about a hundred feet away from the largest curled up, snoring dinosaur that I'd ever seen. It was the sort of dinosaur that would make Governor Fredrick jealous, even after he slayed the Tyrannosaurus near Whitesberg.

I supposed the beast didn't have any predators. Or at least, I hoped it didn't. As big as this creature was, it'd take a trio of Maxim machine guns to finish off.

Something shifted in the trees. Glancing up, I saw a black raven turn its head sideways to look down at me.

Odd.

Behind me I could hear horses and men approaching fast through the forest. They were racing down the beaten trike path, knowing full well that we were unarmed except for my weapons and a few swords and no risk to them.

Well, maybe we weren't. But this big ass dinosaur would be.

Drawing a pistol, I fired a shot into the air to wake the ugly sleeping beast.

It twitched but didn't wake.

Sighing, I began to unsling my ten-gauge Auto-5 shotgun. That should wake it.

A loud crack split the sky as a lightning bolt slammed into the towering forest a couple hundred yards away. The boom shook the forest. My mount jerked at the reins, and I had to fight it to a standstill.

Thank you, Thor.

The beast stirred, the long tail unwinding from around its alligator face as it shook itself awake. I waited, impatiently, as my horse trembled beneath me. The massive dinosaur stood, stretching forward on its haunches like a dog, before fixing its eyes on me. The sound of horse hooves was growing louder. The Roman cavalry was almost upon us.

The bottom dropped out on the storm and rain cascaded down, soaking through the chain mail and cloth shirt, making me shiver.

This time, I slung the shotgun on my back, and fired a shot at its underbelly with my pistol.

Just to make it mad.

I whipped the horse around with the reins and bolted in the direction of crushed vegetation from the path of the trikes. Heading back in the direction of the Roman encampment.

With an angry growl, the dinosaur gave chase.

The horse panicked beneath me, fear giving his hooves wings, and we whipped in and out of towering trees and barreled through brush and ferns in the direction we'd come. The Auto-5 slammed into my back over and over again, sending agonizing pain shooting along my spine as it pounded bruises into my flesh.

Crashing through a thick screen of slightly trampled ferns, I was among them.

There had to be about thirty of them, riding in a column after us at a quick trot.

A Decurion was leading the way. It wasn't Livianus, but another one with a fancy helmet.

He looked very surprised at my sudden appearance.

My left pistol leapt into my hand, and my first bullet hit him in the throat. Grasping helplessly at the small hole, he toppled from his saddle as I jerked the reins and moved to the right side of the column of men and horses.

His men were disciplined. I'd give them that.

Several spears were thrust at me as I rode past firing indiscriminately into the armored men within arm's reach.

One of the steel tips nicked the neck of my horse, while another slid off my chain mail shirt.

I pulled the horse to the right, moving further away from the column of mounted men and reach of their weapons.

Behind me, the dinosaur attacked the mounted column with an ear-piercing roar.

The Romans were brave, I'll give them that too. They didn't scatter, instead they charged forward in unison.

Which meant their horses were either braver or better trained than anything I'd ever seen before. Because they rushed forward into the gaping maws and claws of the beast that towered a good ten feet over them.

I shot my pistol empty, knocking two more riders off their horses as the cavalry split around the dinosaur. As they passed, each rider hurled their spear at the monstrosity, piercing its hide and peppering it with pointed shafts.

Wheeling my horse around, I holstered the left pistol, flipped the reins to my other hand, and drew the right one.

I did this just in time to see the beast knock a half dozen spears off its body with a swipe of its long black claws. It appeared the spears hadn't penetrated very deep, just enough to cause rivets of blood to begin flowing, but nothing had hurt any organs or vitals.

Most of the Romans were focused on the bigger threat and ignored me. But four of the men drew their swords, raised their shields, and rode directly at me.

I shot the closest one out of the saddle.

Shifting my aim, I caught a blur out of the side of my peripheral vision a split second before Awshucks' trike rammed its horns through one of the horse's sides and out the other with a spray of blood and a loud bellow.

I fired again, missing the breastplate of the armored man thundering down on me and hitting his horse in the head instead. The beast dropped abruptly, brutally flinging the rider face first into the ground with a sickening thud that I was close enough to hear over the battle around us.

The leader of the apes roared and swung his stone axe, hacking off a Roman rider's arm at the elbow while his trike dragged its blood-covered horns out of the horse corpse.

A couple of dozen feet away, the dinosaur sunk its teeth through a Roman breastplate, then thrashed the screaming man side to side until his lower half flung off into the trees.

A brave Roman hacked at the back legs of the beast from horseback with his sword, slicing open several wounds in the pebbled hide.

The monstrous dinosaur stomped on him, sinking large, clawed toes into flesh, and squeezing. The screams of both man and horse were loud and brief.

I quickly holstered my pistol and unslung the shotgun.

Things were going to all sorts of hell around me, and I was ready to get out of here. But I didn't want to leave Awshucks behind. The big black and bronze haired ape had risked himself by coming back for me, the least I could do was make sure he got away too.

Kicking heels to the horse, the mount surged forward, racing through the chaos to Awshucks and his trike.

With a fiery blast, the ten-gauge buckshot blew the closest cavalry man off his mount as he leaned back to pitch a short spear at the ape.

Another rider shouted, jerked his horse around, and rode towards us with shield and sword raised.

I hesitated, worried about hitting the great ape between us.

The dinosaur snapped the charging man off his mount with a crunch and a splash of blood.

"Go!" I shouted at Awshucks, waving my hand at him to ride away.

For a moment, I worried the ape wasn't going to listen. But he turned his trike with a jerk of reins and kicked flanks to get it running back in the direction of the others.

Twisting my mount to follow, I emptied the shotgun in the general direction of the dinosaur and riders, pelting them with a spray of buckshot, then chased after Awshucks into the forest.

CHAPTER 39

Leaving the carnage behind, I quickly reloaded my guns while traveling after the ape leader. The big ape seemed pleased and gave me a toothy canine grin as I caught up to him.

We'd gotten lucky with coming across that spined beast, and the mess it'd left behind would be a reminder to the Romans coming after us that Prehistoria, or myself, would not be so easily conquered.

An hour later, as the rain tapered off and finally quit, we caught up with the others.

At a shout from one of the axemen glancing behind them, they noticed us approaching.

Elsha pulled her trike to the side and stopped while the others continued moving towards the coastline.

I slowed my horse while pulling abreast of the mounted trike. "Elsha, you look pleased to see me," I told the Viking shield maiden.

She laughed, a harsh but beautiful sound, while her green eyes took me in. "I see you didn't get eaten. That is good. We may have need of your guns again."

"They are at your service," I told her sincerely as we grinned at each other.

She suddenly looked uncomfortable. "We should catch up to the others. You have bought us some time, but we need to make it to the boats if we want to live." With that, she urged her trike on after the other riders.

I glanced behind us, worried that at any moment more riders would appear. The Legate's order to take us alive may change once he sees what we did to his other men. It gave us an advantage; we could kill while they would only try to wound... but only for so long. I had a feeling the Roman hospitality of taking us alive would probably be over soon.

But then, with the trail the mounted trikes were leaving behind, it would be nothing to track us at their own pace. And it wasn't us they wanted to overcome; it was our civilization.

I rode beside the ape leader, reflecting on that thought.

Our civilization.

I was lumping myself in with the Vikings instead of the gunmen.

I supposed I'd always felt like something of an outsider. I recalled vaguely the Charleston slave docks where Eugene Landry saved my life before I was discarded as useless. After that I was a black child raised by whites. First at the Landry home, then on the road with the Captain, and later by the side of Reydan White as the Captain returned home from the South to reclaim his birthright fortune and build a railroad empire out of it.

But so far, the most I'd ever felt at home was with the axemen. As a professional gunman, I was typically either treated with respect for my abilities or disdain for my race depending on who I was around. With the axemen though, it was general disdain for my meager axe abilities and no thought for my race. A pleasant change.

Or maybe I thought 'our' civilization because I had it bad for Elsha.

I sighed loudly and Awshucks looked at me curiously.

I was a damned fool.

CHAPTER 40

When we reached the coast, we turned and rode south along the rock-covered beach. I thought this would work out well, as Elsha would rather approach them from the open than surprise them coming from the forest with a pair of apes in our midst.

After several hours of riding our trikes and lone horse at a quick pace, I soon realized that Asger and the other Vikings had been busy while we'd been gone.

Where the boats had been was now a fort, similar in design, but inferior, to the Roman encampment. Numerous small trees had been cut down from the area, leaving the largest and most difficult to cut still standing. Those small trees, which would be normal size compared to what we had on the other side of the Shimmer, had been cut into length, sharpened, and planted to build a solid palisade. Around the palisade, rows of sharpened spikes had been planted, jutting outward at an angle to stop anything trying to attack directly at the fort.

It looked impressive, but I knew it wouldn't be enough to stop thousands of angry Romans.

"Hail the fort!" shouted Elsha as we approached.

"Welcome back!" Thur cried from his position by the entrance. "And what have you there? A pair of ape prisoners?"

"A pair of friends," Sif shouted back.

"Sif? Is that you?" he called, moving forward on foot with his spear in hand to greet us.

"It's me, you old goat."

"And Leif? He's not with you?" he asked, rubbing the scar across his throat while looking behind us at the other mounted Vikings.

"No. He feasts in Valhalla."

Thur's shoulders drooped slightly, but he gave a quick nod then lifted his head. "As is where he belongs."

Asger came around the gate with Janse close behind. The beastly axeman pointed his great axe at the apes. "What are you doing with these two?"

"Long story," Helga said as she dismounted.

"No worries. I'll dispatch them now to their foul god," Janse strode forward and Awshucks quickly dropped from his mount with stone axe in hand to accept the challenge.

As much as I'd love to see the two of them battle it out, and hopefully Awshucks win, Elsha put a stop to it. "Leave them. They are friends."

"Apes are not friends," Asger said with a skeptical eye appraising the two hairy men.

"They are today," I replied. "They saved our lives."

Janse looked at the other axemen and women behind us, "Where is Ingrid?"

"She too feasts in Valhalla. Along with everyone else not with us," Elsha said as her trike sidestepped away from the giant axeman.

Janse carefully reached out, placed his hand on the trike, and patted it with a gentler and calmer manner than I'd ever seen the man display before. "Nice mount, Elsha."

She passed him the reins and slid down from the horned mount. "He is yours if you want him."

Janse grinned broadly as he looked over the trike. "It is large, like me. I think it will work."

"That's nice and all, but we've got an enemy coming for us," I told Asger. "And this fort ain't shit to stop them."

The black bearded Viking leader glanced behind us for any approaching threats.

"How soon will they be here?"

"Soon," Elsha replied as she ran a hand through her hair in frustration. "Very soon."

"Best come inside and tell us of it."

"And the apes?" Sif asked.

"Bring them."

"Asger! They're apes. We can't bring them inside," Janse said in outrage. "They'll see our defenses!"

"We can if I command it," he warned the giant. "And I command it. Besides, there's only two. Surely, we can handle two apes? And the trikes, take care of them. Don't let them wander, as we may need them soon." He turned back to us, sizing up the apes. After a moment, he seemed to make up his mind, "Can they speak our language?"

"A handful of words."

"Why are they with you?"

"Not really sure." I glanced back at Awshucks and Thathas, who were watching us with what looked like amusement. "They saved us, and then stuck around. Seemed curious about what we're going to do with the Romans."

"Romans? What sort of dinosaur is that?" Thur asked.

"They're not dinosaurs, they're people."

"People? Of what sort?"

"The angry sort that will stop at nothing to rule everything and everyone."

"That's a problem," Asger said. "Novagant will be ruled by no one but our Jarl."

I eyed the forest to the front. There were a lot of big trees still standing, that could go either way with the Romans. It might slow them down, or it might give them cover to move closer. I didn't know which way it'd go; I was no military strategist. I was just a trigger puller.

So, to me, trees meant cover. Which was bad. Especially when the trees were thick ones that could soak up a lot of bullets.

"Well," Asger waved at the apes to come forward. They glanced at each other but didn't move.

"Helga, you try. They seem to like you," Elsha told the shield maiden.

Helga walked back to the apes, spread both her arms out at the encampment and said, "Fort."

Awshucks repeated the word, close enough to be understood.

"Come with us, inside," she said, waving an arm and hand in invitation.

Thathas grumbled something to Awshucks, and the leader of the apes grunted back and dismounted. He left his spears strapped to the trike but brought his large stone axe with him.

"What'd he say?" Asger called.

"No idea," Helga said as Awshucks walked forward towards us while Thathas stayed seated on his trike. "Looks like only one of them is coming in."

"That is fine. Janse, watch the other."

"I'll kill him if I need to," the giant axeman replied.

"Please don't," Helga said.

"Janse, only if necessary," Asger warned.

Leading the way, Thur walked inside the encampment. By now the palisade was lined with axemen watching the apes interact with their fellow Vikings. Their faces were a range of amusement to disgust and sheer hatred.

"We need to be careful with Awshucks. Apes and axemen have been enemies a long time," I told Elsha.

She rested a hand on my arm, and I tried to suppress the shiver that ran through me from her touch. "Relax, they won't do anything unless Asger allows them to."

"I hope you're right," I mumbled as she moved her hand away and stepped forward quicker to catch up with Asger, while I fell behind the towering ape that swaggered between the upright spikes and into the fort.

CHAPTER 41

Inside the fort was nothing much. The four longships had been pulled inside. There were multiple cooking fires and shelters built from fallen trees thatched with thick ferns to give the axemen shade from the blistering sun. Several axemen were wading in the ocean, spears in hand, shouting at each other in laughter as they tried to spear fish.

As we passed one of the fires, I realized they had a medium-sized pterodactyl skewered across the flames to roast. A Viking poked the body with a stick, then ladled something out of a simmering bowl and poured it over the corpse.

Whatever seasonings they were using, the smell made my stomach growl with lust.

As the surviving axemen and women from the previous expedition fell out of our crowd to be greeted by the others, our group dwindled until it was Elsha and Sif, Awshucks, and myself following Thur and Asger to a rectangular open-air tent. It was formed from angled logs notched together with a large piece of dinosaur hide draped over the top for shelter.

Awshucks had to bend over to fit under the hide, and we all sat down together with the ape crossing his hairy legs Indian style, which I found to be rather amusing and strange at the same time.

I sat next to him as I was the last to sit, but everyone else made sure to give him plenty of room.

Asger shifted his sword on his hip and looked at Elsha's sister. "Tell me everything. Starting with you, Sif."

"I think you need to get everyone ready for battle first," the shield maiden warned. "And we need to see about getting the boats loaded and in the water."

"That bad?" Asger grumbled, before turning to look at the four longships resting in the clumps of grass amidst the sand hill the fort was built on.

"Yes," I said. "It's bad. You're far outnumbered, perhaps fifty to one."

He cursed something in Viking tongue under his breath that I couldn't make out before shouting at Gundar the Wrathful who was sitting by the closest fire, sharpening his sword with a whetstone.

"Gundar! Prepare the men for battle. Send some out to Janse to mount the trikes. Tell them to keep away from the ape."

"Yes, Asger!" he called back as he scrambled to his feet. Then the old Viking hesitated a moment, looking at Awshucks, before asking, "Is it hairy men or lizards, sir?"

"Men."

Gundar dipped his head in acknowledgement and began shouting at various axemen nearby. The fort began to bustle with energy as men moved and made ready for a fight. Within seconds the cooking pterodactyl was jerked off the skewer and torn apart in chunks to be devoured on the move.

I wondered what it tasted like.

"Now, tell me who these Romans are," Asger demanded with a snarl on his bearded face.

"They are from a place called Rome," I began. "They are fierce warriors and known for conquering nearby tribes and expanding their lands."

"They sound like us," Thur said.

"Yes. But there's a lot more of them than you. From what Awshucks has been able to tell us, it sounds like they wiped out all the apes around here. Just him and his band is all that's left."

"Awshucks? The apes have names?" Thur grumbled.

Asger ignored Thur. "Why'd the apes save you? And what from?" he asked quietly, a frown growing across his face.

"I suppose it's because we don't look like Romans. And they saved us from a buscha ambush. Buschas are those damned lizards we fought in the water. They're smart, lethal, and somehow the Romans have them under their thumb. They used them to help defeat the apes."

"We sent scouts out; they never came back and we couldn't find them."

"It was likely the buschas. I believe they take and eat the dead. They killed Ingrid. Or it may have been that finned dinosaur we keep running into."

"We saw the tracks of it, but no sign of it eating anyone," Thur said. "That's why we built our walls so tall… we were afraid it would come around hungry."

"I don't think you have to worry about it anymore," Elsha said with a sly grin. "Cato led it to the Romans, and they killed each other."

"I'm pretty sure that giant spined beast is still alive. But hopefully it's occupied with the Romans instead of tracking us down," I rebutted.

"Clever," Thur gave me a hard slap on the back.

Awshucks grumbled and looked like he was about to get up and kill Thur for touching me. I waved at him and said, "Friends."

The ape leader looked around and repeated, "Friends."

"By Odin's spear, he can speak our language," Asger said in shock.

"Yeah, he's learning." I clapped Awshucks on the shoulder like Thur did to me.

The ape leader looked down at me, then slapped me hard enough to nearly topple me forward.

Sif barked a laugh as I straightened up with what dignity I could muster.

Asger stared at Awshucks for a moment before turning to Elsha. "Who speaks the hairy man tongue best?"

"Helga."

"Have Helga work with them more, I want them speaking as much as possible as quickly as possible. And I want her to ask that whatever apes are left to help us."

"No one is going to like that," Elsha warned, jerking her head to signal the camp around us.

"They don't have to like it; they just have to obey me. If we are outnumbered as Cato says, fifty to one, we need allies. And Awshucks is looking like an ally."

"We can't fight fifty to one, unless there are thousands of apes who can help us." I protested. "We need to leave. Get in the boats, sail back across the sea, and prepare Novagant and Whitesberg for an invasion."

"We can't, Cato. Not until the tide is high enough to clear the rocks," Thur said, looking past me at the water beyond the fortification.

I turned to look. We'd come in on high tide, and I hadn't noticed any rocks previously. But sure enough, there they were. Jagged ones, the sort that would dash a man or boat to pieces. Waves were pounding against them, sending water spraying six feet high. There was no way we could get the boats over that until the water rose again.

Damn.

"Let's hope the high tide gets here before the damned Romans," I growled.

CHAPTER 42

Awshucks sent Thathas to get the other remaining apes. I was willing to bet that they were nearby, keeping an eye on the fort while staying out of sight. Viking sentries were sent out in three directions to keep an eye out for any advancing Romans.

Axemen began stacking spare spears and quivers full of arrows around the palisade, while others began preparing the boats for departure. Sea chests were packed, oars checked and prepared, and the boats moved down towards the high-water mark.

If the Romans got here before the tide, it'd be a fight for the boats.

"Did you take that chain mail off a dead axeman?" a gruff voice asked, shaking me from my thoughts.

Ajar the Mad turned Bold was walking towards me, the Jarl's jeweled seax strapped to his front. I glanced down at the interwoven armor shirt I was wearing.

"No, Elsha found it in one of the boats. I believe it came from a man named Erikson."

"Ah, yes, I knew Erikson well. He lived to see this place but was killed by the lizards soon after."

"You think he'd mind me using it?" I asked, without really caring.

"He's in Valhalla, likely naked with a horn of mead in one hand and an axe in the other. Too busy fighting to care."

I grinned. Reverend would have a hard time converting these pagan heathens to Christianity.

A shout of warning came from one of the axemen standing guard along the wall near the forest side of the fort. Ajar and I jogged over to the palisade and saw one of the sentries running back in our direction. Behind him followed a pair of buschas, loping along on all fours.

"That's not a good sign," Ajar mumbled. "Run faster, Eif, run…"

We watched, helpless, as Janse and the other trike riders rode forward to intercept the chased sentry. There was no way they'd reach him in time.

The closest lizard leapt at Eif with claws out reached.

Eif dropped and rolled, his axe slashing up and disemboweling the buscha in a smooth stroke.

The second lizard paused, hesitating, as it watched the other lizard tremble and die as Eif stood.

The lone sentry raised his axe and took a step forward.

An arrow pierced the buscha through the shoulder. Spinning, it turned towards the new threat just in time for Thathas to trample the beast under his trike.

"Maybe these hairy men aren't so bad after all," Ajar said with a slight smile.

"The enemy of our enemy is our friend," I replied.

Thathas spun his trike around and lumbered it towards the fort while Eif jogged back.

Reaching the palisade wall, the sentry bent over, gasping for breath and pointing a finger towards the forest. "Romans coming. And lizards," he called out.

"Well done, Eif!" Asger shouted from the entrance. "Now get back in here and prepare for battle."

Eif grinned and raised his bloodied axe in a mock salute.

Awshucks and his band of merry apes rushed out of the forest. Somehow, they'd all managed to find time to apply war paint to themselves. Green, red, yellow, and white, splashed all over their bodies in intricate designs and patterns.

Thathas caught up with them, and they ran their trikes around the palisade to join Janse and the other mounted axemen.

"That's a bit more like it," Sif said from behind me.

I glanced over my shoulder and saw she'd approached with Thur. They were both armed to the teeth, and Sif still carried Dominic's sword.

Seeing it made me frown. I wondered where the brother to the Legate had gotten too. He didn't look like the sort to allow me to kill his twin without retribution. I'd fully expected him to be leading the cavalry charge after us. But it'd been someone else.

Shame.

Then he could have been eaten too.

"Never thought I'd fight side by side with an ape," Thur grumbled.

"How about side by side with a friend?" Sif asked as she ran the tip of her sword along one of the palisade stakes, carving off a thin slice of bark.

"Nope, still a hairy man ape. Only good one is a dead one."

They both laughed.

"Thur," I said, recalling what I'd been carrying with me. I pulled out the trike handled blade and passed it to him. "Elsha found this." I didn't mention she'd found it with a severed and gnawed upon arm.

"Ah, yes." He looked over the six-inch-long forged knife. "Leif loved this blade. He skinned many a dinosaur with it. I once saw him ram it through an ape's eye socket as well." He chuckled. "The ape had him by the shoulder and was picking him up to throw… he jerked this out and slipped it right into the hairy man's brain."

Sif patted Thur on the back as she looked over the blade. "He was a good man. He'd want his brother to have this."

"What do the runes mean?" I asked.

Sif smiled sadly. "It's his name. I gave it to him when we wed."

We were silent as Thur turned the blade over and ran his thumb along the carved runes in the trike handle. "Was it the lizards?" he asked.

"We don't know," I replied "But whether it was the buschas or the Romans, we'll make them both bleed for what they did."

"No one crosses swords with axes and gets away without a cut," Thur rumbled. "Fifty to one is a lot, but that just means there's plenty of them for us to kill."

"Agreed," Sif said as the shield maiden wrapped an arm around Thur and gave him a gentle hug.

"Here comes your chance," I said as a column of Romans began to march out of the forest and into the partially cleared opening ahead of us.

I looked behind us. Damn, the tide still wasn't high enough. But it was creeping up there, one splashing wave after another.

"Stand by with bows," Asger called out. "As soon as they are within arrow distance, let loose. We'll not let the pale skinned bastards prepare themselves before we hit."

The Roman infantry began to move to the right, marching in unison and flowing around the uncut trees from the encampment.

Several arrows were launched and fell well short of the men.

Laughter and cat calls came from around me, as the axemen and women shamed those who thought they could score hits already.

Asger shook his head in disgust as he walked over to our position. "Screw this. Janse! Hit and retreat!" he shouted to the giant axeman waiting on the left side of the fort with the apes.

I realized at some point the mounted axemen had all gotten torches and lit them. An odd thing since the sun was still high in the sky and there was no fog rolling in on us.

"For Odin!" Janse screamed, raising his burning torch overhead and kicking heels to his trike.

Awshucks let out a louder roar, one full of menace and anger, and the apes rushed around the big axeman.

"Eager to kill," Gundar grunted. "Good on them."

Thirty mounted trikes ran, their large feet trampling the forest ground as they thundered forward.

"What are the torches for?" I asked, baffled.

Asger grinned evilly. "Elsha told us what you did with the buschas to try and save Ingrid. We thought we'd do the same to slow down the Romans."

The infantry column stopped abruptly and turned to face the charge. Together, they raised their red and yellow rectangle shields, pointed their spears forward in unison, and braced themselves for the hit.

The apes rode to the right, circling wide as they rode between the remaining trees that still stood.

Mounted axemen rode to the left, riding fifty feet or so in front of the infantry column. Together, they slipped to the side on their trikes, lowering themselves, and began dragging the torches through the underbrush.

Behind them flames leapt and began sending rising swirls of smoke.

The Romans' formation shifted, rotating to protect both side and front with spears. The movement thinned both fronts of spear points but gave them some protection on each side.

"Where are the apes going?" Sif asked. "Fleeing?"

They abruptly turned left, the trikes almost skidding their feet as they moved quickly. Rushing forward the mounted apes hit the column of planted shields on their flank. Awshucks was at the front of the charge; his trike lowered its horns and plowed through the braced shields, flinging men with a bellow and toss of the horns. The other trikes trampled through, crushing men underfoot and impaling or knocking them aside with horns.

"The apes told Helga they wanted to try something new. Seems they've learned some hard lessons fighting the Romans," Asger said grimly.

The trikes made it through the infantry column. Two of them were riderless, and another trike was bogged down by Romans who were swarming over it, stabbing with sword and spear.

"Lost three," Gundar muttered.

"Ja, but look at what they did," Thur said in awe.

The trail of carnage the trike charge left behind was stunning, crushed men and shields lay scattered about with broken spears. Many more were wounded and trying to rise, broken limbs and ribs slowing them down. Even from this distance we could hear the cries of the wounded and dying.

Awshucks led the mounted trikes back towards us in a run as a mass of cavalry broke through the forest and chased after them.

"When in range, let loose!" Asger shouted with a wave of his bow.

The trikes rushed through the rows of flames, trampling fire and sending burning twigs and leaves flying. Behind them the mounted horses leapt over the flames, eager as the riders were to kill the remaining apes.

Arrows let loose around us. Asger, Gundar, and Thur all drawing and releasing fluidly. As the thin, fletched arrows began to pelt the Roman cavalry, they raised their shields and continued on, even as their mounts and men began to fall.

I desperately wished I held a rifle instead of a shotgun. At this range, it'd be a turkey shoot.

Then I recalled I had a horse.

"What are you doing?" Elsha shouted as I pulled the reins free from where I'd tied them and leapt onto the back of the horse. Once again, I found myself wishing the silly Romans had invented stirrups by the time we ran into each other.

In front of us the Roman cavalry charge faltered as they started taking heavy casualties. The ape mounted trikes continued around to the right of our encampment, safe from any pursuit while the Romans turned and retreated behind the other infantry columns marching into the cleared forest. A few wounded riders on foot tried to make their way back but were soon pin cushioned with arrows by the axemen.

I watched the columns of infantry growing for a moment before looking down at Elsha. "There's a bunch of them."

"And what is one man on a horse going to do?"

I looked at the tide. It was almost high enough to ride the boats out on. If they came at us now, we'd be in trouble.

"I'm going to delay them. Tell Asger to get everyone ready to rush the boats and row out of here."

"What about you?"

I unslung the Auto-5 and passed the shotgun to her. "I'll catch up. Don't let that get wet."

CHAPTER 43

Kicking heels to flanks, I rode out of the encampment and past where Janse and the other apes and men waited on the backs of their trikes. Some of them were tending to fresh wounds, others readying weapons for another attack if the need should arise.

Janse looked at me with a frown, but I gave him a wink and kept riding.

Flames between the encampment and the Romans were growing in some places and dying in others. I supposed it all depended on how wet the spots got during the rainstorm. Finding a large break in the fire, I rode into the blackened growth and stopped the horse.

Immediately, a Roman in a fancy helmet rode forward followed by three other riders. Their armor looked expensive and pretty, I took that to mean they were either royalty or in charge.

Either way, they'd do.

As they rode closer, I realized the rider with the fancy helmet was Dominic. The Legate's remaining brother looked angry and fearsome in his get up. Even his partially armored black horse looked mean.

Stretching casually, I snuck a glance over my shoulder and saw that the apes and axemen were dismounting their trikes and making their way into the hastily erected fort.

"Cato of the Black Plague!" came a shout from before me.

Looking back to the front, a gust of wind swirled black smoke and gray ash across the field. After a moment, it settled, and revealed the four Romans stopped a dozen paces in front of me. Their horses snorted in dislike of the scent of fire.

"What did I tell the Legate?" I called back over the crackle of nearby flames. "If you came after me, I'd burn Rome to the ground." Sweeping an arm across the battlefield to show the dead men and horses, I warned, "This is only the beginning."

Dominic laughed, a mean and cruel sound. He looked around him as the others joined in his laughter.

"You black skinned fool. You cannot defeat the greatness of Rome. We will chase you to the ends of the earth then throw you off the edges as you beg for mercy. And there will be none," Dominic mocked. "See behind me? This is but a portion of the men and beasts at our disposal. We are legion."

I froze.

Beasts.

He'd said beasts.

Where the hell were the lizards?

He smiled evilly as he saw the realization settle in. "Yes. Your boats are not safe from Rome. Even now as you delay us to allow your axemen and," he spat on the ground, "hairy men friends to escape... the buscha, and a watery grave, wait for them."

There was no time to waste.

I had to warn them.

"Parleys over assholes," I said as my hands flashed to the pistols still strapped to my sides.

Drawing with both hands, I shot them all.

The two men on the outside took bullets to the chest first, easily punching through their armor at this close of a range, then Dominic and the other Roman next.

A look of shock and awe flashed across the Legate's brother's face as he toppled backwards and fell off his mount.

Kicking heels to my horse, I spun him around and raced back toward the encampment as the entire Roman army surged forward in attack.

Within seconds, I was safely out of their bow range, and had a good head start on their mounted cavalry.

I rode like hell with utter disdain for the life of the horse beneath me.

It was forfeit if I was to save the others.

Riding between the jutting wooden spikes, I entered the fort to see the four boats already farther out in the sea than I'd have liked.

I whipped the reins against the horse and sent him charging into the crashing waves of the rising tide. Leaping, he fought valiantly against the sea, striving to swim and carry my weight to the boats, until he went under, and I was alone swimming for my life towards the fleeing boats.

Fighting to keep my head above the waves, I swam.

Stroke after stroke, I stretched out my arms and cupped handfuls of water, pulling them back against me, knowing all the while that I had little chance of catching up with them. But also knowing I'd likely be crucified if the Romans took me alive.

Which was worse, a watery grave or a cross?

As I sucked down a mouthful of sea water and choked as it burned my lungs, a wooden cross seemed rather appealing.

Something grasped me and lifted me from the water effortlessly.

Flailing, I began to thrash about, trying to fight, only to be thrown onto the floor of one of the boats.

Coughing and retching, my vision cleared, and I saw Janse and Awshucks standing above me.

"Odin should have chosen a champion who could swim," the big axeman grumbled before moving back to his seat to row.

"No!" I coughed. "No."

Forcing myself to sit up, I raised a hand and waved it at him while I tried to catch my breath. We were the last boat. The others were already entering the mist. Had Janse slowed his down to save me? Surely not. But it appeared so.

"What is it now? Do you wish for us to go back for your horse as well?" Janse asked. "It is gone!"

"NO!" I finally managed to scream. "Lizards. The lizards are waiting for us. In the water!"

A scream began and ended abruptly from the fog ahead of us. Then came the sounds of battle followed by a loud BOOM as Elsha fired my Auto-5 shotgun somewhere in the mist.

"Finally!" the giant axeman roared. "Row faster! Valhalla awaits!"

I drew both dripping wet pistols as Awshucks and Janse raised their large axes. The rowers sent us surging forward.

We sped into the mist.

CHAPTER 44

The swirling gray fog surrounded us and ahead we heard screams, shouts, and splashing.

We encountered an axeman first. His throat had been ripped out and he was floating on his back in a spreading pool of reddish water.

There was a loud splash from the front of the boat.

"They got Ivar!" someone shouted.

"Come on, you lizard bastards," Janse muttered as he shifted his stance and leaned over the edge of the boat.

Clawed hands shot out of the water, grasping at him.

With amazing speed and agility, the giant axeman lopped off one of the lizard's hands with a swing of his axe.

The severed limb landed in our boat, bumping against Awshucks' hairy foot.

Janse grinned at the ape as the bronze and black monkey showed his canines in what I assumed was a frown.

Or maybe a grin.

The hell if I knew.

We were attacked on both sides of the boat at the same time. Lizards shot out of the water with bursts of sea water and climbed on board to do battle.

Axemen shouted and thrust and hacked with their blades and spears. Lizards hissed as they were impaled and slashed open.

I shot a lizard that leapt on Awshucks' back. It took two bullets to finally dislodge the snapping buscha as it fought to get at the ape's throat.

Shifting, the ape and Janse moved back to back, fighting the wet slippery beasts on both sides. I kept shooting, occasionally shifting to shoot into the water at movement just below the surface. The damned things were quick swimmers, they'd gain speed and launch themselves at us.

Running dry, I rammed the guns back into their holsters and picked up a fallen axe.

Our boat bumped into another, throwing us all forward at the impact. I dropped to my knees, slipping in the water and blood that sloshed in the bottom of the boat.

A large burst of flame came from the boat we bumped into as a familiar roar echoed through the fog.

My shotgun.

Which meant it was Elsha's boat.

Scrambling to my feet, I ran forward, dodging between swinging axemen and hacking with my axe at every chance I had to strike.

Miraculously making it to the prow of the boat, I leapt into Elsha's longboat.

Falling once again onto my knees, I bounced off a sea chest, and smacked my head against an oar.

Shaking my head to clear the stars dancing in my vision, I found myself under the weight of a heavy, slippery buscha that was trying to rip my face off.

It hissed and slashed with its claws.

Jerking my head away, the beast's hand slid across my chain mail shirt.

I kneed it in the stomach, then hit its face with the backside of the axe. A small white tooth chipped off.

The lizard bit down on my shoulder.

Hard.

Roaring in pain from the crushing pressure, I flailed about with the axe. There was no room to get a good swing and my hits were bouncing off the buscha's slimy hide with little effect.

Letting go of the weapons handle, I grabbed the buscha by the throat with my left hand and with my right jammed my thumb into its eye socket.

The lizard shook its head on my shoulder like a ragdoll, but I kept applying pressure with my thumb.

Releasing me, the buscha screamed in my face as its eyeball popped out. Dangling from corded nerves, I snatched it in my fist and jerked it out of the skull all together. Oily blood dripped on me. Some landed in my open mouth as I began punching the lizard in its hideous face.

It snarled and lunged.

Turning my head, I managed to slip a forearm between us.

The teeth snapped shut inches from my cheek as I pushed with all my strength to keep it away.

Blood sprayed over me as the buscha's forehead split open with the swing of someone's wedged blade.

I let the lizard fall and wiped blood out of my eyes.

Elsha stood above me with Thathas. They were both covered in blood and water. She held my shotgun, and the mottled white ape had a nasty cut across his chest.

Reaching down, he wrenched a Viking axe out of the buscha's skull and inspected the blade for damage.

Helga appeared and slapped him on his hairy back. "Told you it was made good."

Thathas grunted happily but pointed at the short handle and rumbled something.

"We'll get you a bigger one," she promised.

Elsha helped me up. "You need a seax," she said firmly. "For close fights."

"Yeah, no kidding," I replied as I stood in the swaying boat. "Did we win?"

Her face fell and she shrugged with one shoulder while passing my Auto-5 back to me.

Flipping it over, I began pulling shells out of my bandoleer and reloading the shotgun while looking around.

It looked like half of the shield maidens were dead or missing. As I watched, Sif pulled a limp axewoman from the water and began pressing on a wound across her stomach. There were several hairy ape bodies sprawled out on the floor of the boat as well. Thathas looked to be the only living ape on this boat.

Janse was lashing his boat to Elsha's, and I saw they'd lost a lot of men and apes as well. The giant axeman leapt over into our boat and nodded respectfully at Elsha. "Well done." He glanced back at Awshucks who was putting purple fern on one of his ape's wounds. "We'd never have made it without the apes," he admitted grudgingly. "The Romans and buschas didn't expect them to come with us."

"That'll teach them," I said while reloading my pistols and keeping my eyes on the water around us. After that close call, I wasn't eager to clash with a lizard again.

Janse turned to me with a mocking smile. "Still alive, Little Plague?"

I thought about the ramifications of shooting him where he stood.

Tempting.

Very tempting.

But I doubted Asger or the Jarl would like that. And if my guess was correct, Novagant would need him soon.

"Any sign of the other ships?" I asked.

Both Janse and Elsha frowned. "None. We became separated during the fighting. With luck once we are out of this fog, we will see the others," the shield maiden leader replied.

Bending over, I grabbed the dead lizard that almost killed me and began to lift and shove its body over the side. Elsha grabbed the bottom half of the corpse and helped.

"I heard you use the shotgun," I told her with a sly smile as the corpse splashed into the ocean.

"It was… useful," she admitted.

"Still believe it to be a dishonorable weapon?" I teased.

"Yes. It is too easy to kill with."

"That's the point."

"You don't believe your opponent deserves a chance at a fair fight?"

"No. There is no sense in messing around, killing is killing. The faster you can do it with the less risk to yourself, the better."

"Where is the honor in that?" she asked.

"It comes with living," I replied. "Lots of dead men had honor. They're still dead."

She smiled slightly then frowned. "Sif said the Romans had been preparing to march to the sea and stockpiling wood for boats."

"They'll be coming for us then."

"Yes."

CHAPTER 45

Once we rowed out of the fog, we found the other boats. Pulling alongside each other, we evaluated our casualties.

There were many.

Including Asger.

From the way Gundar told it, the axeman had gone down swinging his axe, teeth bared, against an onslaught of buschas. And while he'd slayed several and wounded many more, there'd just been too many of them.

The ships were quiet as we loaded our dead onto Asger's boat. It would be pulled behind Janse's, the new leader of this failed expedition, as we returned the bodies to Novagant for a funeral pyre or burial.

For the next few days, we sailed quietly. Gone was the laughter and boasts of strength, power, and glory... the recent defeat weighed heavily on the Vikings' minds.

The wind was in our favor, and we made good time making it back to Prehistoria. Once the sandy beaches were in sight, we quickly rowed until we reached the axeman town.

A horn blared as we drew close. Onlookers rushed to the shore to seek out their friends and loved ones. They gasped as they saw how few of us returned. And I saw more than one bow drawn and pointed in the direction of the apes as we reached the dock.

We sat in the boats, letting the sun beat down on us, keeping watch on Awshucks and his apes, while Janse walked down the dock to deliver a report of the failed expedition to the Jarl.

Women and children called out to him, asking if someone had made it back. And I watched the giant's back as his head shook over and over. He'd been strangely quiet, usually sitting off by himself or with Ajar, deep in discussion. The quiet rumors that made their way around the ships was that he'd gone mad himself and had only Ajar who could understand him.

But from time to time, he had stood and given orders to row, or work the sail, or to shut the hell up or he'd throw you into the ocean.

So, I took no stock in the tales of his mind having gone.

I believed he was simply a man who'd never witnessed defeat before.

After a while, the Jarl turned back to the crowd and spoke loudly. He told them that Awshucks and his apes were welcome, and that they were not the ones the axemen and their ancestors had been fighting since the founding of their town. But that they were valuable allies we'd soon need.

I barely listened.

It was the same old story since the dawn of time.

Men make enemies. Men make allies. Men make war.

And where there was killing, I'd be needed.

I glanced at Elsha; she was sitting with her sister Sif. She met my eyes with her own, smiled sadly, then looked away.

The Jarl finished, and Janse walked back to us.

Thur stood, patted me on the shoulder, and picked up his belongings to disembark.

I stayed, waiting as the axemen unloaded and the wailing of many women and children grew louder.

There was no one waiting for me.

No Reydan White. No Eugene Landry. Not even that asshole Jed and all his friends.

Picking up the Auto-5, I slung it over my shoulder.

"Cato." I glanced up. Thur had come back to the boat and was standing over me. "The Jarl wants to see you." He jerked a thumb over his shoulder towards the shield maiden's boat where the apes still waited, unsure of what to do with themselves. "He says to bring your hairy friends with you."

"I'll need Helga then," I said, standing. "She speaks ape better than anyone."

Thur nodded. "She's standing at the end of the dock, making it well known that if anyone intends to go near them, they'll deal with her first."

I stepped onto the dock and waved at Awshucks. "Come. We go, talk," I said first in axeman, then repeated the go and talk in my best ape impersonation.

"That's terrible," Helga told me as she strode down the dock.

"I'm not as good as you. At least not in ape."

"You aren't that good in my tongue either," she reminded me. "You have a terrible accent."

I laughed and started walking. After making it several steps, I paused and unslung the shotgun.

Just in case some axemen get ornery over an ape in their midst.

A 10-gauge blast into the air should persuade them to stop.

After that, I supposed I could try to buttstroke one to give them pause without getting in too much trouble.

CHAPTER 46

We made it to the Great House on the hill above Novagant with little trouble.

And by that, I mean... little trouble. Some Viking kid smacked Thathas with a wooden sword on the way.

The way the ape roared and sent him scurrying off, I'd dare say that kid learned to use something sharper next time.

Thur opened the twin doors for us, and I entered the room first. The apes followed, ducking their heads to make it inside. Helga brought up the rear, her fierce scarred face keeping any more kids wanting to cause trouble at bay.

The Jarl and Janse were at the far end; Jarl Mikah sitting on his wooden throne, and Janse standing before him. The giant room was quiet.

Thur whispered good luck to me, then closed the door behind us. I walked with the apes and Helga through the empty tables and benches and stopped beside Janse with the apes pausing slightly further back. They still carried their weapons, and at a word from Helga, began to set them down and lean them on the tables with all sorts of ruckus.

Jarl waited impatiently, tapping the point of his sword on the ground before him.

"Cato," he spoke finally as the room went quiet. "How did Ingrid die?"

I froze for a moment, not expecting such a question.

"I shot her," I finally admitted. "Through the heart."

He stared at me, and I realized the look on his face was one of sadness.

"Why?"

"The buscha... the lizards... they took her. They'd ripped her intestines out and were torturing her to trap us."

"You killed her to ease her pain?"

"She was in great agony."

The Jarl's eyes closed for a moment. "Thank you, Cato."

I didn't know what to say, so I remained silent.

"Tell me, Cato. Of these Romans."

I glanced at Janse beside me. He was still looking forward, ignoring me. I wondered if he'd just gotten his ass chewed for letting the expedition fail. It wasn't really his fault.

"They are a fierce warrior tribe," I said. "Led by a man named Legate Augustus."

"How many does this Legate command?" Jarl Mikah asked.

"Men? Thousands. Horses? Hundreds. Buschas... the lizards... probably hundreds."

His eyes darted behind me. "No apes?"

"No."

"The Romans killed them all off," Helga said. "Only these few remain."

"And you speak for these apes?" Jarl asked her.

"I do. They speak some of our language, but I've learned some of theirs as well."

"These apes before me, who I've allowed within Novagant... they mean us no harm?"

"They desire only revenge on the Romans," she replied.

The Jarl chewed his lower lip. "Janse believes we are safe on this side of the water. Do you agree, Cato?"

My eyes darted towards Janse, then back at the Viking king. "No. From what Sif says, they were already preparing to cross the sea. And now that they've tasted blood, they'll want more. They'll seek us out and make us knuckle under their rule."

"I agree. How long do you think we have?"

"They've begun stockpiling wood for boats, Jarl. We won't have long. Perhaps a week or two. Maybe more once they land to find us. I can't say for certain."

"You think they can build boats so quickly?"

"Yes. They are like ants. A force unlike anything we've ever seen before."

"Then we must begin preparations. But first we must bury our dead brothers and sisters." He fixed the giant axeman beside me with a stare. "We will use Janse's boat, as this failed expedition rests on his shoulders."

I frowned. It wasn't the big asshole's fault we ran into a civilization that conquered a large portion of the world through warfare that outnumbered us fifty to one.

"Jarl-" I started to say.

"Yes, Jarl," Janse spoke loudly, cutting me off.

"You are dismissed, Janse Borison. Find Elsha and Thur. Prepare the bodies and your boat."

The giant beside me dipped his head, turned without looking at me, and with his back straight and head held high, walked out of the Great House.

"Helga," the Jarl said, "you will find somewhere for these apes to stay. And you will gather several of your sisters to watch and protect them. I'll have no further injuries inflicted on my people by the hairy men. Least of all from the ones we brought inside our town."

"Yes, Jarl."

"Cato. Come with me." Mikah stood, sheathed his sword, and walked past me towards the side door he often entered from.

Taking one last look at Awshucks and the others, I followed.

The Jarl walked quickly, not waiting to see if I kept up, and soon I realized we were heading to the wall that surrounded the town. Climbing the stairs, we reached the top platform that lined the interior of the palisade.

Putting his hand on one of the sharpened logs, he looked out at the fields that surrounded Novagant. The sun was setting, and the shadows stretched as Vikings made their way back inside the town. It was a peaceful view. One I wished I could be sharing with Elsha instead of the Jarl.

"What do you see, Cato of the Black Plague?" he asked.

Frowning, I told him the truth. "I see an attack coming. One that we would be hard pressed to survive."

"Will the gunmen of Whitesberg join us in battle?"

"I don't know. But they owe you."

"Yes. I want you to go to them and remind them of that. And I want you to demand that they come to our aid. We will need their guns if we are to fight such overwhelming forces."

"Yes, Jarl." Sensing he had more to say, I lingered, waiting.

After a moment, he turned around and looked inside the walls of Novagant. The market was beginning to close, axemen and women were heading home for supper, and the streets were beginning to empty. The loud, boisterous town was becoming quiet.

"I will not have the free people of my town fall to a Roman bastard who leads lizards. Nor will we kneel before a foreigner because he has more men. We will fight. And you will fight with us, Cato of the Black Plague."

"Yes, Jarl," I repeated.

He turned to me with a frown. "We've given you some, but now we ask you much. Do you think I ask this unfairly of you?"

I thought of Elsha, then of Thur and Gundar. "Jarl... I have only the skills that Reydan White gave me. And that's to kill. I'll gladly use them to protect your home."

"Thank you, Cato. Now get some sleep, tomorrow we have work to do. And then, you have a long ride to make."

CHAPTER 47

Thur woke me early the next morning. After the attacks by the buschas, none of us slept well on the boats on the return trip. I barely recalled laying down in my bed before I fell asleep, and only woke when Thur shook me roughly by the shoulder.

"Wake up, sleepy head."

"What is it?" I asked, sitting upright, and pulling a pistol out from under my bedroll that I used as a pillow.

"Nothing to shoot today. We hope. Today is a day for mourning and remembrance of our friends."

An hour later, we were pulling Janse's longboat around the fields of Novagant. It was heavily laden with the bodies of the fallen axemen and all that they would need in the afterlife. The Jarl had picked a spot, at the far end of the fields, for their burial. And that was where we took them.

I had been surprised to see the Reverend taking the thick rope ahead of me and leaning into it as we pulled the boat over rolling logs.

Seeing me, he dipped his head in greetings. "Good morning, Cato Landry."

Rolling my eyes at my full name, I replied, "Morning, Reverend."

"I'm glad to see you've returned from the other side. As will your father and brother be, no doubt."

Not replying, I strained harder against the ropes, enjoying the trickles of sweat dripping down my forehead. I'd always been naturally strong, but after a couple of months with the axemen, I could feel the gains in muscle.

Now would be a good time to fight Jed again.

Especially after his soft ass had been sitting behind a desk with a badge on his chest.

"Still trying to convert the heathens, Reverend? You realize this is a pagan funeral, right?"

"I do. But I plan on saying a few words over them afterwards just the same. Some of them had converted."

"What will your words do for them?"

"Funerals are for the living, Cato."

Thur grumbled behind me. "If you're talking, you're not pulling hard enough."

"Why don't you use trikes?" Reverend asked the axeman.

"They died so we could live. The least we can do is to make their burial as personal as possible."

The Reverend nodded in understanding, then leaned down and grunted as he pulled harder.

By the time we reached where the fields and forest met, the Jarl was waiting for us. Judging by the small size of the trees, this was a field that had recently gone fallow. He pointed at the trees with a finger. "Fell them all. This is where we will enshrine them."

Stretching my back and feeling the ache in my shoulders and hands from the rope, Gundar pulled a pair of axes out of the boat and passed me one and the other to Reverend. "We are just getting started," the old axeman explained.

The trees fell quickly under our axes. I thanked Odin and the good Lord that they were small and reasonable. Some of the trees in Prehistoria would put the great redwoods of the northwest to shame.

Once the trees were down, the boat was moved to the center of the field and logs cut to brace it upright. I worked under Gundar's direction, trimming logs into rough shapes and length while others began to build a sloping ramp from the ground to the edge of the ship.

"What do you think the ramp is for?" I asked Reverend between swings of my axe.

"I believe it's for the trike," he said, looking to the field to our right where a handsome green and yellow streaked trike was being hand fed freshly chopped ferns and grasses.

"Huh," I replied, catching on. I guess the Jarl didn't want the other Vikings to sail off into the afterlife without a mount. Since there was only one, I guessed that Asger would ride it while the others walked to Valhalla.

It was hard to not think of the dead as we worked. The axewomen had prepared the bodies, and the pieces remaining of some, but they still gave off the scent of death. Or perhaps it was just our imagination, knowing what was on board the boat.

I thought of Asger and smiled. He'd have approved of the way he'd gone out fighting. A warrior's death against overwhelming odds. And now he was receiving a fine burial.

The best I could ever hope for would be a shallow grave and a bullet through the back, most likely with no one to miss me.

I glanced at Elsha as she worked to put the final log into place on the ramp into the boat.

She'd warmed up to me a bit across the ocean, but on the way back she barely spoke to me, and I'd heard nothing from her since we'd arrived.

"Watch it!" Thur shouted as my axe struck a glancing blow and the blade nearly hit him in the foot.

I grunted an apology and made myself pay attention to the next swing, the axe cleanly severing a thick branch at the intersection of the trunk.

Women were a distraction, I reminded myself.

That's what Reydan White had always told me when he caught me eyeballing some pretty lady.

I sighed and straightened.

Didn't matter. He was dead now.

Gundar herded the fattened trike up the ramp and onto the boat where Janse waited with his seax unsheathed.

Once the dinosaur was in position, the old Viking tied it off to keep it from moving and upsetting the longboat.

By now, hundreds of axemen, women, and children had gathered. It looked like almost the entire town had come out to watch the burial of their loved ones. Dozens of them began to step forward with bundles and trinkets in their arms. Some carried weapons, others loaves of bread, skins of mead, and other odds and ends. They all walked up the ramp, placed the objects in the boat and stepped back off. The trike bellowed sadly from time to time as it tried to move and couldn't.

Thur leaned in close to me. "Those who died on the first expedition are being remembered. We don't have the bodies, but we send them what they may need in the afterlife."

Sif and Elsha stood a dozen yards away from me. Out of the corner of my eye I saw her staring at me, but when I turned my head, she quickly looked away.

"Odin!" shouted Janse as he raised his seax overhead. "Thank your Valkyries for taking our loved ones home to Valhalla, where they feast and wait for us to join them. And may they watch us destroy the Romans and their savage buschas with great satisfaction. May our offerings of blood and sacrifice please you, as we await our eternal reward on the field of battle." He deftly grabbed the trike by one of its black horns and with a quick slash, slit its throat.

A low groan came from the beast as blood poured from the wound, splashing across the bottom of the boat and the goods that'd been piled in it. Janse didn't move, even though I was sure his leggings and shoes were being soaked.

The dinosaur sagged, straining mightily to stay upright, then collapsed.

Reverend stood behind me, and I heard him whispering a prayer for the deceased Christian Vikings and asking for the forgiveness of the desecration of their bodies.

Janse walked down the ramp as buckets of a black tarry substance were produced, and quickly painted around the entire ship. Both the logs holding it upright, and the ship itself were coated.

By now the sun was lowering itself across the sky. We'd worked all day to build this monument and now we would burn it down.

Four torches were lit, and at a sign from Jarl Mikah, they were touched to the two sides and the prow and rear of the ship. Flames leapt into the sky as families openly wept and held each other. I watched, surrounded by Vikings, yet still alone as those I'd come to know over the short trip across the ocean had their bodies cremated in a massive funeral pyre.

"Cato," a voice said, stirring me from my dark thoughts.

It was the Jarl. He pointed behind him to where another axeman stood with a saddled black horse with three white stockings. "Tonight, there will be a feast as we remember those who we've lost. But not for you. There is no time to lose. We've readied a mount to take you to Whitesberg where your gunman leaders will hear our request for assistance. While you are gone, we will prepare ourselves and Novagant. It is a long trip to Whitesberg, and I know we are asking you to go it alone. But we cannot spare anyone else as we don't know when the Romans will arrive."

"What makes you think they'll listen to me?" I asked. "I'm not the most well thought of gunman."

"You'll have to make them." He placed his hand on my shoulder, and I met his steady gaze. "Novagant needs you."

Not trusting the sudden tightness in my throat, I gave him a nod and walked to the horse. Not only had it been saddled, but my gear stowed on it as well. Even my shotgun scabbard had been mounted. Unslinging the Auto-5, I slid it into the waterproofed holster.

Gundar approached, carrying a sheathed seax. He stopped in front of me and held it out awkwardly.

"What's this?" I asked, taking the weapon from him.

"That old seax you found. I had it cleaned up and a fresh shaft put on it."

I drew the weapon from its sheath. There was the Ouroboros hammered into the metal, just like how I'd found it, matching the tattoo on the back of my hand. The shaft itself was of a dark wood from Prehistoria, smoothed and carved with rune work.

"What does it say?" I asked, rubbing my thumb along the runes.

"Until Valhalla."

I clasped the man on his shoulder. "Thank you."

"Just try not to get any blood on it," he said with a toothy smile.

Chuckling, he stepped away as Elsha approached.

"You're leaving," she said accusingly.

"The Jarl asked me to go to my people, to ask for their help."

A frown crossed her beautiful face. "And you will go, alone?"

"Looks like it."

She spun on her heel and stalked away without another word.

"What'd you say to her?" Thur accused from the other side of the horse.

"Is everyone going to bother me before I leave?" I asked back sarcastically but puzzled at Elsha's actions.

He chuckled and moved around to where I could see him. He patted the black mount on its flanks, and I noticed its brand. A circle with a trike in the center. "Good horse. You saved it from being eaten."

"Where'd it come from?"

"The Heart Eater left it for you. He told the Jarl you may have need for a horse one day."

"Jed," I growled. I should have known that circled trike would be his brand. Being a sheriff must pay well for him to have bought an extra horse and saddle for me.

I mounted the horse, thankful for the stirrups, and gave Thur a nod. "I'll see you in a few days."

"Hurry back, you won't want to miss the Romans."

"I'll do my best." And with that, I touched heels to the horse and rode past the bonfire. Some of the Vikings were already beginning to make their way back towards Novagant, where a feast and plenty of fist fights awaited them.

I'd just ridden past the last field and was turning south to Whitesberg when a trike and its rider appeared out of Novagant's gate. I glanced at it, noting that it was in a hurry. But it wasn't until it drew close that I realized the rider was none other than Elsha.

Pulling back on the reins, I stopped the horse and waited. When she reached us, she wasn't wearing a smile, but rather a frown of disapproval.

"Jarl Mikah should have known better than to send you alone. Do you even know how to get there?"

I pointed at the beach to my right. "Pretty certain I just follow that."

She harumphed but gave me an abrupt nod. "You could, and it'd add time to your ride. Or we could go as the pterodactyl flies and shave off a day."

"Faster is better," I agreed while still looking at her somewhat baffled. "Is that why you're here? To guide me to Whitesberg and back?"

She glanced away for a moment, then turned back with a stern face. "Cato of the Black Plague, you are a fool."

"Yes, yes I am," I muttered to myself as I urged my horse forward.

CHAPTER 48

We made good time, but soon night was falling, and I quickly realized the value of having a companion. While Jarl Mikah did see fit to fill the saddle bags with food, he didn't see fit to provide me with someone who could watch over me and my horse while I slept.

We didn't bother with a fire. The food was dried dinosaur... or perhaps horse... meat and didn't need heating. So, we chewed on the axeman's version of jerky, and tried to make small talk.

"Does the Jarl know you came with me?" I asked.

"No. But I told Sif, she will let him know if he needs me."

"Won't he need you to help prepare?"

"Unlikely. If we can't afford one less person helping in preparation, then we are doomed. And we cannot afford to have you eaten on your way to get help. You know little of this Prehistoria, as you gunmen call it. While we have been here a long time."

I stretched out, pushing some fallen leaves out of the way with my feet to get comfortable. "How did your people get here?"

"Our ancestors left for Greenland. It is said that they sailed their ships through an air that reflected like water as they entered. They thought little of it, until they discovered where Novagant is now. Then they knew that they were not where they were supposed to be."

"I suppose dinosaurs and apes were a big surprise for them."

"Yes. They lost many the first year. But we are strong and resilient. We established our home and our people flourished."

"And now the Romans threaten them."

"Sif told me what you did. That you killed the raptors in the pit, and then you killed one of the Legate's brothers."

"Both of them actually, the other I shot while you were escaping in the boats."

"The Legate will seek revenge."

I grunted dismissively. "That's fine. Others have tried and failed."

Elsha chewed on a corner of a piece of dried meat thoughtfully.

We were quiet. Her eating, and me... well, I was studying her face. I'd never met or seen anyone like her before. She had such grace and beauty, but under it all was a fierce warrior woman. Or maybe it was the other way around.

"Stop looking at me," she demanded as her eyes met mine.

A chittering erupted from behind several ferns in front of us.

Before I knew it, a pistol was in my hand and pointed in that direction.

"It's okay," Elsha said as she tore off a piece of her jerky and tossed it in the direction the sound came from.

It landed with a thud, followed by a thump as something pounced.

"What is it?" I asked, not moving my gun from the location it was pointed at.

"What the gunmen call a compy." She broke another piece off and tossed it closer this time. It landed on this side of the ferns.

The leaves shook for a moment, stilled, and then a small green head poked out. The black eyes stared at us, unmoving.

Then, with a quick snap, it grabbed the morsel of food and ducked back out of sight.

"Cute," I muttered, while wondering if it could kill us. I didn't know much about dinosaurs, except that they all seemed lethal in some way.

The little green beast stepped back out of the ferns cautiously.

"Your turn," Elsha said.

I picked up a small piece of dried meat and tossed it between us.

It chittered, bounced forward and picked up the piece between its teeth. Tossing its head back, the little lizard gulped it down then cocked its head sideways at us, as if expecting more.

"Is it dangerous?" I asked.

"Only if you are wounded or dying. They are scavengers."

"They?"

"Oh yes. There's a bunch of them back there, they travel in small packs."

I cocked the hammer on the pistol. "Should I pop this one to get the others to leave?"

"No. Just stop feeding it and it'll leave us alone."

"What about when we sleep?"

Elsha looked thoughtfully at the little dinosaur. "We should be okay, as long as one of us is awake."

"Should be..." I muttered to myself.

"You take first watch," Elsha said abruptly, settling herself into a dip in the ground and trying to get comfortable. "Don't shoot anything unless you wake me first."

"Ok."

The little compy chittered, looked disappointed that we didn't throw any more food at it, and bounded off into the brush.

CHAPTER 49

A firm push woke me from my slumber. "You sleep like a log," Elsha hissed angrily in my ear.

"What is it?" I whispered softly, ignoring the barb, as I tried to see any threats.

"I don't know... But it's circling us."

A stick snapped, muffled by a weight on top of it, but enough to be noticeable in the sudden quiet of the night.

Something huffed softly in the darkness.

My horse nickered softly, and I saw the trike shuffle slightly turning to face the direction of the unknown thing stalking us.

Quickly pushing myself upright, I snatched up the Auto-5 while Elsha raised her shield and axe.

"We can't let it get the mounts."

"Or us," Elsha replied as she lifted her weapon in a fighting stance.

I nodded slightly at the obvious statement.

A heavy weight slammed into me from behind as the shield maiden let loose with a battle cry and flung her axe at me.

Falling forward, I ate dirt as the spinning axe thunked into something meaty above me. A sharp hiss came from the buscha that'd tackled me as Elsha's edged blade found its mark in the lizard's chest.

I shoved the dead weight off me and rolled over in time for another buscha to lop out of the darkness on all fours and leap towards me.

Twisting, I brought the shotgun up and jammed the muzzle into the lizard's stomach like a spear. Pulling the trigger, I was rewarded with a shower of meat and blood spraying out the back of the animal.

Another buscha grabbed the shotgun. Wrapping its nasty black claws around the stock and barrel, the scaly beast scratched and gouged the wood stock trying to pull it from my grasp. I could smell the stink of ocean and fish on the beast. And twisting its thin mouth into a snarl, it snapped the jagged teeth at me. "Meat," it hissed evilly.

Realizing the lizard was far stronger than I, I let go of the Auto-5, and grabbed the handle of the new seax at my waist. Jerking the short blade free of its sheath, I slashed it across the chest of the lizard.

Blood splashed across me.

Raising the blade overhead, I hacked sideways, driving it deep into the scaled flesh where shoulder met neck.

The lizard screeched and pulled backwards, still clutching my shotgun to its bloodied chest with one good arm.

Hissing at me, it backed up and began to run away.

I drew a pistol and shot the wounded beast in the back.

Throwing its claws up, the buscha toppled forward, dropping my shotgun, and began twitching in death throes.

Glancing to my side, I saw Elsha resting on one knee. Her head was bowed, and the shield maiden was breathing hard. Two lizards lay before her, and her painted shield was splattered with gore and her seax was stabbed into the ground to help support her weight.

Looking at me, her face ghostly white, she tried to speak and slowly toppled to the side.

I scrambled over to her side.

Grabbing her about the waist, I rolled her onto her back to look for wounds.

There was a terrible rip across her stomach. Ragged white flesh peeked through her hardened leather armor and dark fluid that I knew to be blood trickled down from the wound.

"I'll be fine. Just a moment," she said as her eyes fluttered open and shut.

"You're not fine." I looked around wildly.

The buschas had attacked our mounts as well. My horse was mortally wounded, a wicked rip across its throat and the body of the mount lay trembling as it bled out. The trike appeared okay though; it nudged its beaked mouth against a dead lizard. One buscha was nothing for a three horned prehistoric dinosaur to deal with.

Running over, I drew my pistol and quickly shot the horse through the skull. Then rummaging through the saddlebags, I found what I was looking for. Bandages and purple fern leaves tucked into the very bottom.

Pulling them out, I moved to Elsha and began removing her leather armor. One of the straps had been cut through, and it was easy work to pull the rest over her head. Leaving her cloth shirt on, I moved it aside and looked at the wound.

I was no Doc, but it looked bad.

Real bad.

Stuffing the ferns in my mouth, I began chewing as I'd seen the apes do.

The taste was awful, and it took effort to not gag as my saliva mixed with the leaves to make it into a mush.

Using my fingers, I dug the wad out of my mouth and began to pack the wound.

Elsha moaned painfully and I whispered I was sorry as my fingers pushed the purple ferns deep into the ragged gash.

Once the poultice was in, I wrapped her stomach with bandages, tying the ends tightly around her waist.

Lifting her with both arms, I carried the wounded shield maiden to the trike and sat her on the beast's back.

"Why?" she muttered. "Why lizards?"

"Scouts. The Romans sent them as scouts," I told her before picking up my Auto-5 shotgun and slinging it across my back. I looked at the trike and frowned. I had no idea how I was going to ride this thing, but I was going to have to make it work.

"Where's my axe?" she asked softly.

I ran back to the lizard she'd killed with it and with a boot on the corpse, jerked her weapon free of the body with a sucking sound.

Running back to the trike, I gently slipped the rune-carved shaft into the metal baldric she wore on her belt. "Try not to throw it this time," I warned.

She smiled faintly as I climbed onto the trike behind her awkwardly.

Wrapping my arm around the wounded shield maiden, I picked up the leather reins.

"I need you to stay with me. We have to get to Whitesberg."

"Why?" she moaned, leaning back against me. The piece of blue cloth in her hair fluttered slightly against my cheek.

"Because you'll die otherwise."

I didn't know how the pterodactyl flew in Prehistoria... but I knew that the beach was to our right and once I hit that, we could go north and follow it to the gunman town.

And that's what we did. We rode and I learned along the way how to make the beast obey. Elsha had periods of waking before falling back asleep, and during these she would mumble odd bits and phrases in both English and axeman. Usually making absolutely no sense. But I did hear my name a couple of times. Fear for her life made me urge the trike to move faster.

CHAPTER 50

The moment I spied Whitesberg in the distance, I ran the trike the rest of the way. It was breathing hard, the beast's sides heaving as it sucked in air when we reached the northern gate to the town.

Holding Elsha upright, I shouted at the guards on top of the palisade for directions to Doc's house. One of the men was helpful enough to run down the stairs, mount his horse, and lead me to him.

I rode the trike after him, letting the big beast push its way through the wide streets. There were all sorts of folks everywhere. Shaynee Indian, Shayana tribesmen, some axemen, and a lot of gunmen.

That almost brought a chuckle to my throat, gunmen. The word had a different meaning between the Vikings and Americans.

Overhead I heard a pair of Breehas screech as they flapped their wings and flew to the large rocks the Shayana used to rest them on when they visited. And there were a few mounted trikes we passed in the street along the way, but most of them seemed to be confined outside of the town in large corrals.

Elsha moaned pitifully as the guard took me down a pair of side streets and then stopped at a building with a DOCTOR sign over the boardwalk.

The man quickly dismounted and helped me as I passed the wounded shield maiden down to him.

Sliding down from the trike's back, I groaned in pain at the movements of my legs. The horned dinosaurs were wider beasts than a horse, and really stretched you out.

Carefully taking Elsha from the guard, I thanked him and shoved the Doctor's door open with my foot. The shield maiden's face had grown pale and clammy, and I worried she'd lost too much blood to survive.

"Doc!" I shouted. "Got a wounded woman here."

"Bring her in! Room to the left," came the call from back inside the house.

I maneuvered her through the foyer, and into the room the voice had told me to use. There was a bed in the center of the room, a couple of tables with basins and pitchers of water, and a stack of folded sheets to the side.

Carefully, I laid her on the bed and stroked the red hair out of her face. The small bit of blue ribbon, I touched lightly with my fingertips before kneeling down next to the bed.

"Easy, Elsha," I whispered. "We made it. Doc will get you patched up."

Her cracked lips moved slightly, but I couldn't make out the words.

"What's the trouble?" came the voice as an older gentleman barged into the room carrying a leather medical bag. He glanced at me and froze for a moment, before gathering his composure and moving to the side of the bed.

"What did this?" he asked, beginning to untie the bandages.

"Buscha."

"What's that?"

"Kind of like a lizard person," I tried to explain, the words failing me.

"Lizard people? Prehistoria is one messed up place," Doc muttered as he pulled the bandages aside and peered into the wound. "The wounds I see today are worse than the War Between the States. And believe me, it's a damn war outside these walls. Savage beast versus man, and often the beast wins." He reached his fingers into the wound and pulled out part of my poultice. "Ah, I see you used the purple ferns. Good, that's real good. Their healing properties are incredible."

Without looking at me, he began washing his hands in a basin of water. "Now get, let me work on this young lady."

"Shield maiden," I mumbled while drawing my pistol.

"What?"

Cocking the hammer back, I pointed it at his back. "She's a shield maiden of the axemen. Her name is Elsha. And if she dies. You die."

Turning, he saw the gun pointed at him and swallowed. Then his face turned from fearful to glaring. "Mister. I know who you are. And if you want her to live, you need to leave me be and let me work on your Elsha."

"...his Elsha," she muttered as her eyelids flickered.

I reached down and gave her arm a gentle squeeze, then forced myself to walk out the door and close it gently behind me.

Holstering my pistol, I tried to sit outside the room and wait. I really did. But I couldn't stay still. Possibilities of what might happen to Elsha ran wild through my mind.

I needed a drink.

But first, I needed to talk to the Governor.

Finding the Governor's office was easy. I'd been there before. Hell, I'd been shooting from there when the apes breached the walls of Whitesberg and came flooding in.

Lost in my thoughts, I tied off the trike and began walking. Soon I found myself staring at a set of steps leading to the top of the wall that ringed the large town.

I looked towards the top of the walkway.

This was where Reydan White and I'd fought together in our final moments, before the dragon fell from the sky and knocked us and our Maxim machine gun off the wall. Ultimately leading to Mr. White's death, and my being found by the axemen.

I began climbing the steps, recalling the sights and sounds of the battle. There had been hellacious fighting. And fire, so damned much fire. During the battle, Mr. White had been working the Maxim while we were trying to keep the apes off him. It'd been touch and go a few times, with us narrowly being overrun by the hairy monkeys.

Reaching the top, I looked at the repaired portion of the wall that'd fallen with us. New posts had been set, and they hadn't faded from the sun enough to match the others. I put a hand on one sharpened point and leaned over to look.

It was a long way down. Incredible that I'd survived at all. I wondered where Mr. White had landed. Somewhere below me in the hard packed sand and clumps of grass, Jed Smith had watched him die without offering aid.

Not that I could fault him, I supposed.

They were enemies. Trying to kill each other is what they were meant to do.

I looked around, wondering where Elsha had fought. I'd never thought to ask her.

Sighing, I turned away and a thought struck me.

What would I have been like if it hadn't been for Mr. White raising me?

How would I have turned out?

Without thinking, I ran a hand over my arm, feeling the burn marks beneath the shirt from when I'd disappointed him.

Gritting my teeth, I shoved away from the wall and quickly walked down the steps to the ground. It didn't matter. I was what I was, and the past was over.

This is who I was, a killer of man, apes, and beasts.

And proud of it.

CHAPTER 51

Governor Fredrick's office was a two-story building at a corner along Main Street. A big, whitewashed building, with sufficient imposing grandeur to be tasteful. And a balcony on the top floor that I knew entered into the Governor's office. On the porch was a pair of rocking chairs, empty at the moment.

I opened the door and stepped into the wallpapered waiting room.

Across from me was a giant gaudy picture of the Governor standing next to a slain tyrannosaurus. He was a man who loved his renown and the sort to brag of his accomplishments.

To the right of the painting was a pair of cowboys sitting on a bench with hats in hand. Awaiting an audience with the Governor no doubt over something of less importance than what I was bringing to his table.

I walked past them, up the stairs and opened the double doors leading into the Governor's office.

A dinosaur hide rug was spread out on the floor. Guessing, I'd say a trike. But with this man, you never knew. His giant desk stood at the other side of the room, deep hack marks pocketed the stained wood and a bleached raptor skull rested on top. A large, bodied man stood before it, shuffling through a stack of papers.

"Good evening, sir. How can I-" Governor Fredrick von Holsak said turning, then pausing with his mouth slightly open as he took me in.

"I need your help."

"Cato." He said it simply, but the words carried great weight in his voice. He looked me over, taking in my chain mail shirt, leather pants and shoes, and black cowboy hat. "I'd heard you were living with the axemen. Never expected you to show up here again."

I squinted at him, worried. "Am I wanted?"

"No, Cato. You are not a wanted man. But your brother is Sheriff and Reydan White is dead. That spells trouble."

"I know. We've already butted heads and fists over it. But that's why I came to you. I need the Pinkertons." As soon as I said it, I realized in my hurry to get Elsha to the doctor, I hadn't fully noticed the lack of black suited men with badges.

"They work for the East-West railroad now that Reydan is gone. Which means they just protect the train. I hold no sway over them," Fredrick said.

Thinking, I rubbed a hand across the beard I'd grown over the past few weeks. It was shaggy and needed a trim or to be shaved off.

"Then the Army."

"What do you need them for? What sort of trouble are you in?" the Governor asked accusingly.

"It's the axemen, they're going to be attacked... by Romans."

Fredrick swore and dropped his head. Without looking up, he sighed, then asked, "Romans... as in... from Rome?"

"Yes," I said simply.

The Governor moved behind his battered desk and pointed at a chair. "Better have a seat and tell me the whole story."

CHAPTER 52

Fredrick ran a hand through his thick hair and adjusted the glasses resting on his nose, "Here's the problem, Cato. I have to protect Whitesberg, it's the hub for everything in Prehistoria now."

"You're tasked with protecting all of Prehistoria, not just Whitesberg," I replied impatiently. Telling the story had taken longer than I thought, and I was anxious to get back to the Doc's to check on Elsha.

"And I don't have the men to do it. The best I can do is protect Whitesberg in case this Legate that you pissed off decides to hit us instead of Novagant. And even then, if they hit us with an entire legion of infantry, cavalry, and these lizard people... I don't know that we can fend them off."

"Then how are the axemen to survive?"

"Cato," Fredrick looked strained. "I can ask for more soldiers, but raising an army takes time. After the defeat of the apes, the U.S Government withdrew a large number of men and equipment. Decided it wasn't worth the cost of stationing them here if there was no immediate threat."

"That was stupid. We've no idea what we face on this side of the Shimmer."

"Your Roman legion proves that." The Governor flicked open a case on his desk and pulled out a cigar. "Smoke?" he offered.

"No."

Tearing off the end, he then puffed on it while lighting the wrapped tobacco stick with a match.

"The axemen helped when Whitesberg was under attack. This town owes them," I argued.

"This town owes everyone. Shaynee, Shayana, axemen, Rough Raiders, and everyone who was on this side of the Shimmer during the battle. We can't repay all of our debts."

"Then give me the Rough Raiders."

"They've been disbanded. With the apes whipped, there was no further use for them."

I swore and stood angrily. "Dammit man! Then be of a little use and help me get the word out, the Jarl wants all axemen to return to Novagant immediately to prepare for their extinction."

The Governor raised his cigar and waved it at me, "Cato, calm down. I'm sure there's something we can come up with."

"Can you pay for volunteers? We'll take anyone."

"I can do that. With the booming trade with the Shayana, there's a lot of gold in our coffers." He fixed me with a stare. "Even with Reydan dead, there's no way you can get the Pinkertons to assist?"

"No," I said firmly. I knew better than to try and get the Pinkertons to help. With the death of Reydan White, their only purpose would be to defend the railroad. And the stakeholders in the railroad would be too busy fighting over the scraps of Mr. White's empire to make a decision in time to help.

"Then I'll get the word out. All axemen and women are to return to Novagant, and anyone looking for a fight will be well rewarded."

"Thanks." I turned to go, disgusted with how the meeting had gone.

"Cato..." Fredrick began.

"What?"

"You can try the jail. There's some men in there that might be willing to help."

"You mean, the Sheriff's jail?" I asked with a sudden distaste in my mouth.

"Yes."

I walked away.

CHAPTER 53

Before dealing with my brother, I went back to the Doctor's house to check on Elsha.

I knocked this time, and an older woman I assumed to be the Doc's wife answered the door.

"You must be Cato," she said kindly.

"Yes, ma'am."

"Come on in. My husband will want to see you."

Taking off my hat, I entered the house and even though I'd already been there, I let her show me into Elsha's room.

The old Doc was sitting in a chair beside her bed, watching her sleep. She didn't look very peaceful. Her eyes were flicking back and forth under her eyelids as she dreamed of killing apes or something, and her body trembled under a blanket even though it was warm in the room. Seeing me, he raised a finger to his lips and crossed the room. "Outside," he whispered in my ear.

Following him, I closed the door behind us.

"How is she?" I asked.

"She's still in a lot of trouble, and pain. That lizard thing did a number on her, but luckily it seems whatever armor she was wearing helped blunt most of the attack. I got her patched up the best I could; if she survives there will be some nasty scarring. But considering what I know of these Vikings, she'll be thrilled with that."

"You said she's in a lot of trouble?"

"Infection. She's running a high fever and burning up. Those purple leaves seem to help with that, so I made her a tea with them and managed to get some down into her while she was awake." He stared at me. "That cut on your face will likely need some stitching as well."

I gingerly touched the clawed cut. I'd forgotten all about it. It was scabbing over and hurt, but not as bad as I expected. "It'll be fine. Like you said, axemen love scars."

"Well, don't worry about Elsha. I'll keep an eye on her. But it'll probably be a week or more before she can be up and about."

She wouldn't be happy about that, I thought. She'd miss out on the Romans.

"Thanks, Doc." I shook his hand and handed him a couple of gold eagles that I'd had hidden in my belt. "Is there anything else she needs? I'll be leaving town shortly to return to Novagant."

"This will more than cover any costs."

"I want the best care for her."

"She'll have it. You have my word."

"Thanks, Doc," I repeated before leaving the house. It was time to deal with Jed and his bullshit to try and get some help. I figured at this point, every warm body that could pull a trigger or swing an axe would be of help.

Chapter 54

Jed was walking Skyla around on that trike of theirs when I walked up to the corral beside the Sheriff's office. The lawman was holding the reins while Skyla rode on the back, and it looked like the dinosaur was doing well listening to her commands.

Resting my forearms on the top rail, I watched for a moment while waiting for them to see me.

I'd seen a lot of various types of trikes among the axemen, and Jed's wasn't one of the prettiest. But, judging from its size, it was still a young one. Maybe it'd blossom as it grew.

It only took a few moments before Jed saw me, frowned, and said something to Skyla before passing her the reins.

The trike bellowed softly as the Sheriff sauntered over.

"Cato," he said calmly.

"Jed."

"I see you haven't lost the Auto-5 yet," he said, holding his hand out.

I unslung the shotgun and passed it over the fence to him. He ran his hands over the stock, pausing at the teeth and claw marks gouged into the wood. "Damn, don't let Carson Skinner see this, or he may live up to his name and skin you alive."

"He the one that provided it?"

Jed nodded and handed it back. "He's got an in with John Moses Browning. He's where I got the *Eighty-Six* from."

"And where is your legendary rifle?"

"Is it legendary now?" He smiled at the compliment. "It's in the office above the door, with a new stock. Old one got ruined during the battle here."

I swallowed some pride and looked down at my feet. "I need your help."

"You've got it."

"That simple?" I asked suspiciously. "You don't even know what it is?"

"Father told me I'd better start treating you like the brother you are instead of the asshole you've become." He grunted and rubbed his chin. "I'm trying."

I chuckled. "I guess you can't get mad at me for killing that horse you left in Novagant then."

His face soured, "You killed Jack?"

"Aw hell, I didn't know you named him. But yeah, Jack got his throat ripped out by a buscha. I had to put him down."

"Thank you for that kindness... what's a buscha?"

"A lizard... person..."

Skyla dismounted and tied the trike off next to us. "A lizard person?" she asked.

"The apes call them buschas."

"You speak ape now?"

I sighed and rubbed a hand on my beard in frustration. "Can we go inside and sit down? Get out of this heat while I tell you what's going on? I just went through this with the Governor."

"So, you need help and you went to the Governor... is this legal trouble? Do we need to get our sister involved?" Jed asked.

"Depends, how many US Marshals can she summon?"

"Just her for the moment. The other two are on the other side of the Shimmer. They got chewed up dealing with an Allosaurus, likely one of them won't make it."

I sighed.

Skyla spoke up, "Let's go inside as the man suggested, Jed."

"Alright, go ahead. I'll turn Sara loose first," he said, reaching for the reins.

His paleontologist wife dropped low and slid between the two horizontal rails, coming out on my side. She looked at me suspiciously and lowered her voice. "Whatever you are up to, if you get my husband killed, I will shoot you in the back some random day and you'll never see it coming."

Hiding a smile, I nodded. "Yes, ma'am."

She pointed at the building next to the corral, "Now come on into the office, we have some coffee on."

Entering the building, I was greeted with three cells across the room with two white men and an axeman inside. There was a neat and orderly desk to my right. And a newly made table was in the middle of the room.

Noticing something on the wall, I stepped over and looked at the crude bullseye. Touching one of the bullet holes curiously, I looked over my shoulder as Jed entered the room.

"Practicing shooting in here?"

"Not me. The drunk Pinkertons who had this office before me were."

"Good, 'cause it's pretty bad shooting."

CHAPTER 55

"Thanks for the coffee," I told Mr. and Mrs. Smith. "But what do you think?"

Jed looked thoughtfully at the prisoners in their cells.

"What about it, gents? Wanna go to war?"

"Hell naw!" said the big bald one immediately. His partner hesitated for a moment, but once he was shoved by the bigger one, he shook his head and looked away.

The axeman looked up from where he was sitting on the cot and just nodded simply.

"Well, that's one more. Not that he had a choice with his Jarl demanding he return." Jed stared at the white men. "Tell you what, if you two fight, I won't turn you over to the Shayana." He glanced at me. "They tried to steal a Breeha."

I looked at the prisoners in surprise. "What for?"

"To ride," the bald one said.

"We were drunk," said the other as he looked down and scuffed the floor with his boot.

"Well, that explains it," I said, then asked Jed, "What will the Shayana do to them?"

"Likely drop them from a very high place. They are protective of their mounts. Just like we are."

"I'll go," said the one with a full head of hair.

"I won't," said the bald one.

"That's fine," Jed replied. "I'll just take you with me. After all," he grinned, "you're too... dangerous... to be left here alone. Once we get there, you won't have much of a choice left anyways. It'll be fight or die."

"Hey now-" he started to object.

"You're going? Then so am I!" Skyla declared.

Jed looked at her with a smile. "Of course, you are. Just don't get hurt. Or else I'll have to shoot Cato in the back someday."

"You heard that?" she asked accusingly.

"Yup."

"Can we stop talking about shooting me in the back? It's making my skin crawl," I muttered.

Jed chuckled. "Alright, that's five folks."

"Better make it six. Once Father hears, he'll be joining us," Skyla said as she pulled down the heavy *Eighty-Six* rifle and handed it to Jed.

"We can't all go. I'll need someone to hold down the fort here and keep the peace," Jed protested.

She laughed, "You try to tell him that. Besides, your U.S. Marshal sister won't be back from the Shimmer until tomorrow. She'll be mad you left her behind, but she can take care of things here."

Jed sighed.

"What about that gun slinger you hang out with... Wesley?" I asked.

"We can ask him, but he's probably too mercenary to come unless there's something in it for him." Jed stood from his chair. "Let's go to the bar and ask him. Might find some other down on their luck suckers as well."

"Wait, what about me? You can't make me go!" cried the bald prisoner in his cell as he clenched the steel bars angrily.

"Yes, I can," Jed grabbed his hat and rifle as Skyla opened the door.

I followed the two out and pulled the door shut behind me.

CHAPTER 56

Reydan White was too respectable to go into a common bar. He preferred to sip his fine whiskeys and smoke his cigars in the solitude of his office or armored railcar.

Which meant going into the Crystal Palace was a new experience for me. Not that I let it show, but as I took the place in, I looked for any threats. And realized, the damn place was full of them. Whiskey and men were typically an awful combination, leading to lots of fights, stabbings, and shootings. Men seemed to puff up their chests easier when drunk instead of knowing when to back down gracefully while they still breathed.

I'd killed more inebriated men than sober, I was willing to bet.

I thought for a second.

Well, maybe not.

Anyways, the bar was full of men drowning their sorrows and ladies of ill repute seeking out customers. And then there were the gamblers out to take everyone else's money. Back in the far corner, with his back to the wall, sat Wesley. His hat was pulled low, a lit cigarillo dangled between his lips as he stared at his cards.

"McGinnis," Jed called to the barkeep. "How's he doing?"

The bartender stalked over, an angry scowl on his face. "He's taking everyone's money. Which means they aren't spending it on drinks or women." Then he saw Skyla standing behind me. "Sorry, ma'am, I meant... spending it on drinks and... and..."

She waved a hand dismissively at him. "I'm well aware of what the women here do for money."

McGinnis blushed and began polishing an empty glass with a rag.

"Ladies and gentlemen!" Jed shouted as he pulled a chair over to the bar and stood on it.

The room quieted down, and I noticed Wesley's hat tip back slightly as he looked up.

"What is it, Sheriff?" an older gentleman by the door hollered back.

"I've come before you with a proposition from the Governor!"

"What's a proposition?" a rough-looking fellow with a ragged beard and suspenders over a dirty shirt asked.

"It's an offer. Novagant is about to be attacked. You come and fight with us, and he'll pay you in gold."

"Apes?" the older man who shouted before asked.

"Romans. An entire legion of them. Allied with some ungodly lizard people."

The rough looking fellow guffawed and looked around the room. "He's pulling our leg."

Jed stared down at him dangerously. "Mister, I assure you I am not bluffing." He looked back up at the room. "I should warn you, there's a handful of apes fighting with us."

Several men and women in the room laughed at that.

"Now I know you're full of it," the fellow stood, hitching his pants higher about his waist and sticking thumbs into his suspenders. "Lizard people? Fighting with apes? And Romans? Whatever the hell they are... I think you're having fun at our expense, Sheriff. And I don't appreciate it."

I was closest to him, so I drew my pistol and thumped him over the head with it.

He toppled into a pile on the floor, clutching his crumpled hat to his bleeding scalp.

Pointing the pistol at him, I cocked the hammer.

"Holy shit! That's the Black Plague!" someone shouted as they recognized me. I guess the chain mail armor, shotgun, and scruffy beard had them fooled.

Wesley carefully folded his cards and looked up. Our eyes met for a moment, and he dipped his head respectfully.

I wondered if I was faster than him.

Probably.

Jed looked around the room. "Spread the word. Axemen are required by their Jarl to return to Novagant immediately. Anyone else willing to fight, and get paid for it, we ride from the northern gate at dawn."

The Sheriff stepped down from the chair and pushed it back under a table.

"What about the Shaynee and Shayana?" Skyla asked him.

"The Shayana won't risk any more of their Breehas, they've lost too many fighting the dragons. And the Shaynee... maybe. They like to fight, but their numbers are dwindling. If they keep it up, their tribe will be extinct."

"Aren't there more pockets of Shaynees scattered out in the New West?" I asked.

"Yeah, but not Chief Toko's. And those are the only ones I care about."

"Where's your scarred Indian friend anyways? The big, ugly one that follows you around like a puppy," I asked.

"Otto? He's on the other side of the Shimmer, rounding up more Shaynees to bring back here."

"Well, we need someone. If we don't get defenders for Novagant, the axemen will be extinct," I argued.

"I know, Cato." Jed sighed and ran a hand through his black hair. "Let's go ask Carson Skinner, maybe he's got something up his sleeve that will help. He usually does."

"Didn't he steal some Gatling guns from the Army that you used at the Battle of the Apes in Granite Falls?"

"Stealing is a harsh word. More like… he found 'em."

CHAPTER 57

Leaving the saloon, we walked down the street. It still took a lot of getting used to the strangeness of Prehistoria. There were all sorts of oddly dressed individuals moving about, which I supposed included me in my mix of western and Viking attire.

Carson Skinner's store was a two-story building built like it was expecting a siege. Stepping onto the boardwalk, I reached out and tapped the end of an ape arrow shaft jutting from the wall. There were a bunch of them decorating the front of the building, mostly centered around the iron barred windows. It looked like someone took an axe to them and left little sharpened shaft pieces sticking out instead of carving them down flush.

Stepping inside and out of the heat, I was met at the entrance by a tall, gaunt looking man who was moving a stuffed raptor mount into position in front of the door. We weren't the only people in the store; a pair of axemen and a Shaynee brave were looking over goods inside.

The thin man looked up at us and straightened with his hands on hips.

"Jed, Skyla, nice to see you again. And this is the legendary Cato armed with the only 10-gauge Auto-5 shotgun in existence," he said, looking at me before I could be introduced. His jaw worked slightly as he chewed on the inside of his cheek. "Your reputation proceeds you," he said in a way that sounded like disgust.

"I don't work for Mr. White anymore."

"Yes, because he's dead," the man said bluntly. I felt my right eyelid twitch slightly as I choked down a response.

"It's okay, Carson. He's with me," Jed said.

"I know, your father has told me all about him. Or should I say, a little about him." The weapons dealer fixed me with a stare. "A gunman with a mysterious past… you wouldn't be the first nor the last."

"I'm just here to see if you can help Novagant defend itself."

"Yes, I've heard," Carson Skinner muttered. "The Governor stopped by earlier. Romans. How interesting."

"Thousands of them. With supporting cavalry and lizard people. We need something to even the odds," Jed told him as he walked down the tables, looking over the weapons. In addition to firearms, the store was full of other, more dated weaponry. I spied steel axes, shields, spear shafts and tips, even a table with a half dozen plain swords laying on a draped animal hide.

"I don't have the vast fortune or world-wide contacts that Mr. White had. He got lucky with getting those Maxim machine guns that we used so well recently." Carson paused and smiled crookedly, "But I do have my own sources." He walked over to the Prehistorian patrons and ushered them out of the building. The Shaynee brave didn't want to leave, but Jed spoke rapidly to him in their own tongue and the man left. Indian was a language I'd never bothered to learn. Too many dialects and of no use for Mr. White.

After closing and locking the door, he flipped the OPEN sign to CLOSED in the window. Then waved at us to follow him around the wooden bar that stretched across the back of the room. "Come with me, lady and gents."

I let Skyla go first, then followed her around the bar and to a bolted door. Carson grunted as he lifted the heavy steel bar across the door and pushed it open. The door led to the back of his shop, where a large barn-like structure was built, giving cover to whatever oddities the man found and hid back here covered with canvas tarps.

"I'm assuming that used weapons won't bother you any?" Carson asked me in a voice that told me he didn't really care if it did.

"As long as they can kill, we can use them."

"Oh, these can do that." He walked around the closest canvas tarp, grabbed an edge, and pulled it off.

"What is it? A cannon?" Skyla asked as we looked over the twin wheel mounted weapon. It looked like one, but there was a strange thick metal band around the back end of the weapon, giving the weapon an odd, bulky look. And it looked like it'd been through the wringer. There were chips and dents in the barrel and around the carriage, with lead smears that made it look like they were from bullets.

"It's a twenty pounder Parrott rifle from the War Between the States."

"This is a *rifle*?" I asked, my jaw dropping slightly.

"That's pretty old, Carson," Jed said with concern. "How do we know it'll still work?"

"Because I'm older and I still work," the gun dealer replied with a snort. "It's like the inventor, Robert Parrott, said himself. 'I do not profess to think that they are the best guns in the world, but I think they were the best practical thing that could be got at the time.' And Cato, this is the best I've got right now."

"We'll take it then. What sort of… cartridges do you have?" I didn't know spit about artillery, much less giant rifles mounted on wheels, but I did know that there were different types of ammunition they could use.

"Shell and cannister shot," he pointed at a large pair of locked chests.

"How much does this thing weigh?" Jed asked. "And how many horses does it take to pull it?"

"Well, that's one of the downsides to the Parrott rifle," Carson admitted. "It weighs about 1,800 pounds and takes six horses to move."

"We'll never get it to Novagant in time," I said, kicking one of the iron-wrapped wheels in frustration.

"You can if you use trikes," Skyla suggested. "They're bigger, stronger, and just as fast as a horse. You wouldn't need six of them."

"Lucky for you, I know someone who has been working on a trike harness. One of the guards is confident the dinosaurs will replace mules soon. I'll ask to borrow it," Carson offered. "And there's still a lot of rounded up trikes left over from the battle. I'm sure the Governor would let you borrow as many as you want, just to stop paying to feed the big beasts."

"What else do you have?" Jed asked with a sly grin. "I know you're sandbagging on us with this old war rifle. You've got something up your sleeve, don't you?"

Carson chuckled and walked around a wall portioning off part of the barn. We followed him and saw something that took my breath away.

"This is more like it," I said, reaching out to touch it. It looked like a giant Gatling gun mounted on a pair of wheels and carriage. The five rotating barrels were thicker, and there was a large vertical metal plate giving protection to the user from any bullets headed his way.

"That is a one-pounder Hotchkiss revolving cannon. Manufactured in France by an American and given to West Point for testing. They decided it needed some real-world usage, so they shipped it to the Governor thinking he'd find something worth blowing away out here. And then he could report back afterwards on how well it performed."

"How do you use it?" I asked, looking at the pile of wooden crates stacked beside it.

Carson pried open one of the crates and pulled out a stack of ten large bullets mounted together in some sort of a straight walled box contraption. "This is a feeder magazine that holds ten rounds. You put these exploding shells in, like so," he lifted the obviously heavy magazine and lowered it into position on top of the weapon.

"Whoa," Jed said. "Exploding shells?"

"Yes. Just like artillery. Except… repeating." Carson winked then pulled the magazine away and set it aside. "Then," he grabbed the crank on the right side of the contraption, "you turn this." He rotated the crank, and I watched as a barrel moved into place, then stayed there as he finished rotating the crank all the way around. Once it was back in position, another barrel moved.

"That's... strange," I muttered. "Is it broken?"

"No. The Hotchkiss has one large bolt for five barrels. While the Gatling has a bolt per barrel. As you rotate the crank, it puts a single barrel in position, fires, and then waits for you to finish the rotation before moving another into position to fire again. This mitigates damage from potential hang fires and increases accuracy. Besides, it's not sending bullets downrange. It's sending explosive shells. Instead of a single bullet hitting a Roman legionnaire in the face, it's exploding on impact and hitting several of them at once."

I rested a hand on one of the wheels and tried not to grin. "This will be very useful."

"How many people does it take to use this?" Jed asked.

"Three. One to work the crank and turn the elevation and windage knobs, one to load the ammunition, and one poor sap to haul the ammunition to the loader."

"I suppose you have just the one?" I asked.

"Yes. Only one on this continent..." he paused, "Well, and in Prehistoria. And it comes with two hundred shells."

"What about guns?" Skyla asked as she looked around the barn. "Lots and lots of guns."

I shook my head. "Won't work. Only a few of them know how to use one. They'd be more risk to themselves than the Romans if we just dump a few cases of rifles on 'em."

"Then this is it... whoever we can scrounge up plus these two weapons," Jed said as he glanced sideways at Carson. "Don't suppose you'd be interested?"

"As much fun as the last fight was, I do believe I'll pass. I've a business to run," the southern gun dealer told us wryly. "But if you survive, do bring me some of the dead Romans' weapons and armor for study and sale."

"Do you have a place to stay, Cato?" Skyla asked abruptly.

"No."

"Reydan's armored railcar is still here. Just waiting on the new East-West railroad owners to claim it," Jed told me while thumbing towards the rail yard.

"That'll do. I thought it was gone by now. But it has my belongings in it."

Carson slapped the Hotchkiss. "I'll have it ready to go by dawn. With the Parrott rifle."

"Thank you," I told him sincerely as we shook hands.

"Just don't let the bastard Romans win. Then they'll use it against us." He raised a finger, "If you start losing, blow it with dynamite."

"We'll be needing some of that as well."

"We've got you covered there. Plenty here and at the office," Jed said with a wink. "I've always been a fan of blowing things up."

After Carson's store, I parted ways with my brother and his wife. They headed back to the hotel as their house was still under construction in town. And I walked to the rail yard to find Reydan's car.

The big steel behemoth beckoned me to the far tracks where it'd been pushed. There was plenty of dust on the steps and rear balcony so I could tell no one had been messing around with it.

Walking around to the back side, I rested the shotgun against one of the wheels and after making sure no one was watching, reached underneath.

Reydan had hidden a spare key under it. Or rather, had me hide a spare key. He wasn't about to get dirty doing something like that. Not when he had me.

Which meant I knew right where to go to find it.

After sliding a small fake metal bottom aside, the key dropped out of its special compartment and into my hand.

Standing, I picked up my shotgun. So far, in the diminishing light, no one had seen me or was paying attention to this abandoned car.

Walking up the wrought metal steps to the balcony, I unlocked the door and entered.

CHAPTER 58

Grabbing a lantern from where it hung on the wall, I lit it with a match and looked around. The interior was just how we'd left it when the apes attacked Whitesberg.

Reydan's papers were scattered over his desk. I shuffled them around, looking. They were proposed routes for tracks through known Prehistoria, some of them were going to run towards Novagant, while others would be laid in the direction of the Shayana and their gold. There were also stacks of payroll documents for the Pinkertons. A burned-out cigar was left in the ashtray, Reydan's final one before he was knocked off the wall to his death.

A picture on the wall caught my eye. It was framed above his desk, showing a young, smiling Mr. White and myself a short distance behind him. I remembered the day. It was when we returned to the North-East after he grew tired of working over the South. His Senator father had welcomed him back with open arms. The war hero son, returning to take the reins of the East-West railroad to run steel tracks across the continent to unify the western territories to the states.

At least, that's how the papers had run the story.

I often wondered why this picture. Of all the ones that had been taken of Mr. White. Why did he hang this one?

And I felt like, in my heart, it was because I was in it with him. Every once in a while, he'd tell me how proud he was of me. Especially after I killed someone for him. I was like the son he should have had, he'd say.

Sighing, I moved to the back of the car. This was where the sleeping compartments were. I slid back the red sheet hanging from a rod and looked into Reydan's. The ornate brass bed was neatly made with military-like discipline. The drawers in his dresser were closed. A pitcher and wash basin sat on top, near a large oval mirror. A closet was at the far end, where numerous tailored suits hung waiting for a man who'd never come back to wear them.

I slid the fabric closed and turned to the other side where a much smaller compartment awaited my return.

Moving the curtain aside, I stepped into the little room.

There was only room for a cot just large enough for me with a pair of blankets folded at the end, a half dresser tucked into the side full of matching black shirts and pants. Above the cot, mounted to the wall was a rack of guns and boxes of cartridges stacked neatly.

I sighed contently and sat on the edge of the small bed.

This was my home.

CHAPTER 59

A loud banging on the armored door woke me. I'd fallen asleep half-dressed on my cot, the exhaustion of the past few weeks making me sleep like the dead.

Fumbling upright, I slung the gun belt about my waist and moved through the dark railcar to the door.

With pistol in hand, I yanked it open.

Jed was there, an annoyed look on his face. There was a glimmer of light peeking over the horizon that told me dawn would be here soon. And we'd be on the move to Novagant with however many men we could swindle into risking their lives for the axemen.

The Sheriff straightened, his eyes growing large as he looked at me.

"What?" I glanced down, realizing that my chain mail and shirt was still lying on the floor of my sleeping compartment.

"What the hell is that?" Jed demanded, staring at the scarring that peppered my chest and arms.

"Nothing," I told him while turning away to get my things.

He grabbed me by the shoulder and jerked me around, his eyes ablaze with anger.

"Nothing, my ass. Someone burned holes in you. ALL over you," he shouted. "It was that Reydan bastard, wasn't it? This how he made you who you are? Putting out cigars all over your body when you didn't do as he asked?"

I twisted free of his grasp as he followed me into the railcar. "A boy's got to learn to be a man, Orville," I sneered with a taunt. "You should know that. It wasn't easy to raise me."

"You don't make a boy into a man by torturing him!"

"Yes! Yes, you do!" I snapped, pointing a finger at the picture on the wall of Mr. White and myself. "That man took me in! He cared for me, taught me, raised me! I'd be nothing without him!"

BOOM!

The railcar echoed the gunshot as Jed put a bullet through the picture, breaking the glass and shattering pieces onto the floor.

I ducked as splinters of glass, wood paneling, and bits of splattered lead ricocheted through the room.

"Are you crazy?" I shouted at him. "You could have killed one of us."

"No," he said as he holstered his Peacemaker. "This is the opposite of crazy." He picked up the lantern and turned the wick up, sending bright light through the car. With a wild-eyed stare, he raised the lantern overhead in preparation to throw it. "You'd better get out. I'm burning this sumbitch to the ground."

My pistol leapt into my hands, and I cocked the hammer as the barrel lined up on his face.

"Don't," I warned.

"HEY!" a loud female voice yelled from the entrance.

Moving my head slightly, I looked past Jed and saw Skyla standing at the entrance with a rifle cradled in her hands. "Will you two knock it off? We've a battle coming."

Jed seemed to get a grip on himself and after a moment, turned down the wick, darkening the room as he did so. "Fine." He set the lantern on the desk. "We'll deal with this later."

"Yes, we will," I told him while carefully lowering the pistol and uncocking the hammer.

"Got a horse for you outside," Jed said. "Why don't you get dressed, and we'll get this show on the road."

"Thanks."

"Please don't shoot this one."

"It got a name?"

"Henry."

CHAPTER 60

Throwing my clothes and weapons on, I was outside and taking the reins to Henry from Skyla. The horse was black with three white sock feet. Nothing special about it. As for the lawman himself, he had already left to fetch the prisoners he was coercing into fighting for us.

"I've an errand to run, I'll meet you at the gate in ten," I told Jed's wife.

"I heard you brought a wounded axewoman in with you," she said, not exactly smiling, but with a knowing look.

"Yeah. I need to check on her."

"What's her name?"

"Elsha."

"Pretty name... is she pretty?" Skyla asked, this time smiling.

"Does that matter?"

"Usually."

"She's beautiful," I said, thinking as I mounted the borrowed horse. "And bold, brave, fearless... she's a shield maiden. A woman warrior of the axemen."

"Sounds like quite the catch." Skyla turned her dapple-gray horse around, "I've got to see the Governor before we leave. I'll catch up to you all."

I rode away from her, thinking about what she'd said. *Sounds like quite the catch.* Yeah, she was. But I didn't know if it was possible to catch a woman as free as Elsha.

Reaching Doc's house, I dismounted and tied off Henry. This horse had a different brand on it, a bar over a C instead of the circled trike that was Jed's. That was curious. I'd have to ask him about it later and make sure I didn't have to shoot this one since it was someone else's.

I knocked on the door and a few moments later the Doc's wife opened it. She smiled when she saw me.

"Come on in, Cato. Elsha's awake and asking about you."

That made me feel a thousand bucks, and when I entered the room the shield maiden was leaning back on a couple of pillows and sipping from a bowl. The scent of a beef and vegetable broth in the air made my stomach jump in hunger.

The shield maiden smiled weakly when she saw me and lowered her bowl.

"Cato…"

"Elsha…"

Seeing the chair in the corner by the bed, I sat and looked her over. Her color looked bad, her lips were cracked and chapped, and her hair was plastered across her forehead from dried sweat, but she still looked amazing.

"The fever broke last night," came a voice from the doorway.

It was Doc. He nodded in greeting. "Those purple ferns saved her, I'm betting. If you find more, bring me some live plants and I'll reward you handsomely. They can save a lot of lives."

"I will, Doc. Thank you for taking care of her."

"She's been a great patient, except for this morning when she tried to get out of bed to find you."

I looked at Elsha.

"We've a fight coming. I'm no good here," she said as if she hadn't just been eviscerated by a lizard humanoid the day before.

"You'll be no good in Novagant either. You'll tie your people up taking care of you when they could be fighting," Doc reprimanded her softly.

"He's right. You barely made it here," I told her.

She handed me the bowl, and as our hands touched, she grabbed one of them and held onto it tightly.

"Don't let my people lose, Cato. Whatever it takes, whatever you have to do. Don't let them be wiped out."

I ran my thumb over the back of her hand, enjoying the feeling of her touch.

"I promise."

She pulled away from me and reaching into her hair, pulled free the strip of blue ribbon that tied it back. She pressed it into my hand with a slight smile. "Then get going. And kill them all for me."

CHAPTER 61

Ten minutes later, right on time, I rode Henry through the northern gate to Whitesberg.

There was a better turnout than I expected. A couple dozen gunmen were mounted on horses, a few Shaynee braves mixed in, and then a lot of axemen and a few axewomen on trikes. Not a single stinking Shayana in sight though. Father saw me and gave me a wave, but appeared busy talking to a pair of men and didn't ride over. There was also a half dozen wagons readied with teams.

"Not a bad turnout," I told Carson as he worked with another man to adjust the trike harness for the Parrott rifle. The steel clap wheels were already cutting deep into the soil from the weight of the gun, and I knew it was going to be a bear to move it across any loose sand.

The other man looked up at me and grinned crookedly. "How's your lady axeman friend?" he asked in a friendly tone.

It took me a moment to recognize him as the guard who'd helped me find Doc's house yesterday.

"She's recovering," I told him, reaching my hand out to shake his. "Thanks again for your help."

"Not a problem. My name is Bill Argave, and I'll be riding to Novagant with you. I've actually got a little bit of experience with this Parrott rifle, so I'll be manning that if you don't mind."

I looked him over suspiciously, "Don't take this the wrong way, but you look a little young to have been in the War Between the States."

"I lied about my age, joined at 13. Wanted to see battle."

Carson glanced at me and nodded, confirming that he had served.

"Was it everything you thought it'd be?" I asked.

"Not a damn bit. No glory, no honor, just blood, misery, disease, and death." Frowning, he tightened the harness and tugged on it to make sure it was good. "Lost a brother to the south, and two brothers to the north. One of them at Gettysburg... I was there too. And it haunts me to this day that I might have been the one to have killed him."

"Odds are highly against that," Carson said, standing up to arc his back with his hands on hips. He stretched, a grim look on his face.

"Doesn't mean it wasn't possible."

"That's a guilt you don't need to carry," he told Bill gently. "And anyways, you're probably going to be slaughtered by Romans soon.

Keep what I told you in mind. You start losing, you blow this big rifle to hell. Don't let them take it intact."

He patted a bag that was resting on the carriage between one of the wheels and the giant rifle. "Yes, sir."

I thought of all the returning soldiers we'd killed as Reydan raided the South. None of them I recalled as well as the first that he'd had me shoot. After a few weeks, the faces had just blurred together into mindless killing as I did as I was commanded.

"Cato," Carson said softly, and I realized they were both looking at me.

"Cato," he repeated, "You okay?"

"Yeah," I said briskly.

"You had a terrible look on your face," Bill said, staring at me. "I've seen that before from people who've remembered too much at once."

"I'm fine." I raised myself in the saddle and looked for Jed. He was riding to the front of the group on that dun-colored horse he favored so much. Carbine, I reminded myself. That was its name.

"Cato!" He looked around and saw me. "Hey, come up here!"

I touched heels to Henry's flanks and trotted him through the crowd. "Yeah?"

The lawman nodded at the large group. "Say something."

"You're the Sheriff, you do it," I told him accusingly.

"They aren't risking their lives for me. Except for the inmates I'm bringing along. Everyone else is here for you, and your axe friends. You do it."

"And I'm sure the gold's got nothing to do with it either," I muttered to myself as I rolled my eyes. Raising my voice, I called out over the loud murmur of voices. "Listen up!

"We're headed to Novagant to help the axemen fight off the Romans. If you don't know who they are, they're a bunch of stuck-up fancy pants in armor who think they are better than everyone else. But don't let that fool you. Their discipline and unit cohesion are incredible. Their savagery, unequaled. They may not be apes, but they will kill you and think nothing of it. Romans live for battle and conquest, and now they've fixed their eyes on conquering Prehistoria. We won't let that happen. We are going to stop them at Novagant, and we are going to wade through their blood and corpses to victory. Let's ride!"

Amid the whoops, gunshots, and thunderous shouts, Jed looked at me in surprise. "Well, that was.... grim."

"If you're going to give a speech, I figure you might as well go all out," I retorted as we began to ride ahead of the group.

Twenty minutes later, Skyla raced up alongside us, her dapple-gray horse easily catching up. "Easy, Smoke," she said as she held back on the reins to slow the mare down. She looked around. "I missed the speech, how was it?"

"Dark," Jed muttered.

"It went fine," I told her.

"Well, Fredrick sends his regards, along with those wagons filled with provisions and dynamite to get us to Novagant."

"I hadn't thought of feeding everyone," I admitted.

"Me neither. But it is a two day ride. And folks got to eat," Jed said as he patted his horse.

Father ran his horse and caught up to us. He nodded at Jed's wife. "Darling, do you mind if I have a moment with the boys here?"

Skyla glanced at Jed before replying, "Not at all." She pulled back on the reins and let Smoke fall behind to the strung-out ragged column behind us.

He twisted in the saddle a bit to stare at us. "Look, lads. I know you two have had your differences. But I don't want anyone shooting the other in the middle of a battle against a common enemy. We don't have time for either of your shit. Act professional. All these men and women behind us are looking to you for guidance, and if you start feuding and brawling it's going to make them regret coming along for the fight. If they sour on following you, they may leave and get eaten. That will be on you." He nodded, his tin deputy badge twinkling in the sun. "Then you will have to explain to a widow and her children why Billy Bob didn't come home. Or worse, you'll have to explain to the good Lord after this life that you failed to defend Novagant because of your damned bickering."

He jerked a thumb behind him. "Carson Skinner and Governor Fredrick may not be here with us in person, but they are in spirit. Fredrick had all the forges working last night to make a neat little toy that will confound the hell out of the Romans. And Carson sent us a pair of artillery rifles. We'll make good use of it all, and maybe we'll stand a chance."

"Yes, Father," Jed said sincerely.

I tipped my hat in agreement, unsure about calling him my father just yet. After all, the man who really raised me was dead. Wasn't he more of a father than Eugene Landry?

I didn't know.

As we rode, I thought about trying to recover the saddle from Jed's dead horse that I'd shot, but when I mentioned it, he told me corpses and leather didn't last long in the wild around here. By now the horse would have been devoured and the saddle made useless by the scavengers. That made me think of the compys that I'd seen with Elsha, and wonder how she was doing. I was willing to bet she was giving the Doc hell trying to get healed to make it to the battle in time. But I knew he wouldn't let her go until she was ready. And I really hoped she wouldn't resort to thumping him with her axe to get away.

Towards dusk we rode past a large herd of strange, humped back dinosaurs eating in a marsh, with their mouths resembling duck bills.

"What are they?" I asked Skyla.

She raised an eyebrow at me. "Irving says they are hadrosaurs."

"Who's Irving? And are they?"

"They are. And he's our new paleontologist."

Jed unslung his *Eighty-Six* and dropped one with a quick pair of shots.

"And they are delicious," he added. "But don't tell Irving if you see him. He's not much for us slaughtering the local wildlife."

"Who is going to butcher that big beast?" I asked.

"Them." Father pointed at the axemen who were already riding towards the downed dinosaur as the rest of the herd began to slowly move away from the encroaching trikes.

"Should be enough to feed all of us tonight," Jed mused as he reloaded his fancy rifle.

"And where do we camp?" I asked, looking around at the wet grass-soaked marsh to our right and the ocean to our left. We were moving down a strip of packed sand that looked like it had been pushed inland by a giant storm.

"Half a mile past this is the Thirsty Wench," the lawman replied. "We'll camp there for the night."

"Is that a bar?" I asked, incredulous.

Jed and Skyla laughed, before my brother responded, "Not quite. But we left something there from your former employer that I'd like to pick up on the way."

I grunted in response but didn't bother asking what the hell he was talking about. There was a lot to Prehistoria that I didn't know.

The axemen and women made short work of the hadrosaur, piling large chunks of fresh meat in the back of several wagons. It looked like we'd be feasting well tonight. And if I knew anything about the Vikings, there'd be plenty of mead to go around as well.

CHAPTER 62

We reached the Thirsty Wench about an hour later. By then I was exhausted and covered in muck up to my waist from helping Bill dig the Parrott rifle free when we ran out of sand, and it bogged down beside the marsh. Once we broke it free, it was okay as long as we kept moving. But every time the trikes stopped, the iron-clad wheels would begin to sink into the wet ground deeper and deeper until we moved again.

And the Wench wasn't a bar or saloon. But a pirate ship of some sort.

It was a big wooden thing with two towering masts that had strips of rotting canvas draping off them. It leaned on its side slightly and looked as though the same great storm that'd moved the strip of sand earlier had pushed this well past the high tide mark. The ship had circular marks that crisscrossed the exposed underside and the railing at the top was splintered in places.

"This thing has been through it," I muttered.

"You've no idea," Jed chuckled. "It was attacked by a kraken. A giant sea beast, kind of like an octopus."

We circled the wagons in the long shadow of the ship. The trikes and horses we pulled inside and staked on the side of the circle the ship made, and a couple of fires were quickly put together from driftwood. Jed and Skyla, and a couple of others climbed to the top of the ship to get the Gatling gun free and to post a look out over those of us below.

Once we'd arrived, Jed had explained how Reydan White sent a group of Pinkertons with the Gatling to try and assassinate Jed and his friends.

The attack failed, and Jed ended up with a crew served weapon packed away for a stormy day after killing and hanging the Pinkertons.

I remembered the day that Jed had confronted Mr. White about it.

Hell.

I remembered the day that Mr. White had devised the plan.

It was strange to think how far my brother and I had come since then. Not that I'd been hoping for his death, at the time it just didn't matter any. If Mr. White had asked me to kill him, I would have.

But now...

Well, I'm just a big jumble of emotions these days.

I skewered a piece of hadrosaur on my plate with my knife and bit into it. The meat was juicy, cooked to red tinted perfection, and seasoned well with salt.

Drops of grease dribbled down into my beard as I chewed. That was the problem with a beard I was coming to realize, it was a bear to keep clean. Food was always getting into it.

"Something's coming from the water!" someone shouted from the top of the ship, followed by, "Lots of somethings!"

Setting my tin plate aside, I grabbed up the Auto-5 shotgun and ran to the farthest wagon. I'd been sitting on the side of the wagon circle that was nearest to the forest and had to run around a couple of cook fires of roasting hadrosaur. But when I reached the wagon nearest the water, I knew right away what was coming at us.

"Buschas!" I shouted. There were a lot of them crawling on all fours out of the water, and even from this distance in the fading light I could see their lizard faces flicking tongues out of toothy maws.

From above me, I heard Jed yell faintly at someone to help him move the Gatling.

"Behind us! More of them lizard things!" I heard Bill call out.

"Don't wait! Start shooting them!" I yelled as several of the gunmen and Shaynees did just that. They all had rifles, but with the shotgun I was forced to wait for the buschas to come closer.

Arrows whistled overhead as the Vikings got into it as well.

Lizards started dropping in the sand, kicking and thrashing from bullets and arrows. Realizing that most of us were on this side, I turned and ran back to the forested side of the wagon circle.

Sliding up against a wagon wheel, I saw Bill next to me. The man was using an older revolving carbine. Basically, a pistol with a rifle stock and longer barrel.

I peeked over the wagon and saw he was being surgical with it. Every time he fired a lizard took a bullet.

And Lord, there were a lot of buschas headed this way. More than were coming from the water, which must have been a feint to draw us away so they could hit us from behind.

Damn, I hated smart opponents.

Standing behind the wheel, I rested the Auto-5 shotgun and quickly emptied all five buckshot shells at the mob of lizards racing towards us on all fours. I wasn't doing much at this distance, mainly trying to just wound them some.

"Get the Parrott going," I told Bill as I plucked shells from the bandoleer across my chain mail shirt and began reloading.

"Too close! And they'd overrun us by the time we get it aimed!" he shouted back over the gunfire and growing hiss and shrieks of the approaching lizards.

Pop-Pop-Pop-Pop!

Bullets stitched a line across the attacking lizards in front of us as Jed got the Gatling gun going from on top of the pirate ship.

None of us had been expecting that. And the buschas actually slowed for a moment, looking around for where the bullets were coming from, before renewing their attack as more of them were slayed.

Finished loading, I flipped the shotgun over and stood back up as a lizard leapt over the wagon at me with claws outstretched.

Firing from the hip, I blasted it out of the air, sending the corpse smacking into the side of the wagon with a thud.

I glanced at Bill. He was still firing his revolving carbine and should have warned me.

"You missed one," I told him.

"Figured you had it," he replied grimly without looking at me.

Grunting, I dropped to a knee and shot a lizard that was crawling beneath the wagon to get to us. At this range, the buckshot blew multiple holes into its face and body.

"We need to fall back!" Bill cried out as a claw slashed within inches of ripping his arm apart. He fired, and the lizard fell backwards to be replaced with another.

I quick fired the shotgun as fast as I could, emptying the remaining rounds from beneath the wagon. Several lizards dropped, but more kept coming.

"Can't! There's dynamite in the wagon. We hit it, it goes boom," I told him while dropping the shotgun and drawing a pistol in one hand and my newly rehandled Ouroboros seax in the other.

A claw reached towards me from beneath the wagon, and I slashed the blade, nearly severing the hand at the wrist. It jerked back with an agonizing shriek.

Bill tossed the carbine on top of the crates in the back of the wagon and drew a pistol from his waist.

A lizard tackled him and knocked him backwards towards one of the cookfires.

Twisting around, I lined up the shot to help him.

Before I could pull the trigger, something grabbed me from beneath the wagon and jerked me down.

Curling my body upwards, I fired a shot between my knees into the pair of lizards that were grabbing at me. The pistol bucked in my hand, the bullet striking one of the buschas.

The dying lizard let go of my leg and clawed at the bullet hole in its throat.

With my leg freed, I began kicking the other over and over about the face and torso.

"Let. Me. Go. You scaly sumbitch!"

Twisting my seax about, I thrust with the point, slicing off part of the nose and through the cheek of the lizard beast.

The clawed hand let its tight grip on my leg drop.

Giving it one last kick in the face to add insult to injury, I scrambled on my back out from under the wagon.

"They're retreating!" someone shouted.

"Keep killing them!" I yelled back, then switched to the axeman language and repeated the command.

The Vikings didn't need the command though. They were already leaping over and rushing around wagons, chasing after the buschas.

A dozen lizards dropped from thrown axes and spears, and a couple more from arrows through the back.

Looking around, I noticed the gunmen were more reluctant. A few shooting, but most were either standing around taking in the carnage or tending to each other's wounds.

Swearing at the modern-day chivalry that would leave more enemies for Novagant to fight, I looked around for any surviving buscha.

There was one trying to crawl away.

Boom!

One of the other gunmen got to it first.

Nevermind.

I looked for another before I heard a slight hissing sound from beneath the wagon. Squatting, I found myself face to face with the one whose nose I'd cut off.

"Still here?" I asked it in Latin.

It hissed at me, the sound odd and strange since its face was all cut up.

Looking behind it, I saw a bullet wound through its back. A big one.

I glanced up at the pirate ship towering over us. If they'd shot that close to the wagon, they would be risking a lot. Including blowing me sky high.

Jed was looking down over the edge. Skyla waved at me.

I waved back, then grabbed the wounded lizard and dragged it out from under the wagon. It tried to swipe at me feebly, and I knocked its claws aside then smacked it over the head with the barrel of my pistol.

"Stop it," I told the scaly lizard person thing.

"Die, Cato!" it replied.

"Did you just talk to that thing?" Bill said, casually leaning against the wagon and reloading his pistol carbine.

"Yeah."

"And it said your name..."

"Yeah."

"How's something like that know your name?"

I shrugged with one shoulder before pulling the rest of the lizard out. I'd been wrong; not only had it been shot through the back, but it'd also taken a bullet through its foot as well.

Dragging the lizard closer to the fire, I dropped it and took a quick look around. A fair amount of buschas had made it into the circle, but from what I'd seen, a lot more died outside of it. The wagons had helped keep them at bay.

"If we hadn't circled the wagons, we'd have lost a lot more men," Father said as he strode up to the cooking fire. The dinosaur meat on the spit was burning now, and I pulled it away from the flames.

"Where were you?" I asked. "Missing all the fun?"

"Killing lizard people a couple wagons to your right. You looked to be doing okay with that shotgun, didn't seem to need my help."

"I got dragged under a wagon," I said accusingly.

"Yeah, I missed that part. I was a bit busy." He pointed at a ragged tear in his shirt. "They almost overwhelmed us before the Gatling drove them back."

"How many did we lose?" Bill asked, sauntering up to the fire with his long barreled revolving carbine slung over his shoulder. He handed me my Auto-5. "You dropped this."

"Thanks." I glanced at the weapon for any damage. It looked alright, just a little sand on it. I'd have to clean it now.

"Don't know yet for sure... but looks like six or seven. Pretty good considering how many of the buschas we killed," Father said as he squatted beside the captured lizard and poked it with a finger.

"Not good enough. As outnumbered as we are, we can't afford to lose anyone."

"Stay positive, Cato," Jed said as he calmly walked up with Skyla behind him. She was still carrying her Winchester rifle in her hands, but he'd slung his *Eighty-Six* across his back.

"You got a little close with that Gatling," I groused. "Any closer and you'd have hit the dynamite."

"You survived, didn't ya?"

I rolled my eyes and looked at the wounded lizard.

It stared back defiantly.

"What are you going to do with this one?" Skyla asked. I could tell the paleontologist in her was fascinated with the creature, especially up close and alive.

Grabbing the lizard's wounded foot, I held it to the flames where it sizzled, and scales popped.

Shrieking, the buscha tried to jerk away but I held it firm.

"What are you doing?" Skyla cried out as she tried to grab my arm.

I let her pull me back and bring the foot out of the fire.

"Ready to talk?" I said in Latin to the beast.

"You speak Latin?" Skyla asked, astonished.

"Way to go, son," Father admitted. "I know a few phases but always wanted to learn more of that myself."

The lizard person hissed at me.

"How many of you?"

Lunging slightly, its teeth snapped at me and missed.

This time I punched it in the face. "Stop."

"Maybe this one will help a bit better!" came a gruff voice from behind us.

It was one of the axemen, and he pushed a Roman ahead of him. The man's face was bloodied, and it looked like he'd taken a beating.

"Where'd you find him?" Father asked.

The axeman pointed towards the forest. "He was out there, watching. He couldn't run as fast as the buschas."

Grinning evilly at the new opportunity, I drew my pistol and shot the wounded lizard through the skull. It burst open, and an eyeball popped out, landing a few feet away from the kneeling Roman captive.

"You speak English. What's your name?" I asked the axeman.

"Egil."

"Well, Egil, thank you for this gift."

The bearded Viking nodded and squatted down beside the prisoner, the Roman's sword held in his hands.

Stepping forward, I bent over and flicked the lizard eye at the Roman with the barrel of my pistol. The sand-covered orb with bits and pieces of brain dangling from it landed in his lap.

The Roman calmly reached down with one of his hands, picked up the eyeball and tossed it into the fire where it popped and sizzled.

I grinned at him.

"Cato, maybe I should do this," Jed offered as he drew his Bowie knife.

"You speak Latin?"

"Not really," he admitted.

"Then I'll do it."

Jed offered me the blade, but I shook my head.

I had other plans if necessary. But if it went that way, Skyla would need to go somewhere else.

"What's your name?" I asked in Latin.

"Centurio Felix Antonius Glavius," he said fearlessly.

"And what do you do for the Legate, Felix?"

"I command a contingent of the... buschas... as you call them."

"The lizard people."

"Yes."

"Why did you attack us?"

"Opportunity to deprive an enemy of reinforcements."

I frowned. Had they killed us all, Novagant might have been fine, as few in number as we were... but they would have certainly fallen without the Parrott and Hotchkiss guns.

"Are you going to attack Novagant?"

"The barbarian town? Yes."

"You speak freely," I told him.

"I want to live," he replied honestly.

"When do you attack?"

"We will be within siege distance in three days."

"What's he saying?" Jed demanded, as he toyed with his Bowie knife.

Changing to English, I told him, "He's answering everything I'm asking. They will attack Novagant in three days."

"He may be lying," Father said.

"No, I think he just wants to live."

"So, he's a coward," Jed muttered.

I shook my head slightly, "No, I think he thinks he's smarter than us. He's been looking around while sitting here, probably counting numbers and observing what we have... Probably hopes we'll let him go so he can report on us." I looked the Roman over. Had he been standing he would have been shorter than me, but broader about the shoulders. A sharp nose and dark cut of short hair completed the look. Not much stood out about him, but then, I didn't really care.

Felix looked back fearlessly.

"How many men, horses, and buschas?" I finally asked in his language.

"Four thousand men, two hundred horses, and two hundred lizard people," the Centurio glanced around in what looked like amusement as folks began dragging corpses out of our wagon circle. "Give or take a few. We already lost a lot defeating the hairy men."

I repeated his numbers to the others.

Father guffawed, and Bill looked sick to his stomach. Jed's jaw tightened, and I could tell he was weighing what the cost would be to fight such a force.

"We can't handle that many," Skyla said. "Even with the two crew-served guns and the Gatling…"

"Not in open battle, but perhaps from a defended position…" Father's voice trailed off.

"Doesn't matter, we fight," I told them sternly. I'd made my promise to Elsha. And I'd keep it.

"Strip him, tie him up, and put a watch on him. He knows a lot. And we need to know what he knows."

Egil started to happily strip the legionnaire of his armor. Within minutes he was wearing nothing but cotton undergarments. I stopped the overzealous Viking there. "Leave him some dignity but check him for weapons."

Grunting in response, Egil searched him thoroughly and found a small knife strapped to the inside of his thigh. The axeman tested the blade carefully with the underside of his thumb, and smiled in approval when it sliced a thin line in the skin.

I stared at Felix. "The more you talk, the more likely you'll live. Remember that."

"I'll talk," he said earnestly.

"Good, we will. Everyone else, post guards and get some sleep. We move at dawn."

CHAPTER 63

The night was uneventful, except for the triumphant return of the trio of Shaynee braves who had taken it upon themselves to sneak out of the camp and hunt down any straggler buschas. They seemed very disappointed that there wasn't any hair to scalp on them, so instead resorted to knocking out one of the fangs on each of them instead.

One of the braves, a short and stocky fellow with an attitude problem, named Runs With Dogs, had an entire pocketful of bloodied teeth.

Once I saw that, I promised them that Jarl Mikah would reward them well for their kills and encouraged them to get as many as they could. Be it man or lizard.

After restlessly sleeping for another couple of hours, at dawn we were awakened by a small flock of pterodactyls catching fish out past the waves.

I watched them as I packed away my blankets and made sure my Auto-5 was clean of any sand or debris. These must be the peaceful kind, I assumed. I'd heard of big ones, bigger than the Shayana's breehas that they flew. Big enough to rip a man's limbs off his body. And right now, I wished we had some of those on our side. Or one of the ape's dragons. Those flame breathing monstrosities were fearful to behold. I supposed the Romans never encountered one with Awshucks' apes on the other side of the water. Or if they did, I wondered how they managed to take it down with their outdated weapons.

Shrugging to myself, I went to help Bill get the Parrott rifle ready to move. His idea, with Carson's help, of using the trikes had been a godsend. Without the dinosaurs, I don't think we'd ever have been able to move them short of using a train.

Thirty minutes later, we were leaving the Thirsty Wench behind and on our way, our column just a little longer with the new Gatling gun and Roman leader in tow.

As we moved, we tried to stay in the open as much as possible, fearful of another buscha attack.

But we kept the three Shaynee braves riding on the outskirts to keep an eye out for any more of the lizards, or Romans that might be leading them.

After a few hours, we crossed the corpse of a giant shark that'd been pulled onto land and ripped apart savagely. Dozens of small green whip-tailed compys were hopping over the corpse along with several pterodactyls, nipping and tugging at pieces of flesh.

I dismounted with Skyla and Jed as the column of men and women rode past. They watched in awe and wonder. But the axemen seemed familiar with the beast and looked happy at its death.

"What do you think it is?" Jed asked as we approached the head of the beast. A large chunk had been bitten out of it, taking an eye and part of the lower jaw.

"Prehistoric shark," Skyla said with a smile.

"No kidding," I muttered as I got closer and realized just how massive the dinosaur was. It had to be forty feet long. Even with part of its tail missing.

"The Smithsonian just received part of a shark fossil," Skyla said as she squatted down and looked at the off white and almost tan colored teeth. "The jaws alone were large enough to fit a man standing upright. And the teeth..." she reached out and touched one of them. They were giant. Some of them were larger than both of her hands put together. "The teeth," she repeated, "were like this. Not to say it's the same sort of shark, but they'd already taken to calling the fossil, Otodus Megalodon... which stands for big tooth."

"Look at this," Jed had moved to the other side, and we followed him.

There was a great big harpoon jutting from the shark's back. No rope was attached to the end, whatever it'd been attached to was long gone. But it'd certainly helped with the beast's demise.

The Sheriff frowned as we looked at the giant steel spear, "That's something new. We don't even have any boats at Whitesberg yet, so it didn't come from us."

"It's modern though," Skyla replied.

"Yes, it is. Which means there are some folks like us out there, with boats, and hunting sea beasts."

"More people to keep an eye out for. Prehistoria is filling up fast. We need to hope they are friendly."

While they were talking, I was busy staring at the large footprints around the carcass.

Three large toes with straight claws on the end... and a smaller toe on the backside.

"What is it, Cato?" Skyla asked, noticing my stares.

"These footprints… These are the same ones that came from the giant dinosaur on the other side of the water. From the giant beast I lured into fighting the Romans."

Jed walked closer to the water. "Look," he pointed. "You can see where that thing of Cato's dragged the shark out of the water." He looked back at us. "Can that dinosaur swim? Did it survive the fight?"

"Shit if I know," I muttered. Then louder, "No idea."

Skyla moved closer. "Draw it in the sand for me."

Sighing, I bent over and used the tip of my finger to begin sketching in the dry sand. As I did, I talked, "Had a head like an alligator. Long snout, full of long teeth. Two eyes up high. Kind of a curved head that turned into a muscular neck, but as soon as it hit its back there was a giant fin-type thing sticking up that ran to its big back legs. Had two front arms that were kind of small, but still long enough to kill people with. Also had a really long tail that reminded me again of a gator."

"That sounds like a Spinosaurus," Jed said, looking over my shoulder at the drawing.

"How do you know what that is?" Skyla asked in astonishment.

"Irving told me he found a skull of one once on a mission trip with his folks or something. I asked him if he knew what the rest of it looked like and he described it kind of like that," he pointed at the sand.

"We may have a problem then," she said. "Because it's a giant carnivore, and the only thing around here that might have been able to fend it off would have been that tyrannosaurus that you all killed with Fredrick a while back. It'll likely make its home around here and we'll have to worry about it eating people until it's taken care of."

"Well, good for it," I said as I dusted my finger off and stood back up. "But it's not here so let's focus on the problem at hand. Killing the Romans."

"You know we don't have to kill them all, right Cato?" Jed said with a sideways glance at Skyla.

"Of course," I lied smoothly. They didn't know my promise to Elsha, and I meant it. These Roman bastards had been playing sport with the lives of axemen and women in a pit filled with raptors. I wasn't going to let that slide.

"Jed, would you be so kind as to cut a couple of the bigger teeth out? I'd like to send them back to the Smithsonian for cataloging. And maybe knock out a big one for Irving too, he'd like that."

"Yes, ma'am," he replied while moving to the front of the shark and drawing his Bowie knife.

I walked to Henry, grabbed the saddle pommel and pulled myself up. I was itching to get these big guns to Novagant and see what they'd come up with for a defense plan.

CHAPTER 64

We reached Novagant with little fuss. Just lots of heat and humidity soaking through our clothes and making us miserable and ornery. An axeman knocked out a Shaynee brave over a misunderstanding, and it took a lot of effort to keep the Indians from killing an axeman in retaliation.

Savages and savages, I thought. We're not so unalike.

"I never get tired of the natural beauty of this place. The Vikings have everything so nicely laid out and defended," Father mentioned as we rode side by side towards the large axeman town.

"They aren't strangers to hardships," I reminded him.

"That's a fact."

A trio of mounted trikes rode from the entrance, lumbering along at a lazy run until they stopped before us.

Jarl Mikah smiled as he looked over the caravan of wagons, men, and weapons we'd brought. The axemen and women who'd returned with us dipped their heads respectfully as they rode past and left our column to join the preparations. "You did well, Black Plague," he told me in English.

"Jarl, if you will show us what you have planned for defenses, we'll help get the big guns set up where they can do the most help," Father replied.

The one-armed Jarl spoke to one of the axemen behind him, and he rode forward. He was shorter than most of the Vikings, but still stocky and his bare arms were covered with intricate inkings that put the two small tattoos on the backs of my hands to shame.

"Geir will help you place the big guns," Jarl said. "He speaks some English, and your Reverend is waiting inside the walls of Novagant to help you speak to the others."

I motioned to the Roman behind me. "This is Centurio Felix Glavius. He led a buscha attack on us and one of your axemen captured him."

As I was speaking, the axeman Egil strutted by carrying the Roman's armor. He grinned at the Jarl and handed over the Centurio's sword.

Mikah held it in his hand and turned it over, looking at the blade. "Good craftsmanship. As good if not better than what we make." He passed the blade back to Egil. "Use it well," he told the axeman.

The Jarl moved forward and looked over the Roman curiously. "Does he speak axeman or gunman?"

"No, he only speaks Latin."

"Should we kill him?" he asked, stepping towards the man and looking at his enemy's face.

"No. He's been very helpful in telling us what the Romans have planned and what their weapons and tactics are."

"He's a traitor to his people," Jarl said simply.

"He wants to live," I told him. "I told him that is dependent upon the information he gives us."

"Very well. Bring him and let us see what this Centurio has to say." Jarl stepped back and turned to Skyla and frowned slightly. "This is no place for a gun woman. But we thank you for your help."

I repeated it in English to her. She nodded her head respectfully.

"We brought everyone we could, Jarl. Governor Fredrick is paying the gunmen and Shaynee in gold to help."

"I see no Shayannas or their breeha riders," he replied wryly as he looked down the column.

"They are sitting this one out. They don't have many breehas left."

"A shame they are cowards. But such is their people."

I didn't reply to that. I knew there was some animosity between the Shayanna and the Vikings, just as there was between the gunmen and the tribe of English and Shaynee ancestors. They put their own interests first, and I couldn't blame them there. We all did.

Jed and Skyla moved aside as one of the wagons rolled to a stop beside us. Bill looked down from the seat. "Where's this stuff going?" he asked.

I pointed at the short, heavily tattooed axeman who was inspecting Egil's new sword. "Geir will show you."

Jed leaned over on his horse and slapped the side of the wagon. "This is going to be quite a surprise for the Romans. Let's stop talking and get it ready."

"Indeed," I muttered as we dismounted. "Let's get ready."

CHAPTER 65

For the next two days, we worked like mad to prepare our defenses. Governor Fredrick's nasty little surprise was heavily talked about, as the Jarl didn't want to use it. But eventually he gave in to our persuasion and let us deploy it where we figured it would do the most good.

But I noted the area well, and decided that if we won this battle, I surely would not be riding a horse or walking through there anytime soon.

And finally, as we lay resting on the floor of my hut with Skyla using the lone bed, we felt like we were as prepared as we could be.

"Those apes are something else," Jed was saying. "Stronger than a bear, and smart too. No wonder they've been such nasty enemies. But Awshucks, I like him. He can growl and grumble all he wants, but he's a warrior through and through."

"Are you thinking we should maybe reach out to the remaining apes over here, see about peace?" Father asked as he contorted his back a bit to get more comfortable on his bare blanket on the floor.

"We should try," Skyla replied. "If we can end the killing, we should."

"Whose killing?" I asked bluntly. "People killing apes or apes killing people?"

"Both sorts," Jed replied.

"Peace is hard to come by. But I wish you luck," I told him sincerely.

"Me? What do you think you'll be doing after all this?" Jed asked, waving his hand in a big circle to imply all of Novagant and the approaching army. We had axemen scouts watching them now. There'd already been several small skirmishes between scouts with our side coming out the victor. But those were small numbers of Romans dead, we were going to need a whole lot more to win.

"I hadn't thought of it," I lied. I had thought of it a lot. But the problem was, every time I thought about my future, my thoughts tended to go towards Elsha. I felt like I didn't have a place in either Prehistoria or on the other side of the Shimmer. My world had collapsed with the death of Mr. White, and now I was adrift. And the only place that I even remotely felt like belonging was with Jarl Mikah's people.

That just seemed odd for a gunman of my stature and abilities. But maybe that's why. This was a place where my reputation meant little and the opportunity to start over had already started for me. I'd been making myself a place here since I woke up months ago with tattooed hands and bruised ribs.

"Maybe I'll stay here," I finally admitted.

"If that's where you feel like you belong, then you should," Father added. "The Jarl seems to like you well enough. And we won't be too far away should you need us."

I didn't say anything. I was still feeling a little unease towards my... family. It also felt strange to call them that. I hadn't had a family in a long time, not since I'd been taken by Mr. White. But here we all were, once again in the same room. Except for our sister. I couldn't believe she was a US Marshal now. But then again, she'd always been the one to break up Jed and my fights.

"So, you don't think I made the wrong choice? Bringing the apes here?" I asked to change the subject.

"Sounds like the Romans would have slaughtered them if you'd left them behind. Your only option was to bring them after everything you'd been through together. It will take some doing, but I think fighting side by side with a former enemy sort will go leagues in helping us come to peace with the apes on this side. Maybe these apes you brought can help smooth things over. After the whooping we put on them at Whitesberg, I'm sure they're ready to take a break for a bit," Father drawled as he pondered the question.

"We'll do just that. Maybe after this battle, we can go with Awshucks and his friends to find the others and ask for some peace," Jed said firmly. "But they're going to have to knock off that eating people's hearts in rituals and stuff."

"Assuming we survive this battle," Skyla mumbled.

"Easy there, darling. Don't worry, we're going to live. We've come too far in Prehistoria to have it taken away by a bunch of Romans," Father told her sternly.

"I've been hearing a rumor about you, Cato." Jed said. "They've been mentioning you as Odin's champion. I get that Odin is some pagan god of theirs, but what's this about you being a champion?"

"Thur and Gundar had finally told me while we were preparing defenses. When they found me, there was a raven nearby watching. Ravens are Odin's bird of choice for keeping an eye on mortals."

"There was a bird from the other side of the Shimmer... here?" Skyla asked.

"Strange, huh? Thur saw it and came up with this Odin's champion thing. I think he just wanted to use it as leverage to get his people to accept me so I could help them. He saw me as a boon to the axemen. A trained gunman who could teach the Vikings how to use guns and bridge the way between our people."

"Clever man," Jed snorted. "I'm glad it worked out that way."

"I haven't taught them much about guns yet. But they've taught me a lot about their weapons. I think they were hoping to get some guns before crossing the ocean, but it was a timing issue. The Jarl needed to find out about the survivors, and we couldn't wait any longer in case they were stranded somewhere."

Father rolled onto his side. "They taught you to use that short sword you carry?"

"They call it a seax. This one saved my life a couple of times, so I'm partial to it. And the shield, well, that should come in handy tomorrow."

"Let's not worry about what tomorrow brings," Father replied. "It will have plenty of troubles. Let's just enjoy tonight that we are safe, alive, and in a Viking town."

Jed laughed, reached over, and picked up the lantern that'd we'd found in one of the wagons from Whitesberg. He turned the wick down to a low glow.

"Goodnight."

CHAPTER 66

I slept terribly, often lying awake and listening to Jed and Father snore. How Skyla managed to sleep in here was beyond me. But the noises were loud and grating on my ears.

After a while, I gave up and eased myself out of my makeshift bed. Quietly, I took my gun belt with seax and strapped it around my waist.

I paused at the door for a moment, knowing by the silence that Jed and Father were awake now. Not knowing what to say, I pushed through the slab door and stepped into the night.

Today was the day.

Axeman scouts had confirmed that the Romans would reach us today. Jarl Mikah hoped it wouldn't turn into a siege but had assured us there were plenty of provisions put away if that happened.

But that'd only happen if I failed in my task.

I would be part of the trike cavalry charge. I was, as Jarl had planned, a special weapon of a sort. The killer who only needed to get within striking distance to kill again. And with luck, my guns would end this battle.

But the chances of me making it out alive were slim and depended completely on the axemen who'd be riding with me.

I spied the Reverend, off to the side by a small fire, praying with a gathering of converted axemen. Today was the big day. They might meet their maker.

Finishing the prayer, he looked up, made eye contact with me and gave me a smile and a nod before turning away to talk to Christ's followers.

For a moment I considered wandering over and listening in, but I hadn't been in any kind of church since I was a boy. Pre-Reydan White days, that is. Mr. White didn't care too much for religion unless he was using it to manipulate folks. Then you'd catch him in the front of church, dressed in his finest, giving large tithes where the newspapermen could see him. I'd be in the back, of course, waiting to shoot someone should the need arise. It never did, thankfully.

Turning away, I froze for a moment as Elsha stood beside me. For the briefest of seconds. Then I realized it was Sif, her sister.

"You're a quiet one," I told her as I noted she was still carrying the Roman sword she'd taken from her captor.

"You were distracted," she replied. "That will get you killed."

"Ja," I told her in agreement. "Can't sleep?" I asked.

"Never before a fight. Elsha always said it was because I was too eager."

I grinned, thinking of her sister. I wished she was here.

"Where will you be?" I asked.

"On the wall, with bow and arrow, and sword at the ready for the fiends to try and take Novagant." She jerked her head towards the hut behind us. "You bid your friends farewell?"

"No."

She stared at me for a moment before responding, "You will probably die, Cato of the Black Plague."

"Yup," I told her sincerely. I was taking a big risk, but it'd been part of the plan. And I'd volunteered for it. At first, I thought it'd come to blows with Janse, he wanted the honor. But the Jarl put that down fast when he pointed out I had guns.

With luck, that'd be the deciding factor.

"Good luck," I told Sif.

"May Thor be on your side," she replied before leaving me alone as she walked away.

I turned and walked down the beaten path between huts, past the Great House, and to the southern entrance to Novagant.

At the bridge over the moat, Thur sat with his feet dangling over the edge. In his hands he held his brother's knife and whittled away at a thin piece of wood. Beside him stood Gundar the Wrathful, casually tossing scraps of meat into the murky water below. With each small splash, something in the trench ate.

"Good morning, Cato. Can't sleep?" Thur greeted me with a sly smile.

"You're dulling your knife," I warned him while leaning over the edge to look below. "And you talk of not sleeping, but here you and Gundar are, feeding the fishes."

The old Viking laughed and threw a piece of raw flesh further out. A long, toothy snout rose from the water and snapped it out of the air before it could land. "I call that one, Old One Eye. He's been in there since I was a boy. You can't see now in the darkness, but there is a scar across its snout that ripped an eye from its socket. He's an angry one and always quick to fight or eat anything smaller in the moat. He will feast today."

"Not if he's full," I scolded the older axeman.

A thumping came from the end of the bridge.

Turning, we saw Helga and her band of merry apes sauntering across. Awshucks grumbled a hello. As he moved past leading the way, I noted instead of his typical stone axe, he now carried a massive, forged battle axe. The metal glinted in the moonlight and flickering of torches the apes carried. They were all painted in streaks and swirls of green, yellow, and red. They looked like monsters from children's tales come to life to do battle.

"Holy hells. You've armed them," I said, realizing that they were all carrying forged weapons and stout rounded Viking shields with metal embossed centers.

"It was the Jarl's idea," Helga said with a sly grin. "With some help from myself."

"They'll be damned near unstoppable," Thur said, tossing his stick into the water below and standing.

"That's the idea," the shield maiden told him. "We didn't have time to make them any armor, so they will still die. But until then, they'll be a force."

"You make it sound like a suicide attempt," I told her with a frown as I waved to Thur and Gundar and followed Helga after the apes.

"It may be. But if it is, the Valkyries will carry us with songs to Valhalla." She squinted side-eyed at me. "But what about you Christians? If you die, who will carry you to this Heaven of yours?"

"I suppose the angels." I gestured ahead of us at the backs of Thathas and another ape. "And I suppose something, or someone will carry their souls to whatever dark god they worship. They seem pretty happy right now though."

"That's because we let them sacrifice Felix."

"You did what?" I nearly shouted as I came to an abrupt stop.

She shrugged and kept going. "We didn't need him anymore. And you can't trust a traitor. What better purpose could he have served after telling us of the Roman ways of war?" she called over her shoulder.

I jogged to her side, shaking my head.

It made sense I supposed. But sounded cold blooded.

Ahead of us I heard the soft bellow of trikes. We were a bit early, but I was certain that Janse was already waiting for us. He probably slept beside his trike, with his axe for a pillow.

I hoped today would be a glorious day of victory. But I had my doubts.

CHAPTER 67

The Romans weren't playing around.

We knelt in the shade from a small stand of trees and watched from a distance through Jed's borrowed telescope as the enormous mass of men moved south into the open fields of Novagant, fully equipped with siege weapons from another time.

"There are so many," Ajar the Bold muttered as he passed the telescope back to me.

"We will kill them by the dozens," Janse replied firmly.

"We will need to kill them by the hundreds to break the Legate's army," I told him.

"Then by Odin's spear, we shall."

I changed the subject to what we were looking for, "Any sign of the Legate?"

"They all look the same," Ajar grumbled as he swatted a prehistoric fly off his arm.

"Fancy armor and helmet, scarlet cloak…. Not much to go on." Janse spat to the side.

"We need to find him. He's the key to all of this."

Small catapult-looking things were moved into position in front of the rows of troops who stood baking in the prehistoric sun. "Onagers," I muttered grimly.

Janse held his hand out for the telescope, and I passed it over.

"The captive Roman spoke the truth," he said as he looked through the long brass tube.

Ajar chuckled. "I've never heard of a blood eagle being performed on a person. But the threat of having one's ribs severed from the spine and lungs pulled out their back is a good way to inspire someone to talk. And he knows if he tells us false, he will suffer greatly."

I glanced at him. "Have you not heard? The apes sacrificed him last night."

The axeman stared at me for a moment before laughing. "No. No, I had not. But if it makes the apes on our side happy, so be it."

"Sure, for this fight. But what about the next?"

"We'll have to capture another Roman," he said simply.

"Surely they cannot throw so far?" Janse asked, bringing us back to the matter at hand, as the soldiers began to crank down the slings on the weapons.

I frowned. Felix hadn't said how far they could throw or how accurate they were. But the siege weapons had to be roughly four hundred yards from the swampy moat and earthen reinforced walls of Novagant. "We'll see soon enough."

Large rocks were moved forward, piled beside the weapons and the small teams manning them. It was nerve wracking to watch the speed and efficiency of the Romans. Within minutes the slings were loaded, and the first small boulders hurled through the air.

Several landed short as the distance was sorted out. But they still sent great gouts of dirt, grass, and grain from the fields flying.

Quickly, by the third shot they were nailing the walls; each successive hit sent an explosion of earth, wood, and occasionally people into the air.

I felt helpless watching the reinforced walls being battered. I hoped Jed and Skyla were keeping their heads down. Father too.

Ajar the Bold leaned over and gripped me by the shoulder with understanding. "Do not worry about those in Novagant, they are doing their part and soon we will do ours."

"And right now their part is to stay alive," Janse replied.

A loud boom echoed up from the town and an onager erupted in a spray of splinters and death. Half of the eight Romans manning the weapon fell dead while the others were all wounded to some degree. The small catapult weapon appeared destroyed. Several men crawled away as another staggered upright.

"That is one less," Janse chuckled.

"First shot as well! Well done." The team of axemen and gunmen working the large rifle had trained endlessly over the past couple of days to sight it in and reload. Once poor Felix had told us about their siege weapons, we decided to move the large rifle into the Great House. From there it would be unseen and have the highest view of the battlefield while being centered in the middle of Novagant and hopefully out of the Romans' siege weapon ranges.

Another shot from our side and another hit. This time the fired shell must have hit the loaded boulder, because it shifted out of the sling and the entire catapult contraption flipped end over end backwards into the mass of men standing behind it.

"And here come the scorpios," Ajar told us as we watched legionaries rush between the blocks of troops while pulling the weapons on wheeled carts. There were dozens of them, I tried to count but lost the number as they aligned themselves in neat groups behind the onagers but in front of the shielded phalanxes of men.

"Are they accurate at this distance?" Janse asked with a frown as the giant crossbows were cranked back by hand and a large iron-tipped bolt set in the firing slot.

"Felix said they were very accurate."

At a shout, the scorpios fired. Dozens of the bolts shot through the air, falling well inside Novagant on any unlucky defenders in the open.

"Damn," I swore to myself.

"Let us go," Janse said angrily. "We should be fighting. Not crouching here like hiding children."

"It is not yet time. We hit them now, they'll surround us and kill us. We need them divided," I reminded him.

"Doesn't mean I have to like it," he muttered, gripping his giant axe tightly.

Another volley of giant arrows flew through the air, as the Parrott rifle destroyed another onager.

We watched, all of us tense and eager to do our part, as the Roman boulders were coated with a liquid substance scooped from great bowls and lit on fire with torches.

Now flaming rocks were hurled into Novagant, seeking to destroy or burn whatever mystery gunman weapon was hitting the Legate's siege weapons. Smoke billowed overhead, and the wind gently pushed it out to sea.

This lasted for seemingly hours as arrows and rocks went one way, and large explosive shells went the other.

"Look, they move," Ajar said suddenly.

We watched as buschas came from between the neatly formed Roman phalanxes. They moved with ease, hissing, and snapping as they lopped through the beaten down fields.

"Finally," I muttered.

"Let the real battle be joined," Janse replied eagerly.

The big lizards left the protection of the Roman legionnaires and began to run towards Novagant in a large mass. I heard the distant popping of gunfire as Jed and the others with firearms opened up, and soon the sky was full of arrows as the Vikings began loosening their bows. Then I heard the repetitive popping noise as the recovered Gatling from the ship joined the battle with its higher rate of fire.

Dozens of buschas dropped, shot, or pinned through with arrows.

The rest kept moving forward.

Then they hit the caltrops hidden amongst the knee-high grass.

Those were Governor Fredrick's nasty little surprise that he'd had the forges of Whitesberg making all through the night before we left. A simple thing to make of metal, no matter how it was dropped or thrown, once it landed there would always be at least one sharpened point sticking up.

Lizards toppled over, snapping and biting, as they stepped on and then fell into the devious pointed little weapons.

Bullets and arrows kept raining amongst them as they rose and fought to get out of the killing zone of pointy death.

We didn't have nearly as many of the caltrops as we would have liked. But we had enough to do some hurting on the scaly little buscha bastards and to slow them down. They worked like a charm too. Through the telescope I watched the lizards crawling and dragging impaled limbs as the defenders of Novagant chewed them up.

But even now, the Hotchkiss cannon remained silent. I hoped this was because we were keeping it in reserve, and not that it'd been destroyed in the bombardment of burning boulders slung over the walls.

As the surviving lizards came closer to the moat and walls, the Roman phalanxes began moving forward as well.

"It is almost time for us to join," Ajar muttered anxiously.

"Odin be praised," Janse replied.

The lizards hit the moat. It didn't stop them. They leapt into the water and splashed across. I hoped Thur's mysterious friend, Old One Eye, was ripping them apart beneath the murky brown water.

Behind them, the Romans began to move faster, their shield walls raised as they entered gunfire range. But it didn't appear that anyone shot at them with guns. Everyone with a gun was trying to defend the walls from the lizards as they climbed hand over hand with clawed grip to get at the defenders above.

When they entered arrow range, the axemen behind the walls not engaged with buschas fired volley after volley high into the air to rain down on the marching Romans.

The shielded legionnaires turtled, moving shields overhead and covering each other from the fletched death that fell on them. Soon their rectangular shields were covered in arrows like porcupines.

And still they moved closer.

Reaching the moat, the turtled formations paused, and large wooden ladders were brought forward, raised, and dropped. They landed, giving the legionaries a way across the moat without having to go into the foul bloodied water.

At some unheard command, the Romans lowered their shields and hurled a mass volley of short spears at the defenders.

Both axemen and legionnaires dropped, before the shields turtled back over and Romans moved into place in their groups to quickly cover each other from where the dead had fallen.

A few moments later, they flung another set of short spears upwards at the defenders on top of the wall. The javelins embedded into the battered wall and the flesh of those who defended the top.

Now the entire Roman army was moving forward. Those who'd hurled their spears were rushing across the makeshift bridges, and reforming on the other side. The battle was about to be joined in mass.

"Now. We go," Janse said.

"I haven't spotted the Legate yet," I replied hurriedly, raking the telescope across the field.

The giant Viking lifted his battle axe and waved it towards the fight below us. "The bastard is down there somewhere. We'll find him."

From the back of the Roman army, I saw a small group of men on horses riding between the columns of moving men. The one in the front wore a flowing red cape and a decorated helmet of extreme arrogance and red dyed horse hairs.

"There! There he is! He's moving forward to see the assault on the town."

"Let's go!" Janse growled as I slammed the telescope shut and ran with the axemen back to the waiting trikes.

Grabbing Sleipnir by the bone shield, I climbed onto the red and black trike's back and picked up the reins.

"Asger would want you riding his mount," Thur had told me when we were making plans. "He's a warrior and belongs in battle. As do you."

I silently hoped that Asger would be watching over me today, and I would not fail him, as I checked to make sure my gear was ready. Across my back, strapped tight, was the Auto-5 shotgun.

Janse raised his axe and shouted to be heard to the tens of dozens of trike riders that'd been waiting for us. "Today, Odin and Christ watch over us. Today, Valhalla and Heaven will roar as we battle! Let us not let any god down! Follow us to their leader. Kill all in your way, brothers and sisters, and we will feast afterwards with their skulls for cups!"

The riders roared in agreement, with even the apes joining in to shout guttural cries of bloodlust.

Janse kicked his trike forward, and in a mass, we rode around the hill that concealed our numbers and into the open fields surrounding Novagant.

As big as the Viking town was, we were only able to scrounge about a hundred and twenty trikes and riders for our attack onto the Romans' flank.

It was a good thing that the axemen were born fighting, because we had every man, woman, and child available who could ride a trike with us. I saw youngsters from my axe training group shouting and pushing their trikes to outrace their elders to join the battle first. All the painted and well-armed apes were with us on borrowed mounts. They were too formidable of warriors to leave behind a wall.

But Ajar, Janse, and I pushed the hardest. We were at the point of the attack. The tip of the spear. We were leading the wedge that would penetrate the Romans' forces.

Realizing our cavalry was attacking, several phalanxes of men rotated to take our charge on their shields and lowered their spears. Behind them, I saw mounted Roman troops rush down onto the field as well to intercept our charge.

But they'd never make it.

Inside Novagant, still carefully hidden and heavily protected, the Hotchkiss cannon opened fire with its explosive shells to clear a path.

Thank God it'd survived the Roman bombardment.

Horses and men were flung into the air with every loud boom as earth and flesh was torn by shrapnel and sent flying in every direction.

The rate of fire wasn't impressive by any means. But the steady bombardment of the Roman cavalry charge stopped it dead in its tracks as the horses and men scattered to flee the madness and slaughter.

To our distant left, the attacking infantry and buschas renewed their assault on Novagant, urged on to take the city and destroy the weapons that were wreaking havoc on the men behind them. I could see the Romans in the distance climbing over the walls as the Vikings' outer defenses crumbled and fell back inside the town under the onslaught.

Now the fighting would take place in the streets, between buildings and trader stalls, with the women and children and every damned pointy stick we could find. The axemen were ready for this, they'd been expecting their walls to fall.

The Romans would pay dearly to take the town.

The Hotchkiss went silent, as did the Gatling.

It was hand to hand now inside Novagant.

As hundreds of thousands of pounds of dinosaur flesh hammered towards the braced phalanxes before us, it would become a race to see whose would break first. The Romans and their legion of war, or the Vikings and their Shaynee, gunman, and axeman protected town.

I drew the first of two pistols hanging around the trike's neck in holsters and ducked behind my mount's bone shield as Sleipnir hit the wall of guarded men with his horns forward and a bellow on his beak.

Rectangular red and yellow shields splintered under the impact. Spear points dug along the faces of trikes all along our front, gouging out dinosaur eyes, riding along their thick skulls and breaking as the bone shield snapped them in half.

Armored men were driven backwards into each other, then trampled as our trikes rode over them. Large feet stamped death onto the faces of fallen Romans. Horrific screams came from the men we killed and maimed in our charge. Amongst them was the bellow of pain from dozens of trikes and axemen who were wounded or impaled.

From the corner of my eye I saw Ajar the Bold's mount stumble and fall amongst the legionnaires.

A spear bent then snapped on Sleipnir's bone shield. The metal tip flew off into the charge as something human crunched with a scream beneath Asger's borrowed trike's feet.

The axemen and Awshucks had warned me to keep my mount moving. Any rider or trike who slowed or stopped during the charge would die. The numbers were simply not in our favor. The knot in my guts warned me that what we were doing was foolish, and that we were all going to die in this stupid charge.

But we just had to kill one man.

If we could get to him.

My trike pushed forward, lunging and thrusting, leaping over shields and downed men madly to get through the crush. Around us men jabbed with their spears or slashed with swords. The thick boiled leather armor around my legs protected me from being sliced, but not from the stinging pain of a sharpened flat metal rod being hit across it over and over. If I survived, my legs would be bruised for weeks.

A Roman tried to pull himself onto my trike with sword in hand. I shot him in the face below his helmet. With wide, surprised eyes the corpse fell back into the madness of death around me.

Out of the corner of my eye, I saw Awshucks swing his mighty forged axe and cut through an infantryman's breastplate like it was paper. A severed arm was slung into the battle mix.

I emptied the pistol ahead of us as Sleipnir kept surging forward. After the final shot I flung the empty weapon into the armored face of a man reaching up at me.

Abruptly, we were through the phalanx.

The next assortment of armored men braced themselves and lowered spears.

They were all that stood in our way of the Legate and his guards on the other side. I could see the mounted man shouting orders to try and stop our penetrating attack.

Drawing the second pistol hanging from Sleipnir's neck, I fired it into the overlapping shields ahead of us.

Bullets punched through, and men dropped spears and shields as they fell, opening a gap in their heavily armored formation.

Sleipnir dipped his horns low and jerked them upright as we hit the first man. Flinging him into the air, we crashed into the others.

Somewhere in the madness of death, a spear tip smashed into my chain mail armor, knocking the breath from my lungs, and sending me flying off the back of Asger's trike as the prehistoric world went black.

CHAPTER 68

I gasped, drawing a deep breath, and looking around in shock at the carnage I lay amongst. Dead and wounded men were everywhere. The ground was soaked with blood and filth from emptied bladders and bowels of the scared and dying.

Screams and the sounds of battle still surrounded me. I hadn't been out that long.

Rolling to my side, I narrowly missed being crushed by a trike fleeing the battlefield. Blood streamed down its sides and face from dozens of cuts and gashes. A large red smear showed where the rider had been killed.

Stumbling upright, I drew my pistol and shot a Roman soldier who came running towards me with an upraised sword.

The bullet hit him through the unarmored throat and knocked the helmet off the back of his head. Dropping to his knees before me, he grabbed at his neck as life oozed red from between his clenched fingers.

He was young. Wearing only a slight whisp of blonde hairs over his upper lip. Not quite a man yet but doing a man's work.

Letting go of his throat, the dying soldier lurched forward, stabbing at me with a small knife he'd pulled from his belt.

I shot him again and he pitched forward onto his face.

Hell with this, I thought.

A black raven landed on a tilted red and yellow decorated shield and screeched at me.

"Okay, Odin. Let's see who's really your Champion," I muttered while shooting the next pair of infantry men rushing towards me with shields raised.

The first one dropped, but the second who carried a sword took another shot. I dropped the emptied pistol to the ground.

There was no time for reloads. What I had was it.

And I had to get to the Legate.

Nothing else mattered.

I unslung the Auto-5 shotgun from my back and stalked forward around a dead trike and decapitated ape rider.

There.

A small group of mounted Romans with fancy armor were fighting against a pair of trikes.

Janse was one of the trike riders. As I watched, he took a sword blade across the chest and fell. Awshucks was standing on the ground already, his trike gone or dead. He cut the legs out from under a horse bearing down on him with his massive axe, sending the armored rider careening into the ground.

"LEGATE AUGUSTUS!" I screamed at the top of my lungs. I'd lost my hat when knocked off from the trike. Everyone could see my face.

They all knew who I was.

The Legate twirled in his saddle, somehow hearing me over the chaos. The arrogant bastard stared, then removed his helmet so we could glare at each other.

Shouting at the other riders, he snarled and kicked his horse, jumping the armored war beast into Awshucks and sending the painted ape sprawling into a tangled pile of corpses.

The group of horsemen bore down on me.

Legate Augustus raised his shield as I lifted the Auto-5 and emptied the shotgun at the riders. Buckshot peppered them, dropping three of the horses and riders. The Legate's horse was wounded and stumbling, but managed to trample an unlucky legionnaire who didn't move fast enough.

I let go of the empty shotgun and drew my final pistol.

Taking careful aim, I shot the Legate's horse through the head and dropped it.

There was a mere dozen yards between us. A multitude of arrows jutted from the ground mingled amongst corpses, fired from the axemen during the siege. Trampled bodies lay in all sorts of frozen agony from the death my trike friends had inflicted upon them.

Incredibly, Augustus stood back up and raised his shield once more as he walked towards me.

I fired shot after shot into the shield, only to be rewarded with the tiniest of sparks on the final shot as the paint flaked off and revealed the solid metal beneath.

Sonuva bitch was catching on.

And I didn't like that.

I let go of the pistol and grabbed up a fallen Roman shield. It was cracked as though a trike had stomped on it but it would have to do. With a flourish, I drew the Ouroboros-engraved seax from its sheath at my waist.

Stalking forward, I stepped over a dead ape and pair of Romans. Now there was an open area between us.

Legatus lowered his pock-marked shield and grinned evilly. "Silly blackened barbarian. Did you really think I would not learn?"

"Your brothers didn't," I shouted back before rushing forward to slam my shield against his.

He growled, slipped his shield to the side and off mine, then thrust with his sword. The tip slammed against my shield, splintering the wood then sliding off with a deep gouge.

In return, I slashed with my seax. The blade clanged harmlessly against his heavy metal shield and bounced off.

"I did not lie, Cato. I will have you crucified for all of this monstrous world to see," he called out.

I stepped to the right, not bothering to reply. We rotated around each other as I desperately thought of how to kill the Roman army's leader.

He slammed his shield against mine and I felt the wood shudder from the hit.

Glancing behind the Roman leader, I saw legionnaires retreating from Novagant. I suppose their attack did not go well. But now that meant they were headed back in our direction. And all around us was chaos as the remaining trike riders were fighting for their lives. The axemen, not allowing a retreat to grant relief to their enemies, were pouring over the walls now to give chase. At their front was a familiar one-armed berserker turned Jarl.

The Hotchkiss fired once again, its blast a welcome sound amongst the violence. A handful of fleeing Romans were sent spiraling into the air in bits and pieces.

"You've lost, Augustus," I taunted the man opposite me.

He looked over a shoulder quickly then turned back as I dropped to a knee and swung my seax at his foot sticking out below the shield.

The metal shield dropped and pinned my sword to the ground. But not before I'd cut through the hardened leather sandal and lopped off a couple of toes.

As the Legate screamed, I lurched upwards, slamming my shield against his while jerking my blade back to me. It slipped out, bloodied at the tip.

"And now you've lost some toesies," I snarled around my shield.

His metal reinforced shield smashed into me, knocking me backwards as he furiously hammered away at mine. Between bashes, he hacked away at my shield, sending splinters and chunks flying. Desperately, I tried to stay upright as the stronger man whittled both my strength and shield down.

With a final swing of his sword, the remnants of my shield flew from my stinging hand to the ground.

Lurching to the right, I tried to stab around the Roman leader's large rectangular shield and hit only air as the Legate dodged aside.

Twisting the shield about, he slammed the bottom edge into my face as Janse had shown me so long ago. I felt a sickening crunch and piercing pain as my nose broke from the blow. Tears flowed freely and losing my vision, I fell backwards to the ground as the immense pain radiating through my skull threatened to consume me.

Blindly raising the seax before me in defense while trying to blink and wipe away the tears, Augustus swatted it from my grip with a swing of his sword.

With a smile, he tossed his heavy shield aside and held the tip of his sword at my throat. *"Aut vincere, aut mori."*

Grabbing the naked blade with my right hand, I squeezed with all my strength while my left fumbled beside me for anything that could be used as a weapon.

The Legate laughed and leaned forward, pushing the blade closer. I felt it slide through my hand and fingers, slicing the flesh on them open and grating against bone. Blood trickled down my Ouroboros tattooed hand and stained Elsha's blue-ribbon strip tied around my wrist. The skin at my throat parted from the tip of the steel as it pressed home.

I was going to die.

An explosive shell from the Hotchkiss impacted nearby. The blast flung Augustus to the ground, and for a moment I felt as if I was flying before slamming back down on the battlefield myself.

My right hand wasn't working, but my left hand bumped against an arrow sticking from a corpse's armored chest.

Jerking it free, I crawled over the Legate and slammed the bloody pointed tip down into his face.

The arrow sliced a gash down his forehead and slid into his eye socket. For the briefest of seconds, the eyeball rotated backwards sickeningly as I had control of it with the arrow.

Using my body weight, I leaned on the thin carved Viking shaft and thrust the point home into his brain, sending Augustus' body into a spasm beneath me as he died. "Either conquer or die," I whispered into his ear, repeating the Latin phrase he'd spoken over me moments before.

A meaty hand clamped onto my shoulder and lifted me upright effortlessly.

Janse. Covered in blood splatters with a nasty shallow cut across his chest, but alive.

Beside him stood Awshucks. The painted ape still carried his giant war axe, but now you couldn't tell where the paint ended, and blood spray began. His broad black face formed something of a grin as he licked his canines, and they were bloodied as well.

I held back a shudder.

It was a good thing he was on our side.

Around us were Romans and buschas retreating. They ran past us with barely a glance, and the ape leader rumbled a happy sound and chased after them with his big axe swinging like a giant scythe.

Janse and I watched him cut a lizard in two.

The Hotchkiss still fired, sending explosive gouts of dirt and guts as the shells impacted amongst the fleeing. Trikes and horses ran rampant over the battlefield as well, driven mad by the scent of death and noises of battle and destruction. They trampled people and lizard indiscriminately.

I glanced down at my right hand and tried to open it. It wouldn't obey, the fingers still curled inwards around their severed muscles and tendons.

"That looks bad, Little Plague," Janse reached down and tore a strip from his undershirt, then carefully wrapped it around my wound.

"Yeah," I muttered as we watched the attacking axemen approach us with broad grins and shouts of victory on their bearded lips.

CHAPTER 69

We didn't bother rounding up the trikes although I was thrilled to see Sleipnir still alive as he rumbled past us with a corpse impaled on one of his horns.

Instead, Janse and I walked back into Novagant surrounded by a horde of happy and victorious barbarians.

Jed and Skyla met us at the gate. They looked exhausted; their faces were smeared with soot from burning buildings and gun smoke. My brother clapped me on the back in greeting with a grin. "Another battle won. We're on a winning streak, Cato."

Skyla gave me a hug. It felt strange, but also oddly comforting. I hadn't felt a hug since Mr. White took me from my old home.

"Where's Father?" I asked awkwardly as I freed myself from her embrace.

"He lives. And he's with Bill and Thur, by the Parrott rifle in the Great House... or what's left of it."

Looking up towards the highest hill inside Novagant's walls, I saw the smoking ruins of the building. It appeared to have taken a direct hit from several fiery boulders.

Nodding at the married pair, I left them behind and began walking through the town towards where the great rifle had been placed.

"Cato!" I heard Janse call.

With a sigh, I glanced over my shoulder. He dipped his head at me in a customary gunman manner of respect, and said, "Odin's champion? Perhaps not. But certainly favored."

"Thanks, Janse. And for the lessons of shield and axe."

"Why? It didn't do you any good."

I laughed, and it hurt my face and broken nose. Then, with fresh tears rolling down my face from the pain, I walked on.

Thur Thaneson was waiting for me at the top of the hill. He sat on a stool with an axe in hand. Except for some singed clothing and hair, he looked fine, if a bit angry.

"What?" I asked. "You miss the fight?"

"Yes! Gods be damned. Nary a one of the Roman heathens made it up here."

"I'm sorry, Thur. That's an awful thing."

"It is." His face suddenly fell. "Gundar's dead. One of those giant burning rocks tore through the wall and smashed him. It was fast."

"He feasts in Valhalla then," I told my friend.

"Yes," he reached down and plucked a cross necklace from beneath his armor. "And I won't see him again."

I stood there for a moment, thinking about the religious differences and theoreticals of axemen and gunmen... Then shrugged. "Who knows. Maybe when you die, the Valkyries will get you before the angels. Assuming you stop missing out on the fights."

He barked a short laugh.

At a loud gunshot, his head burst apart like a melon. I stood shocked and unarmed as Thur's lifeless body slumped to the ground.

Behind where he sat stood Bill Argave with revolving carbine cradled in both hands. He raised the weapon and pointed it at me.

"What? Why?" I asked, shocked and baffled at the sudden death of my friend.

"You killed Tom. You or one of your damned raider friends. He was my older brother, and he was murdered when he returned home from the War Between the States."

"I don't recall doing that."

"But you raided, didn't you? You and that piece of shit railroad tycoon that the Sheriff killed."

I gritted my teeth and nodded while looking down the barrel of Bill's weapon, accepting my fate. "I did."

"Yes. And I hoped the lizards or Romans would get you... but here you are. Still alive while other, better men, are gone. Get on your knees," he demanded, taking a step closer.

"No," I growled back as I straightened and braced myself for death.

It was finally time to meet my maker.

So damned be it.

A pair of shots rang out. Quick, sounding like one to all but the most trained or accustomed ear.

Bill dropped the carbine as his face spasmed. He stood for a moment, staring at me, before slowly falling forward. With one hand out to stop his fall, he hit the ground with a heavy thud and didn't move.

"I never did trust him," my father said as he stepped out from inside the smoldering Great House while holstering his pistol. "Something about him just felt off."

I stared down at the man's body.

Maybe I had killed his brother. Or been there when it happened. Or maybe it was another outfit; Mr. White wasn't the only one taking advantage of the South.

222

Still. I felt like I had.

"Don't go there, son," Fathersaid as he stepped towards me with a hand lifted. "I've been there, and it's not a pretty place to be. If you don't know if you killed his brother or not, then don't take the weight. We've all enough of wrong doings to suffocate, no need to add to it."

"Yes, sir," I mumbled.

My father kicked Bill's corpse in the side. "That's for Thur."

CHAPTER 70

I stayed in Novagant for a few days. They reset my nose and stitched up my nearly severed fingers the best they could, but it was apparent I'd never be able to pull a trigger again with that hand.

It was a good thing I was ambidextrous. I could still shoot with my left.

And I was confident I'd still be able to grip an axe with my right. Which Janse had promised more lessons were to come after my abysmal performance against the Roman Legate.

I wasn't looking forward to them.

But I was looking forward to seeing Elsha. And when I rode into Whitesberg on the back of Sleipnir, she was waiting for me at the gate.

I'd barely dismounted before she'd grabbed me by the arm and planted a kiss on my lips in front of Jed, Skyla, and everyone else. It was humiliating, but I also hadn't stopped grinning like an idiot since.

We stayed about a week in Whitesberg, letting the gunman Doctor clear the both of us. Personally, I think he just wanted to earn the gold coins I'd given him.

And on the morning I was to return to the Viking town to help them rebuild, I cleaned out the armored railcar of my meager belongings and headed to the graveyard to say goodbye.

It was there that I found my brother by Mr. White's grave. He was staring at the headstone.

"Jed?" I asked as I approached him from behind, ever mindful of a gunman with a lot of enemies who didn't like being surprised.

"Hey, Cato," he replied, glancing back over his shoulder before looking back down.

"Didn't expect to find you here," I stepped beside him.

He chuckled. "I come here from time to time to piss on his grave."

I'm not sure if he was serious or not. But I didn't see a wet mark, so maybe he was joking.

Mr. White's gravestone and burial site was at a place he deserved though, on a nice little hill in the graveyard with a big headstone and a wrought iron fence around it. Oddly though, nothing had grown in the dirt since he'd been laid to rest. It was still as brown as you'd expect from overturned earth.

"Needs some flowers or something," I muttered to myself, even though I knew the dead man didn't care a whip for such things.

"Never. Not for him," Jed replied with a satisfied-looking grin.

"What's that smile about?" I asked.

Jed pointed at the ground. "Night after they buried him, I came up here and salted the earth with a couple fifty-pound bags. It rained the next day and soaked it all in. Nothing will grow here for a hundred years… until this sorry piece of shit is long forgotten."

I looked at him in amazement. "You harbored a lot of hatred for him."

"I did and I do."

"Well, you'd better tighten your gun belt. Because if you think Mr. White was evil, you've yet to meet his son. He's in a whole new category of bad news."

Jed turned towards me; his hands clamped onto his gun belt and his eyes dark. "Don't you worry, Cato. I've already asked around about him. When that little son of a bitch shows up, we'll handle him together."

"Damn right we will," I retorted.

THE END.

Erik Testerman is a veteran grunt of the glorious Marine Corps, a 'faster than he is accurate' competitive shooter, and an admirer of fine arms and armaments. He lives in the mountains of North Carolina with his lovely wife, two rambunctious children, and a slobbery English Mastiff.

To learn more about Erik Testerman or to follow his exploits as he navigates the world of the written word, visit http://GunPowderAndInk.blog or his Facebook page at http://www.facebook.com/AuthorErikTesterman

Check out other great

Dinosaur Thrillers!

John Lee Schneider

AGE OF MONSTERS

Once upon a time, Dinosaurs ruled the Earth.But the Mesozoic era – the Age of Reptiles – came to its cataclysmic end sixty-five million years ago.The Age of Monsters begins tonight.And the world of humankind will crumble. Some will call it Judgment. Some will attempt to fight. Others will simply run. Most will just try and survive. But no one will escape.In the mountains. In the oceans. In the cities and towns. Even up in space.Where were YOU when the world ended?

Gustavo Bondoni

TEST SITE HORROR

Lieutenant Max Alexeyev is a Russian Special Forces soldier. His job is to protect his country's interests at home and abroad, not to rescue overly ambitious reporters who have bitten off stories too big to chew. But when his unit gets called to a press event at a laboratory that has been invaded by dinosaurs, that's exactly what he finds himself doing. Fighting both prehistoric nightmares and the products of modern genetic experiments in the forests of the Ural Mountains, he battles for his own survival as well as that of alluring journalist Marianne Caruso and her peers.Unbeknownst to him, however, shadowy human forces are at work to ensure that no one spills the secrets of the research being done in the area.Will they live to tell the story of the Test Site Horror?

CHECK OUT OTHER GREAT DINOSAUR BOOKS

PRIMORDIA
by **Greig Beck**

Ben Cartwright, former soldier, home to mourn the loss of his father stumbles upon cryptic letters from the past between the author, Arthur Conan Doyle and his great, great grandfather who vanished while exploring the Amazon jungle in 1908.

Amazingly, these letters lead Ben to believe that his ancestor's expedition was the basis for Doyle's fantastical tale of a lost world inhabited by long extinct creatures. As Ben digs some more he finds clues to the whereabouts of a lost notebook that might contain a map to a place that is home to creatures that would rewrite everything known about history, biology and evolution.

But other parties now know about the notebook, and will do anything to obtain it. For Ben and his friends, it becomes a race against time and against ruthless rivals.

In the remotest corners of Venezuela, along winding river trails known only to lost tribes, and through near impenetrable jungle, Ben and his novice team find a forbidden place more terrifying and dangerous than anything they could ever have imagined.

PANGAEA EXILES
by **Jeff Brackett**

Tried and convicted for his crimes, Sean Barrow is sent into temporal exile—banished to a time so far before recorded history that there is no chance that he, or any other criminal sent back, has any chance of altering history.

Now Sean must find a way to survive more than 200 million years in the past, in a world populated by monstrous creatures that would rend him limb from limb if they got the chance. And that's just his fellow prisoners.

The dinosaurs are almost as bad.

SEVEREDPRESS

facebook.com/severedpress

twitter.com/severedpress

CHECK OUT OTHER GREAT DINOSAUR BOOKS

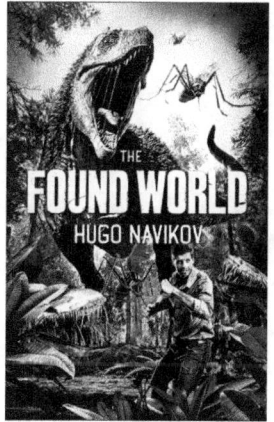

THE FOUND WORLD
by **Hugo Navikov**

A powerful global cabal wants adventurer Brett Russell to retrieve a superweapon stolen by the scientist who built it. To entice him to travel underneath one of the most dangerous volcanoes on Earth to find the scientist, this shadowy organization will pay him the only thing he cares about: information that will allow him to avenge his family's murder.

But before he can get paid, he and his team must enter an underground hellscape of killer plants, giant insects, terrifying dinosaurs, and an army of other predators never previously seen by man.

At the end of this journey awaits a revelation that could alter the fate of mankind ... if they can make it back from this horrifying found world.

HOUSE OF THE GODS
by **Davide Mana**

High above the steamy jungle of the Amazon basin, rise the flat plateaus known as the Tepui, the House of the Gods. Lost worlds of unknown beauty, a naturalistic wonder, each an ecology onto itself, shunned by the local tribes for centuries. The House of the Gods was not made for men.

But now, the crew and passengers of a small charter plane are about to find what was hidden for sixty million years.

Lost on an island in the clouds 10.000 feet above the jungle, surrounded by dinosaurs, hunted by mysterious mercenaries, the survivors of Sligo Air flight 001 will quickly learn the only rule of life on Earth: Extinction.

www.ingramcontent.com/pod-product-compliance
Lightning Source LLC
Chambersburg PA
CBHW060429180626
46817CB00007B/2728